J. Dean says she writes because of her encounters with whales, hurricanes, clown fish, sea snakes, Tuvalu children, dancing dolphins, hitchhiking birds, meditating iguanas, Swami Ram, a baby elephant, a Maori lawyer, the gentle Thai people, and a birthing in Lamu, to name a few. She says her favorite place in the world is mid-ocean in a serenity that is never completely silent, with the purity of nature's power, the beauty of touchable stars, gentle winds, and hellacious storms. She and her husband, Rauf Bolden, spent seven years circumnavigating Earth. 160,000 miles in a 35ft sailboat. The adventures included getting arrested in Yemen when they mistakenly anchored in a PLO training bay at the Gate-of-Tears (Bab-el-Mandeb). She writes from experience and from seafarers' stories gathered along the way, letting fact and fiction freely dance.

For Rauf, my husband and best friend. We share the exciting adventure of life.

J. Dean

SEYCHELLE AND THE CANNABIS YACHTIES

AUSTIN MACAULEY PUBLISHERS™

LONDON * CAMBRIDGE * NEW YORK * SHARJAH

Ordering Information
Quantity sales: Special discounts are available on quantity purchases by corporations, associations, and others. For details, contact the publisher at the address below.

Publisher's Cataloging-in-Publication data
Dean, J.
Seychelle and the Cannabis Yachties

ISBN 9781647504144 (Paperback)
ISBN 9781647504151 (Hardback)
ISBN 9781647504168 (ePub e-book)

Library of Congress Control Number: 2021914574

www.austinmacauley.com/us

First Published (2021)
Austin Macauley Publishers LLC
40 Wall Street, 33rd Floor, Suite 3302
New York, NY 10005
USA

mail-usa@austinmacauley.com
+1 (646) 5125767

One

Chianti crouched on the foredeck, letting another wave break over her, feeling wet fingers find folds and crevices.

"Cheap, useless foul-weather jacket," she growled and again checked her harness was securely attached to the lifeline. The coated wire was swaged at the bow and stern of *Cayenne's* 40 ft. teak deck and there was no corrosion, of that Chianti was sure. She had given her beloved sloop a thorough examination before setting sail from Sint Maarten.

After inspecting *Cayenne's* worn but nearly bulletproof Dacron storm sail, as well as her halyards and sheets, Chianti crawled back to the cockpit. She remained on her knees, inserted the galvanized pipe that served as manual bilge pump handle, and gave thirty firm strokes.

"Blessings be upon you and your dry bilge," she murmured. She had experienced nearly as many failed bilge pumps as efficiently functioning ones during her years at sea, and she knew she would never set sail without at least one backup.

"A manual one," she declared aloud, "and a rebuild kit." She smiled. "So many storms, so many leaking boats, so many adventures."

Standing, Chianti stretched, pleased her body had easily readjusted to life on the boat, that four years locked away had not diminished her physically, though she wasn't sure she could give herself high marks on mental and emotional well-being.

She ran fingers through her short blonde hair, thankful it was growing. The scissor-happy girl who acted as prison hairdresser had said she looked like Twiggy, but when she returned to 'C' Wing the girls had dubbed her 'Skinhead'. She admonished herself with, "Don't go there."

Bracing hands on the aluminum boom that she'd secured amidships, she gasped when a contrary wave splashed her as the boat rounded up. She gave a hoot of laughter and yelled, "Give us your best shot! We love it, *Cayenne* and

I. That's why we came to the Gulf of Mexico!" As if in reply she was again impudently doused as the boat lurched to port. She blinked, wiped salt water from her face and did a slow 360 degree turn, straining to spot the lights of ships or oil rigs. Though waves lifted them, white foam topped the boisterous surrounding sea so the horizon was obscured, blurred by spray. She stepped down and loosened the main a touch, waited. It was difficult to balance with just one reef in the main, but *Cayenne* needed the sail area to power through.

She looked up at the starless cloud-covered sky, shook her head. "Good thing I'm not relying on you for navigation. Hiding, every last one of you, and you took the moon with you! Guess I'll leave my sextant packed away." With a deep sigh she made her way below decks.

Cayenne was damp and stuffy down below. Chianti sweated as she checked, but the RDF was still down. Fresh out of prison, she hadn't enough money to replace old instruments, sails or charts, and had to use all she had to buy the ganja, small load though it was. That wouldn't have been enough to justify this run if Yellowman hadn't fronted her a few extra kilos. Sint Maarten Lagoon Boatyard had maintained *Cayenne*, but she and everything on her needed an overhaul, which was why they had taken that ill-fated Moroccan job. She shrugged. Get this load sold and start replacing everything. It would take two or three more runs, but she would have *Cayenne* ready for some real cruising when Sydney returned. Together they had sailed her around the world, a long slow cruise, and dropped anchor in so many special places.

She heated water on the two-burner gimbaled gas stove, made a strong mug of Nescafe instant coffee and added a heavy dollop of honey. With no radio and unreliable radar pick-up she would get no sleep during these final two days. Approaching land was always tense, so many obstacles, so much danger. She took another look outside before settling into the navigation table seat with her journal. She recorded her position, well, her dead reckoning position, which she was pretty sure was fairly accurate, navigation being one of her strong points. Sydney called it 'guesstimation' and was always amazed by how spot-on she was.

Though she tried to write about the here and now, Chianti could do little more than record positions. Past challenges and adventures pushed her pen, manipulated her thoughts. She smiled, tracing with her finger the one word she had painstakingly tattooed across the cover of her loose-leaf notebook. Fiction.

8

The Guv had acquiesced, had let her keep the notebook and one pen in her cell after her solicitor entered the request.

The British were not so bad, once she understood them. "I am Buddhist, I can't eat meat or dairy," she told them when faced with the meals prepared by prisoners for prisoners. So, peanut butter, white bread, Marmite and black tea had gotten her through incarceration.

She had written about most of their adventures before the Moroccan run and left the incriminating evidence in one of the secret spots they had built into *Cayenne*. While inside she transcribed her memories as children's stories, peopled with animals, created for the U.S. market that was hungry for such stuff. Prison staff had accepted the façade and encouraged developing her talent so she would not return to the life of crime, to smuggling drugs. She had quickly abandoned efforts to explain that grass was not a drug. You either knew or you didn't.

She shook her head, patted the fat binder she had retrieved as soon as she stepped aboard. "You are the guardian, the keeper of secrets, *Cayenne*. Now begins our next chapter."

Remembering, recreating, and repackaging their life at sea had preserved Chianti's enthusiasm and her optimistic view of the future. Only she, and Sydney of course, could unravel the truth, but now she had her original scribbles, as well as the stories, in her overstuffed notebook.

Inside the front cover she had written, "Let me assure you that there is no life to compare with wandering the high seas in a sailboat. Whether wrapped in the energy of a storm or merged into the tranquility of a sunrise or meditating while dolphins dance, being mid-ocean, with no land in sight for hundreds of miles, ensures that one is in love with life. Everything you are about to read is pure fiction. From my imagination and rumors have come these people, events, dates and places. Talk to my lawyer if you have doubts."

Smiling, Chianti flipped to the last page of the book, jotted down her uncensored thoughts and, still smiling, closed her journal, sealed it in its watertight plastic box and returned it to the net bag she kept hanging beside the companionway. Chianti felt the boat lurch, looked up, gasped, and leapt out into the cockpit. Her stomach clenched. There was no time for thought, just reaction.

She threw herself across the cockpit to the tiller, threw off its restraining line, and jammed it to port with her body. Tacking was easy with just a storm sail up, but with so little sail area, there was insufficient momentum to escape the wall that rushed toward her. Cargo ship or tanker, it did not matter. She slammed the throttle forward and pressed the ignition button. One, two, three, the engine turned over but wouldn't catch.

"Bastard!" she bellowed, feeling impotent, frightened. She kept her finger pressed down hard, as if increased pressure would force the little diesel to come alive, as if she could channel her adrenalin-charged energy into it.

Finally, she heard manic revs, but knew it was too late. With a mesmerizing roar the monster's bow displaced a ton of water before it, lifting and pushing, manipulating the little sailboat. With supreme effort Chianti made herself turn left to grab the life raft cord. She yanked without thinking, and was shocked that the raft responded immediately, expanding to force tape that had held its case shut for so many years.

She snatched up the tiller line, snapped it back into the tiller's jam cleat with scant hope it would steer them away from the impending disaster. Chianti fell as *Cayenne* lunged to starboard, scrambled on her knees to the companionway, grabbed her faded orange life jacket and the net bag, threw her body back across the cockpit and shoved them into the expanding raft. She glanced back once and began unwinding the raft's painter from the stainless-steel deck cleat.

The wave caught *Cayenne* at the moment Chianti released the raft's tether. The line shot out of her hand and the bright orange raft was caught, lifted in white foam. She followed, determined to keep it in sight as she dove. She heard nothing but the deafening roar, the power of the sea beyond comprehension.

There was no time for self-recrimination, no time for regrets.

Two

The garish orange alien intruded on the tranquil Gulf Coast scene. And drew her. Nature's subtleties became background.

"I'll not let you beat me to it," Seychelle declared, but she had not the heart to intrude on Beauregard's enthusiasm. She clambered down smooth, bleached rocks to the soft granite sand beach, sure-footed after years of treasure hunting. Today she ignored dream-stimulating debris of past worth.

She stared, barely breathing. The sea had won. The scraped, scarred life raft's collapsed canopy had accumulated a salty puddle, giving the impression of an outgrown, discarded wading pool.

"Beauregard, hush up now!" Seychelle commanded. The Basset ceased charging about, his voluminous bark echoing away with the waves. His brown eyes locked on Seychelle while his tail furiously thumped the raft's still-inflated lower rib.

She approached, wary but vibrating with excited curiosity. Would there be the remains of a lone sailor, dehydrated? Or a couple, their bodies disintegrating as had their dreams and their hopes of rescue?

"Please, no one," she pleaded and reached for the vinyl flap that covered the opening they would have crawled through to escape from the raging sea. Seychelle could see them struggling into the raft, their only hope as their much-loved boat was engulfed by cresting waves.

"Stop it!" she told herself with a nervous laugh. She grabbed a corner and jerked the flap up.

First glance revealed nothing but water. She relaxed, lifted the top with both hands. There were no bodies, just a faded orange floating life jacket. Seychelle stared for a bit, clutched at the thought that perhaps a freighter or fishing boat had rescued them. Holding the canopy up with one hand, she leaned in and picked up the lifejacket. She turned and laid it on a boulder, then stretched in to get a better look, but it was just too dark. Her eyes were slow to adjust from the harsh midday sun. She stepped inside where the warm salt water was about halfway to her knees. Sand shifted underneath the raft's thin floor, making it difficult to support the top and crouch on the slippery surface.

"How long have you been here?" she asked. The stale, old rubber smell and slimy interior coating indicated it had been ashore for a while. It wouldn't have been spotted from the dirt road that curved inland and she had been so involved in her father's funeral she hadn't done her habitual beach wandering for days, weeks. Her eyes began to water. She shook her head, cleared her throat.

Looking around, she shuddered. How long had they lived here? Rough if you're claustrophobic, worse if you're injured. Her arms were aching from supporting the canopy. Had it collapsed while they were alive inside? She turned to climb out, but something bumped her foot. Her heart quickened, she froze, her imagination went into overdrive, but she was glad she was wearing sneakers.

"Now don't y'all go bein' stupid," Seychelle told herself, echoing one of her father's favorite Southern admonitions. She took a deep breath and stated, "Besides, there just might be some little ol' treasure, if only in the form of clues to their saga."

Slowly, careful to keep the canopy elevated so at least some light filtered in, she reached into the water. Her hand found rough netting, like a fisherman's net. She pulled, lifted and slung the net and its heavy cargo outside onto the sunlit beach. Seychelle took a deep breath as she stepped out, relieved to drop the canopy, to vacate the raft's drab interior.

Beauregard, barking and sniffing, approached with care. She laughed, wiped sweat from her face with the sleeve of her white cotton shirt. "It's only a plastic box, Beauregard, but that net bag sure enough does stink. We'll open it when we get home."

She stepped inside once more to check the two self-draining side pockets. Beauregard watched her through the opening, wary of the dark enclosure. Each pocket held a clear, sealed plastic bag and the contents of each looked dry, seeming to have been sealed within the raft before it was containerized.

She stepped out, sat down in the warm sand and hugged the hound, letting him cover her face and neck with slobbery licks, as if she had just returned from sea, had survived nature's wrath. She stared at the bags. One held plastic and aluminum utensils for two, like you'd take camping, a small first-aid kit, sun block and two small bags of glucose-enhanced water. The other contained a flashlight, a flare gun, and fishing gear, as well as a deluxe Swiss army knife.

"All unused," she murmured. "So, whatever happened to them had come to pass before they needed any of this stuff."

Her fingers trembled as she peeled back the wet net bag. "They weren't rescued, Beauregard. Or, if they made it this far, there is just no way in the world they would have left this behind." She stared at the sealed plastic box that held only an overstuffed notebook like she'd used in school.

"It must be a logbook, where they would have recorded navigation details, at least for this voyage. Maybe we can find them!"

She put everything into the wet, smelly, sandy net bag, her questions multiplying.

"Everything seems planned and carefully stored but hasn't been touched. Is that a good sign? Oh, West, I sure wish you had lived long enough to share my discovery."

After a bit she stirred, and realized Beauregard had gone crab chasing, her inactivity having little interest for him. She brushed sand from her cut-offs, threw the net bag over her shoulder and began negotiating the obstacle course to the path she knew so well. With her imagination racing, she was quite unconscious of their 20 minute walk, and didn't return to the present until she opened the front gate.

Seychelle stopped, looked up at the white frame house with its wrap-around porch and ancient oaks whose languorously draped moss hid rain culverts and combined the whole. She was born here, had spent most of her life here, when not away at school, but without her father it held no warmth. For the first time she felt reluctant to mount the wooden steps. So many hours she had spent in the wide slatted swing while West sat in Granddaddy's heavy mahogany rocking chair with its high back and worn leather-covered seat cushion. Gulf Haven was now empty and uninviting.

"What now, West? I've got their logbook, I think, but I have a feeling it's going to give me more questions than answers."

Beauregard's scratching and growling at the screen door interrupted her musing.

"There's no one there to let you in, not anymore. We're completely alone now."

The wet bag had grown heavy. Her shoulders slumped as she walked up the steps and across the porch to enter the silent old house.

Seychelle took a quick shower, towel-dried her thick brown curls, threw on a tee-shirt and clean cut-offs, inserted a Joni Mitchell cassette, and fed Beauregard. She gave a gentle squeeze to some limes on the many trees that wreathed the screened back porch, selected one and wedged it for her sweet tea. She settled on a bench at the long oak kitchen table and Beauregard curled in for a nap by her feet on the linoleum-covered floor.

Had they kept abandon-ship bags ready at all times? She had read that some sailors did that, had thought it a rather fatalistic attitude, but now it made sense.

She took their sealed box from its bag on the floor, shook off sand, dried it with a towel and placed it on the table. She stared at it for a bit, excitement laced with dread, then she grabbed a corner and pulled up, the unsealing creating enough noise to elicit a growl.

Seychelle dipped her head, inhaled. She shrugged, unsure of what she had expected. It smelled a bit like the corner of the living room where West kept his collection of old books, but mostly it just smelled old, as if it had been in storage. The black, over-stuffed loose-leaf notebook was quite worn, like it had been used a lot for a long time. It was not exactly a typical ship's logbook, that much she knew. She studied the neat, even script on the inside of the front cover. Confident, but not bold, a female, she thought. She read the inscription, laughed and declared, "I've gotta find you!"

She flipped through pages with care, resisting the temptation to stop and read. The first quarter looked like a logbook, neatly lined and with most entries in pencil. The rest looked more like a diary or journal, filling every inch of every page on both sides, in the same unadorned hand but written in ink, as if unchangeable was important.

Seychelle returned to the first page, to what she took to be the final entry.

"19:45/ 05.03.1972/ 30.03.26N x 88.27.18W (DR). Just want to write about the past, but must get my head out, at least long enough to fill out the logbook. Tired, but radar down so no sleep allowed. Squall will pass. Cargo is dry. Wind shifts settled from SW. Entering the oil rig area. Down to storm sail, reefed main." Chianti.

Seychelle bit her lip. "Chianti! Hello, Chianti! You are female. Oh, I have just got to get to know you…y'all. Are you alone?" She knew Gulf of Mexico storms could be hellacious but much calmed when they hit land. There had been several spring storms. One around the first of the month had been rated as a gale, force 8, with 34 knot winds and 14 ft. seas, though no hurricane warnings. She had driven West to the hospital for the last time during that one, while sheets of rain blurred vision and lightning illuminated the landscape at irregular intervals.

"The Gods are giving me a fitting send-off," he'd quipped, managing a smile though each word was an effort.

She stood and rushed over to the southeast wall of books in the living room. The Gulf Coast section, composed of old and new books, maps, charts and brochures, filled both bottom shelves. She pulled out several Gulf of Mexico charts that covered the coastal areas of Louisiana, Mississippi, Alabama, and NW Florida. West had taught her to read charts as a child, and during his last few months, after cancer forced his early retirement from the Navy, he used every bit of energy to teach and share before his departure.

Seychelle spread a well-worn chart of the Alabama coast on the table and found their last position was less than 100 miles SW of Dauphin Island. "Did you run into an abandoned oil rig or a container that fell off one of the freighters, or did one of those big old tankers run you down? There must be traffic in that area. Didn't anyone see your life raft? Is there any chance you're still alive?" she demanded. "It's been almost three weeks!"

Clipped to the back of the notebook was a binder with Fiction crudely engraved on its front cover. Was that the name of their boat? The paper was different, the handwriting of Chianti, but not so cramped. She leafed through, shook her head. It looked like stories or chapters, each titled. She stopped at Ms. Frog Goes to Sea. Did you have kids?

She sighed, really missing her father and his wise, experienced observations. He understood her, could give words to her jumbled thoughts. She was not shy, but preferred sharing time with books, or Beauregard, to people. Well, except Geena. Ah, she would call Geena.

She made a tomato sandwich and topped up her tea before returning to focus on their book. "Please tell me where y'all are now," she whispered, studying that final entry with DR clearly noted. "I understand dead reckoning, but didn't you have SSB? You must have gotten fixes from your RDF, or were you using a sextant? You needed clear skies if you were relying on a sextant." She tried to remember what the weather had been of late, but realized with a start that she had no idea.

Seychelle followed the last four noted positions on her chart. "Oh, my goodness, they were coming up from the Caribbean!"

Seychelle had never used the local Coast Guard number West had insisted she enter in her little address book, but the time had come. She told the man who answered about the life raft.

"We'll check all reports and rescues and send someone to see the raft this afternoon. Y'all don't go messin' with anything," was his closing remark.

She frowned, hung up the phone and turned back to the book. Listed positions had Chianti sailing from Sint Maarten to Jamaica and up. "Wow, did you go to a Bob Marley concert? Or, maybe you sailed across to try some righteous weed!" She giggled, sobered.

"Wait, your last log entry was on the first page, but the journal," she bit her lip and flipped the book over, opened the back cover, leafed through a few blank sheets and read the note at the bottom of the last written page.

"I'm told the smuggling of grass is an honorable profession, made necessary by the misconception of governing bodies as to the powers they hold. I'm told as well that those of that calling are sometimes incarcerated, cursed, stoned. At this point I must quote Dylan, 'Everybody must get stoned.'"

"Oh, my goodness!" she gasped and grabbed the phone.

"You have just got to come over here, Geena! Don't ask questions, just come, and spend the night. You are just not going to believe what I have found!"

By the time Seychelle hung up she was convinced she could not give up the book, that she was on to an adventure, a quest of sorts. She turned back to it, and began leafing through. The attached notebook was labeled England and seemed to be lots of children's stories, peppered with notes and sketches. Did Chianti have a family on the boat?

Between the logbook and journal sections there were a few tabbed pages labeled Food, Medical, Tools & Parts, Books, Wine, and Music. The Food section contained lists for stocking the boat for voyages of a week, a month, or three months, but all were for just two people. "I'll read you later," she said.

No section for addresses or dates. "Maybe you are older, like West. He keeps, um, kept addresses and events in his old leather address book and everything else goes, um, into spiral notebooks."

She stopped, shook her head. Later, she thought, later I'll be ready to read things West has written. He had asked her to read his final notes, a memoir of sorts, as soon as she felt up to it, and had given her his key to their bank box, which she hadn't known existed. But she wasn't ready. Not yet.

She gave a deep, long sigh and sipped her tea. Anything like that would have gone down with their boat, or been left at home, if they had a home. Or, if personal stuff was kept in a little address book, like hers, it was probably kept in a pocket. She patted the outside pocket of her blue waterproof North Face backpack. West had started her with backpacks as a child, replacing each as needed. This one, and a larger one she'd used when backpacking around Europe after university, he had picked up on his last trip to California.

Seychelle again read the stoned paragraph and laughed. "Oh, Beauregard, this is going to be great!"

She turned to the thickest, unlabeled section and began leafing through. Fiction? Or, is this your diary? She forced herself to turn pages, to read a few lines and flip. Realizing she was not breathing, she closed the book and sat back.

Funny I've never really thought about the rest of it, that other world. We buy, we smoke, and we share. We know people get busted sometimes so we're careful. Friends tell of friends who have gone to Holland or Mexico and indulged openly. We fantasize about legal weed, unlimited smoking, what a beautiful world it would be. We love Cheech & Chong, The Beatles, Hendrix, Marley, Joni, Stones, Janis. Oh, to have gone to Woodstock!

Seychelle paced, sat. "I didn't tell the Coast Guard fella about the book because," she hesitated, shrugged. "Well, I'll just give it to whoever comes by."

She felt a little like a Peeping Tom, nosing around in someone's private life, something her Southern upbringing prohibited. Bad manners. But there was no turning back now.

"We're going to track them down, Beauregard. Chianti, she, or they might need our help. And, well, maybe I won't miss West so much if I get busy helping, doing something good. Fiction," she said and smiled. "We're going to go find them, yes we are. But don't you go telling folks." His tail thumped the floor in lazy compliance.

Crickets and frogs were making more music than seagulls by the time Sonny Jerken Jr. arrived. Seychelle watched him check over the raft. Middle-aged, cropped graying hair and close-set eyes, though no jowls and only a small overhanging belly, but his exaggerated drawl was there along with an attitude. Add that to the way he looked at her and you had a formula for mistrust. She had dealt with his kind all her life. Her mother's relatives were similar, and she'd avoided them. Even her mother had avoided them, according to West. West had classified such rednecks as just folks, not necessarily bad. He called radicals, like members of the Ku Klux Klan and religious extremists, damned fools.

She smiled. No, she wouldn't give this man Chianti's book. It had no bearing on finding them now and, she was pretty sure from the little she had read, they would be criminals in his eyes.

Back at Gulf Haven she gave him sweet tea on the front porch. "My partner was tellin' me about yer daddy," Sonny Jerken Jr. said as she handed him the survival sacks in the fishnet bag she'd brought back. "Real sorry to hear about him dying."

"Thank you," she murmured.

He pulled out his notepad. As he wrote he wore a wry smile. "This is an older raft, doesn't have a serial number that I could find. Pity. They've gotten a whole lot better, can't scrape the numbers off, easier to track down owners." He put the pen and pad back in his shirt pocket, and looked at her.

"There've been no rescues reported and no calls about missin' boats. Y'all are sure there was nothin' else in that raft?" he asked, studying her face.

Seychelle shrugged. "Not when I got there, but I don't know how long it has been on that beach. With Daddy's funeral, and everything that entails, I've not paid attention to anything else."

"No, no, of course not. I know it's been hard." He gave her a sad smile, stood and gave her his card. "I'll take these little ol' bags with me, get the boys to give 'em a goin' over. Might come back and' take a closer look at the raft, but it's all yours, finders keepers."

He thanked her for tea and for calling and started down the steps. At the bottom he turned to look up at her.

"The chances are good the boat was smugglin' people or drugs, else we probably would've heard somethin'."

"That's quite an assumption, Mr. Jerken," Seychelle stated. He was beginning to irritate her with his callous attitude and insincerity.

"Well," he drawled, "It just seems to be the way of things these days." He gave a slow scratch to short hair at the nape of his neck. "Mysteries tend to point to somethin' illegal."

She watched him walk out to his car, returning his perfunctory wave. Beauregard barked as his car moved away.

"Me too," she sighed, "I hope we don't see him again. Not even slightly interested in saving them or that they might be dead, just in the possibility that they were breaking the law."

She closed and locked the door and returned to the kitchen table, pulled the book out of the oven where she had stashed it, anxious to reenter Chianti's world.

She had formulated a plan by the time Geena arrived. They enlisted the help of everyone they knew in scouring the coast by boat and on foot. Knowledge of Chianti's possible cargo meant they didn't contact the press or police, but the Coast Guard actively searched as well.

After a fruitless week Seychelle presented her Caribbean plan to Geena, whose first reaction was, "Y'all been in the sun too long!"

Seychelle talked and reasoned with her friend for a few days, then presented her with a nonrefundable Delta ticket to Sint Maarten. With that they became co-conspirators, planning and giggling.

They sat on her front porch the night before departure. Seychelle slapped a mosquito that had begun feasting on her knee, ignored the bloody smudge that remained, and lifted her glass.

"To our quest!" she declared with passion. The high-pitched clink as her glass hit Geena's set Beauregard barking and the women laughing.

June's punishing heat had given way to a still, sticky evening. There was little relief from a large overhead fan and movement of the porch swing where they sat seemed to demand too much energy. They drank and stared down at the chart that covered both their laps.

"The Caribbean," Seychelle breathed, "we must take this seriously."

Geena shook her head. "Can't believe I let you talk me into this." They sobered, well as far as they could after over half a bottle of Mount Gay, and were silent for a moment.

"I feel a bit guilty, just locking up the house and taking off, but I've got to follow this up. West would understand and he would want me to find Chianti."

Geena smiled. "Yeah. Actually, he'd probably want to go with us!"

Seychelle threw her head back and laughed, took another long drink and declared, "Roots, Geena, y'all simply must start untangling them!"

"Now you're talking shit," Geena said, shaking her head.

"No, Geena, ya gotta go there! Ya gotta taste the local rum! I'm doing this for YOU!" she declared with a grand sweeping gesture. "You've never met your relatives in the islands!"

"Besides," she said with a sigh, "we've scoured the local area, as has the Coast Guard. Chianti didn't make it this far so we've got to go to the source." She lifted her glass again. "To the source!"

Geena didn't raise her glass. "You just remember tomorrow, not a word about this shit and definitely don't mention the phantom sailboat you're chasing. Mamma would blow an artery. She's already lecturing me about how lucky I am to have you financing my summer vacation with your inheritance. And how hard she's worked to raise five girls single-handed and pay for school for us all, and is saving to get me through this last year of college." She sighed. "And I better not get up to no foolishness!"

"And you've not even confided in her about how you're planning to continue into law school, have you?" Seychelle asked.

"No, and you don't. I'll tell her after I'm awarded that scholarship, but it's going to cost a whole lot more. I will make it work, somehow. Just don't you go giving her anything else to worry about."

"Trust me, my friend, I'll not take a chance on getting kicked out of the finest Sunday dinner in Alabama. Mamma's fried chicken is to die for and nobody can match Mamma's potato salad."

Seychelle drained her glass and recited, "I'm furthering my study of Developing Cultures, which I am, and we're going to visit some of your daddy's relatives, who you've been wanting to meet. After this summer break you'll return and finish your studies. No phantoms, just sun and sex and grass and reggae dancing!"

They both dissolved into uncontrollable laughter and the chart was christened and Mount Gay polished off.

Seychelle would often remember that night and the following day, in spite of her world-class hangover. It felt so good to be included in the closeness, love and friendship of Geena's family. She had been a baby when her own mother had died. As a kid she had fantasized that Geena's family would become hers. That Mamma and West would get married and they would all live together. Yeah, she'd been that naïve.

"See y'all in the fall," Seychelle called as she and Geena climbed into the airport shuttle that afternoon. That would become a mantra of sorts since in truth it was the beginning and the end of so much.

Three

"Il faut aller voir."
Jacques-Yves Cousteau.

Fiction. "Finally, we're connected. Four thousand pounds we'll take from Sint Maarten to Maine. It is just a matter of getting the right boat, and then we'll make the sail up and drop off the bales…approximately ten days, our first open ocean sail! Then, back to the Caribbean. It's a regular highway. Bales of grass are brought up by freighter or fishing boat from Colombia to one of the islands. Shipments are then divided up between boats and delivered Stateside. We've a marvelous collection of characters in the business. Bradford is a Massachusetts blueblood, late 20s, a real preppy with button-down collar and leather deck shoes. Story goes that he off-loaded his first shipment on the small dock of the family mansion on Cape Cod (the servants helped), but his mother insisted that he find other parts of the country thereafter. Big Bad John is a Texan with a massive red beard, a perpetual smile and twinkling blue eyes. He's sort of the main man for putting scams together, well connected. Dolphin Dave, compact and energetic, is a big operator as well and they sometimes work together. He has a boat-building business so can help everyone with repairs or alterations. Dialing for Dollars Dan (DD) lives up on a hill in a fancy villa. He's the laundry man for just about everyone who's made enough money to need his services. He flies regularly to Switzerland, Panama, and various islands in the South Pacific. The crew possibilities are Dirty Darren, Bandaid, Pierre the Frog, All Day Ray, Wolfman, Byron the Poet, Alfredo, and Richard the Heir. They live in the Caribbean through the winter, partying and working on their boats, and then crew or take their own boats Stateside in the summer. It's a great group and the parties are high affairs. There is in common a real enthusiasm for life as well as a love of the product and the business. No one is over 50 and everyone seems to have come up through the ranks. Shifting bales or selling by the ounce is the bottom rung. Of course, there's the element of danger, but that's part of the attraction. There are stories about busts, but not many considering it's been going on for years. I mean, the Caribbean was a grass super-highway in the '60s, and we are late joining in, but looks like the '70s will be more of the same!" Chianti.

Seychelle had gone to the library before they headed south and photocopied some of Chianti's journal, sandwiched the pages in with her Cultural Development research papers and tucked the lot with a couple of textbooks into her backpack. Though Geena refused to read the journal she did not plug her ears when Chianti read aloud.

"Isn't she interesting? Don't you want to find her and learn more, Geena? I mean, she is part of a subculture that has formed because of our laws, because of a lack of understanding. It's like we learned nothing from Prohibition!"

Geena snorted. "Most folks I know grow their own grass or buy from friends." She took a gulp of her Heineken, gave a healthy burp. "You said she did time in an English prison and her boyfriend, husband, whatever, is still there, but they were basing operations in Sint Maarten? So, you reckon you'll just be hangin' out and some old friend of hers will walk up to you and say, 'Hey, I hear you found the life raft that belongs to Chianti (or whatever her real name is) and I want to tell you all about her?'"

"No, the place has changed, gone all touristy. When they returned, after they'd sailed around the world and were in need of work, nothing was going on except the hard stuff. That they wouldn't touch. I just want to be places they were, get a feel for the life they were living. I mean, they had a radical plan."

"I'll give you that," Geena chortled. She waited until the stewardess replaced their empty bottles and moved aft. "I mean, hey, let's move to the Caribbean and see if we can run grass and make enough money to sail around the world. For real?"

"I've gotten to know Chianti and Sydney through her journal and I really like them. You would too. Like you, Sydney is a brain, studies and thinks about everything. Why don't you read it?"

Geena shook her head, the beaded braids around her face adding emphasis as they swirled. "One of us with an obsession is enough. Besides, I have vowed that I will not study until I return to school. I am seriously not serious about anything. I just want it on record that I reckon your Jerken Jr. is probably DEA and you're gonna be in deep shit if they find out you withheld evidence. I'm having nothing to do with the material you stole from that beached raft."

She looked at Seychelle's frown and gave her a wide, mischievous grin. "Y'all can just keep right on reading me sleepy-time stories, as I'm pretty sure it's all fantasy anyway. I mean, even she titled it Fiction."

Seychelle shrugged. "You might be right about him. I'd hate to think he's typical of the Coast Guard 'cause I still believe they wear white hats. But Chianti's stuff just feels true. If she felt hopeless, thought there would be no rescue, she may have sealed her journal in the box and shoved it into the raft 'cause she wanted her story told. I think I would in that situation. But I don't believe she made it into the raft, I think she went down with the ship. I doubt pirates 'cause they wouldn't have left the raft to go off attracting attention and questions. No, something went wrong."

They sat, silent, each distracted with questions and assumptions.

"Anyway," Seychelle continued, "I simply must find out what's going on, what happened, and if she, or someone, needs my help. I honestly do want to research how running grass is morphing into the drug trade. I know there's funding to be had if I can produce some copy about what's really going on now and what was going on that led to current problems. It dramatically affects so many poor countries, as well as our own. Do you realize people our age and younger are being sent to prison for having a few ounces of pot, for a joint or two of a weed that is used for making rope? Rich countries like ours go in and tell some guy who's finally able to feed, clothe and educate his kids that he should give up his cash crop of cannabis or poppies or cocaine and grow soybeans!"

Geena drawled, "It ain't me ya gotta convince, Honey-child. I'll do my part in helping out some poor farmers by purchasing as much local produce as I can smoke. My cousin Yolande wrote that she has a friend who grows fine stuff." Her burst of laughter was infectious and they turned to chatting about sampling locally grown grass and men.

Yolande was waiting for them at the airport. She wasn't as tall as Geena and of lighter skin, a soft fawn coloring, but in facial bone structure and long artistic fingers they were matched. As soon as Beauregard leapt from his travel cage, they became best buddies since she shared her ice water with him.

"Your first time here?" she asked Seychelle as she lit a spliff from the stack she had waiting for them in her car.

"First time in the Caribbean," Seychelle said, smiling as she accepted the joint, "but I may never leave!"

"We live in Phillipsburg, on the Dutch side," Yolande explained as she drove. "That's the southern half of the island. We have our own government but bad roads. The French side has good roads but is run by Guadeloupe. I'll take you over to Marigot while you're here. It's got some good restaurants and bars."

Seychelle was well settled into the back seat, smoking and listening to Yolande's singsong, soft clear voice. Beauregard sat on her lap with his head out the window, long ears flapping in the wind to the great entertainment of all they passed.

"How long have you been here?" Seychelle asked as she leaned forward to pass the joint.

Yolande and Geena looked at each other, burst into laughter. "Girl," Yolande cooed, "we have always been here. The French and Dutch came in 1648. They think they own the place now. Some old families like mine have held onto their land, but the big hotels offer good money. Our place has so many names on the title I'm not sure we could ever get it clear enough to sell if we wanted to. Which we don't," she stated firmly. "Everyone's scattered all over the world, ya know. Geena's family is the only branch I've contact with of the many that live in the U.S." She gave a warm smile and said, "And it is past time to get to know my cousin."

Within a few days Seychelle felt close to Yolande. She shared Seychelle's curiosity and enthusiasm for the adventures of Chianti and Sydney. She even got in touch with her friend, Seagull, who had been in The Business for many years, and he invited them to his place on the lagoon.

The rather shabby wooden house had a corrugated roof and neglected yard. It held appeal because of the mango-laden trees, swaying palms and vibrant pink bougainvillea that overran it. Parked in front were a beat-up rusty car and a brightly painted small bus of the type used to ferry people around the island with music blaring. It was not what Seychelle had expected of someone who was in The Business. Since Chianti hadn't mentioned any West Indians, she wondered if they worked separately, had their own scams.

She liked Seagull immediately. His smile was open and warm when he strolled out to meet them. Tall and skinny, perhaps in his 30s, he had an easygoing attitude but those dark intelligent eyes missed nothing.

"So, a couple of Southern belles have come south. Come on in, y'all." His mocking felt affectionate.

His house was in '60s hippie decor with huge pillows and Indian rugs on rough plank floors. Posters cluttered the walls and batik curtains framed windows and doors. They all relaxed with cold Heinekens and individual spliffs. Bob Marley filled the house, seemed to come from every crack, with depth and quality that could have only been achieved with high-tech sound equipment. Seychelle knew for the first time what experiencing music meant. She was consumed by it. There was no outside world and nothing else to think about. Time disappeared.

At some point Seagull satisfied their munchies with slices of fresh papaya and mango, all juicy and messy and delicious. Later he suggested they move out to the lagoon for sunset. They wandered down to a short pier behind his house, piled into a wooden dinghy and he rowed them to a speedboat that was moored about a hundred meters out.

"Yours?" Geena asked.

Seagull smiled, "Officially no, I'm boat-sitting for a rich American. But, yes."

The lagoon was tranquil. In the distance could be heard traffic, voices, the barking of a dog, a baby crying, gulls screeching. The stark blue midday sky had paled and softened with the acquisition of lush peach and rose streaks. Western horizon was blood red around the golden globe of the sun. Seychelle reflected that nothing seemed worth saying before such awesome beauty. Even Beauregard was subdued.

After a while Yolande broke the silence. "Seagull went to school in Florida. He has traveled and worked in various states, knows his way around," she smiled. "Tell him about your mystery smugglers, Seychelle."

A bit embarrassed, she gave him a quick outline. Seagull was casually listening, his long legs stretched out on the high-gloss aft deck.

"The story is further complicated because she didn't really give dates," Seychelle continued. "When they returned from their world voyage, they found the old gang had dispersed, so they got in touch with a Dutchman they had met in Gibraltar who had asked them to work for him. He wanted a load of hash taken from Morocco to Holland and he would supply the boat. He told them that in Europe grass was too bulky for safe import and not as profitable as hash or hard stuff. Their boat, *Cayenne*, was in bad shape by then so they left her here and flew over. Long story short, when they were sailing the load up, they were busted in the English Channel international shipping lane by the British and thrown into prison in England. They deported Chianti, flew her back to Atlanta after four years. Though they were co-defendants, the British court refused to accept Chianti's claim of equal responsibility, and kept Sydney six months more. I believe I have her journal, which includes children's stories, which she wrote while inside, and detailed accounts of some of their smuggling escapades, which she must have written while they were cruising, before the Moroccan run. She wrote a bit about the prison episode, but mostly about previous adventures."

Seagull's intense gaze belied his flippant, "And fiction is written all over it, names and dates changed, right?"

Geena laughed, "But our girl is a believer."

Seychelle shrugged. "It makes sense that she used fiction labeling and changed names to protect herself and all involved. The fact is that her life raft washed ashore. The Coast Guard said they couldn't trace it and with their drug paranoia you know their search was thorough. Jerken Jr. returned to question me twice after I reported finding it. I'm sure they ran a check on me. The thing is, there is no doubt someone tried to use that raft and I can't live with myself if I don't follow it up. If fiction is fact, Sydney is sitting in prison waiting to hear from her. How would you feel in that position?"

Everyone was quiet for a bit. The night sounds wrapped around them as each pondered the situation.

"What if she landed in the raft," Yolande asked, "and wandered off, amnesia or something?"

Geena gave an exaggerated groan. "That was my contention. Trust me, we recruited everybody for a search of the area as well as checking hospitals and churches. I even had friends from Alabama Southern college searching. One old hunter brought his hound but she was as useless as Beauregard. Most excitement that area has had since the last hurricane."

Seagull stretched, yawned and said, "I'll ask around."

Yolande leaned forward. "You know something, don't you?"

He smiled and stood. "Time to say good night, fine ladies. Me, I got places to go, things to do."

Four

Fiction. "We sold our beloved *Sea Dream* after two years of living and learning to sail on her. The 22 ft. sloop was built on Saint Kitts of marine ply and treated with epoxy resin so she performed like a wooden boat with the low maintenance of fiberglass. We had some marvelous adventures with her. She had none of the conveniences such as toilet, engine, lights, and running water, but we didn't need such frivolous amenities in the Caribbean. We used a bucket as a toilet, lugged water aboard in plastic jugs, bathed in the warm sea and enjoyed a diet based on tomato sandwiches. Life was good. However, we had to get a workable boat before The Boys would take us seriously. We made the down payment on *Cayenne* with ten grand from selling *Sea Dream*, ten saved from crewing on charter boats and from shifting bales, plus ten we'd received up-front for the run. The owners had not taken care of her and had been trying to sell her for years, so were willing to wait for the balance until after our run. *Cayenne* is a 1964 Sparkman & Stevens 40 ft. Swan. The quality design and construction of Swans from that era have earned them quite a reputation, especially in The Business. She came with a limited inventory of sails, old but in good shape, but no fancy electronics. Big Bad John, who organized the run, put on a SSB radio. Bradford gave us a Radio-Direction Finder that was supposed to get regular position fixes from a series of beacons. That was really nice, but one reason we invited Shasta along was that she had a sextant and could navigate in the old fashioned, reliable way. We would learn that valuable skill later, but in the Caribbean, we had simply needed a compass for getting island to island. We were also given some old foul weather gear, just in case. It was a group effort and everyone was great, though some were rather skeptical. It is said that no other couple has made the run, and no one could believe we were taking Australian Shasta as crew. She was new to the business, so we all had quite an adventure ahead of us.

"We anchored off Anguilla, a flat island of few inhabitants that lies NW of French Saint Martin. The small island was again under English rule, though that didn't matter to us on that dark, moonless night. I could just make out the masts of another boat on the other side of the bay. It had not been discussed, the attitude being that ignorance is the best defense in a bust, but I was fairly sure it was *Serendipity*, Bradford's wooden ketch. All was very quiet, the sea calm, but the wait was pure torture. I went below decks and made a final check. The whole of the interior we had covered with heavyweight clear plastic sheets and we used countless rolls of duct tape to securely seal all edges. Shake, the loose seeds and leaves that spill from burlap-wrapped bales, finds cracks and crevices in which to hide and has led to many a bust. The unmistakable smell that permeates everything can also be incriminating evidence. I covered all of the cushions with scented fabric softener sheets beneath the plastic, my innovation.

"I had just rejoined Sydney and Shasta on deck when there was a bump on the starboard side of the boat. We all three charged over. Big Bad John handed Shasta a painter and climbed aboard, followed by Reliable Rachel and Bandaid. They had rowed over in silence and not a word was spoken as we followed Big Bad John below, leaving Shasta, Reliable and Bandaid to keep watch. Sydney and I hovered behind Big Bad John as he sat at the navigation table, dialing and testing until tuned in to the assigned frequency. We listened to growls, static, whistles. We waited, barely breathing. Of a sudden the radio gave a loud crackle, and we all leaned in, attuned, willing communication. Then we heard clearly, 'I will be in your house tonight.'

"Big Bad John tapped the hand-held microphone twice, then three times, replaced it, stood, and returned topside. The three got into their dinghy and moved off into the evening, their departure as silent as had been their arrival. No one spoke above a whisper for the whole of that warm, still night. We waited.

"The big weathered fishing boat entered our bay with a stealth I would never have thought possible. Within minutes we were tied up to their port side, the other boat to starboard. The only sound was a steady hum from the fishing boat's big generator. It's crew, in the inelegant garb of poor fishermen, moved like dancers, in tune with the boat's layout and the job they were doing. Barely did we have time to position ourselves before bales began arriving, passed over from Colombians. Each bale was approximately a square meter, but they were packed by hand, roughly pressed and wrapped, so size and weight varied. Sydney received bales on deck, passed them to Shasta in the companionway, and she handed them down to me. I had scoped out a plan of sorts for where they would fit, but in the mad rush and with the irregular proportions it became a matter of simply stuffing them in wherever they would go. Fast and furious bales came down, the men anxious to leave. The outer burlap was wet on many bales. All were dirty. I was counting, as were Sydney and Shasta, but our tallies varied and I kept thinking that no more would fit, but they did. When the bales finally stopped coming, I was bruised, scratched, itching, sweating, filthy. My eyes burned, my back ached, my arms and legs trembled in exhaustion. Someone whispered, "Hurry, we've been here too long!" The silent bay was disturbed by the growl of diesels as we headed out. I could hardly believe only three hours had passed since we dropped anchor. I was on the bow as lookout, eyes well-adjusted to the dark, as we rounded the point. My heart stopped when I spotted a small inflatable close in by the rocks. I turned to warn Sydney, but the two guys waved, and I remembered there were always eyes posted in strategic spots throughout loadings and everyone was tuned to the same VHF radio frequency. No chitchatting, just strategic words and signs. Insurance.

"We watched and listened and motored due East toward the safety of the Atlantic for a few hours. As soon as we jibed and set sails on course North, we gathered in the cockpit for hot chocolate. We hugged, toasted and laughed. We did it!

"Sydney demanded, 'Did you see Jefe? He never moved, like something from an old black and white movie. He sat on the stern, smoking his small cigar, khaki shirt open to the waist with sleeves rolled up, brimmed hat pulled low. I wouldn't have believed it if I hadn't seen him myself.' Shasta gave a howl, laughed and said, 'I never got a good look at his face, but I'd have had him if we hadn't been in such a rush!' We had a good laugh and went below to do any necessary re-arranging to keep bales balanced. It was of vital importance that the safety and performance of *Cayenne* not be compromised. I longed to take photos of the scene below decks. We shifted and rearranged a bit so we could stand at the base of the companionway and sit at the navigation table. We had left the toilet behind so 4 bales fit in that space. A little muscling around the bales and we had a sleeping platform about three feet below the cabin top.

"We were all tired but Sydney stayed on helm and I kept bow watch as we were still running without navigation lights or sails to lessen visibility. We powered faster than we could sail in the light air so the only sacrifice was of fuel. Shasta slept and kept us fed until we got away from the dangers of land and fishing boats, then we hoisted sails and started taking three-hour solo shifts. We were under way!" Chianti.

Seychelle looked up at her enthralled audience.

Charlie nodded and said, "She was definitely there."

"Were you?" Seychelle asked before she could stop herself. "Sorry, never mind."

The balding, leather skinned, charismatic New Yorker's face closed. He turned towards Seagull. "Walk me to my car." He gave a small nod in her direction and was gone. He'd made it obvious he was only here as a favor to Seagull, who had met her just two days before, and she'd blown it.

Chastising herself, Seychelle went out the back door and down the dock to the end where Yolande sat, leaning against a piling. She had driven Seychelle over for this meeting.

"I'm an amateur," she sighed and plopped down on the rough wooden structure beside Yolande. Immediately there came a bark. Beauregard charged from the bushes and leapt upon her. Laughing, she wrestled with him, accepted his unquestioning affection, bad breath and all.

"What's he like?" Yolande asked in a low, tight voice.

Seychelle sat up, began stroking the dog's long ears to signal rest time. She had felt that Charlie was a kind of Godfather. He wore designer casuals and a Rolex. He had a presence, and seemed to fill the room. She had no doubt he was powerful and that grass was not the only thing in which he dabbled.

"A serious businessman," she said, and didn't feel she should say more. Seagull could answer questions. With Yolande he had avoided naming the friend who was coming and had asked her to wait on the dock before he arrived. The meeting had been just the three of them.

Yolande started to say something, stopped when they heard Seagull coming. He sat down next to them, stared up at the sliver of moon with its crowded bed of stars.

"So, how is your friend, Charlie?" Yolande asked without preamble.

Seagull darted a quick glance at her, and resumed contemplating the night sky. "We were lucky he was on the island since he doesn't come down very

31

often. He did enjoy that recount from the good old days. He was part of that time, but has moved on."

"Hard drugs?" Yolande asked with obvious disgust.

Seagull looked at her. "It is just business. Same as Europe. Grass doesn't pay anymore because of its bulk, too hard to smuggle in, and the sentences for any quantity are about the same as for drugs."

"Did he know her, them?" Seychelle asked impatiently.

"Yes, but not well. I don't know if he worked with them, he didn't say. He thought Chianti and Sydney were their real names. Their radio call sign was Rhythm & Blues. Legends of a sort. First couple to make a run, took only women as crew, made it through a hurricane with the first load, dropped out of the business to sail around the world. And, he was a brother."

Seychelle could see Seagull's smile in the darkness and thought it was a really nice smile. "What was so radical about that?"

He sucked his teeth in that West Indian way she'd tried to imitate the first time they had been to his house. They had been quite stoned and her efforts had them shrieking with laughter. "How many black men have you seen on yachts?" he asked, shaking his head.

She shrugged, embarrassed. "Hadn't really thought about it."

"Well, let me guarantee you that it is rare. Except cleaning and working for other folks doing charters," he said.

Yolande's derisive laugh was harsh. "Same as in almost all businesses. If it weren't for the laws protecting us here, every good job would go to white foreigners."

"What about you?" Seychelle asked Seagull. "What do you do in The Business?"

He chuckled. "You and your questions. I won't run from you like Charlie did, but let's just say I'm a coordinator here."

Seychelle felt her face color. "Sorry. But, was that all Charlie knew?"

"He heard that she was back alone looking for work and that she moved on to Jamaica, that's the best place for grass these days. Some shipments still move through here, but none of their old crowd remains. Everybody was happier when it was just weed coming through, though they didn't make as much money. Nobody got hurt and uniforms just ignored things or helped out."

"They get hurt now by getting hooked on the goods," Yolande flared. "They get hurt cheatin' each other. And they hurt innocent folks. If I caught anyone bringing drugs here, I'd turn them in."

Seychelle was startled by the fierce declaration. It was made more chilling by the passion in her soft voice.

"Go easy, little sister," Seagull said gently.

"One of the boys I was teaching overdosed last year. Thirteen years old. It should never have happened." She stood up. "I need to get home. Ready, Seychelle?"

"Uh, sure," Seychelle said, uneasy. "Seagull, who would I talk to in Jamaica?"

He leaned toward her. "The last I heard, there was a German called Hans based in Port Antonio who organized stateside shipments. I've got a cousin there. I'll call him, see if he can help you."

Seychelle gave him a quick kiss on the cheek. "Thanks."

He chuckled. "If you want to hang out, I can run you back when you're ready to go."

She hesitated, did want to stay, and was trying to think why she shouldn't when Beauregard's barking interrupted. Growling, he charged into the bushes. A loud grunt came from that direction and it was obvious he was chasing a man. Seagull jumped up just as a loud splash was heard above the barking. Seychelle followed him through thick growth that covered the finger of land that jutted out into the lagoon. They had just reached the other side when a large engine started. They watched the powerboat take off, sending up a rooster tail of spray as it banked to starboard.

Seagull's curse was barely above a whisper.

"Who was it?" Seychelle asked as she bent to quiet Beauregard.

"Police boat. They must have been trailing Charlie. I'll have to let him know."

"Why not you?" asked Yolande as she came up behind them.

"French flag. They wouldn't have come into the Dutch side for a local." He stared after the boat that had devastated the tranquility of the lagoon. "You two had better get going."

He walked them to the car. "Fine watchdog," he said with a smile. "If you ever need a sitter, let me know."

33

"I'd like to head for Jamaica as soon as possible," Seychelle told him as she got in.

"I'll come by," he promised.

"Don't come to my house," Yolande snapped without looking at him. She got behind the wheel and slammed her door. "Call if you want to talk to her." Rocks flew as they sped away down the narrow dirt road.

Seychelle was unsure what to say so started looking through the cassettes for something to put on.

Yolande hit the wheel with her fist. "I can't believe he works for that bastard Charlie!"

"But he didn't say he did, he just asked Charlie over to talk to me about Chianti."

"Seychelle, Charlie's a muck-a-muck, top of the heap. No way would he have been at Seagull's house if they were not working together. Just business, he says. I have known Seagull all my life. He's the grass source for everybody I know, but it's never occurred to me that he might handle drugs. I'll have nothing more to do with him."

She looked at Seychelle. "Charlie's trick is to pay the guys that work for him with product. That's mostly crack, though they say he'll handle anything. That is how it gets on the island. I don't care what he does elsewhere, but this is my home, my people."

Neither spoke for a while. Seychelle tried several tapes that wouldn't play. She made innocuous comments about the poor quality of cassettes, the problem with humidity, big business shipping inferior quality products to developing countries. She finally gave up and just stared out the window.

Yolande gripped the wheel, her jaw set firm. When she parked in front of her house, she stated in a flat voice, just above a whisper, "He's gotta be stopped."

Five

Fiction. "The Atlantic welcomed us with a series of storms. Not really a problem except the engine died. We were three days into our 1800-mile voyage, very tired, and all in the dark about repairs. Sydney was the most mechanically inclined so spent the most time standing on his head in efforts to coax the damned thing into action. That meant shifting bales out of the way, not an easy job in a heaving sea in a boat that prefers life at a 45-degree angle. The engine was rather important since it charged the battery that ran the instruments, navigation lights, and radio. Also, getting into Maine and up the river without an engine would not be a piece of cake with coastal traffic and radical tidal flows.

"Wind lessened, and then died, leaving the sails bagging and flopping under burning sun as the undisturbed Atlantic's surface became a desert. We had no awning so stretched a sail over the main cabin to try to keep it cool and moved bales up into the cockpit, allowing room for working on the engine. Dolphins danced around our bow. Graceful, smiling and powerful, they lifted our spirits. Shasta picked a hole in the corner of one of the bales and plucked out some grass for us. I was on helm and… Oh damn! I heard a plane!

"Well, that was a bit of excitement. Three times we hauled out bales and frantically shifted them below again over a two-day stint of no wind and flat seas, but we never saw the planes that we heard. Still no engine but the wind was building. We even put a reef in the mainsail. With no instruments or lights, we kept a close eye on the compass, recording with religious fervor, very aware that dead reckoning was a bit of a coin toss in building seas. It turned out that Shasta had slightly exaggerated her navigational skills, so I did extra time on helm while Sydney worked with her. Luckily, he studied to be an engineer before leaving it all behind to become an adventurer on the high seas, so was able to get his head around the sextant and necessary equations.

"We cheered when rain cooled us and wind filled the sails. They even got an accurate position fix with the sextant and we were only a mile off in our dead reckoning estimate! But the barometer reading dropped as wind increased and the sea began pushing up whitecaps. Aye, we were at sea, pure sailing with naught but a compass, and a storm's a buildin'. Then came the discovery that water was getting into the boat. We did some serious bale shifting as we ferreted around in search of the source, taking turns on the hand pump. Thankfully, it was just around the prop shaft, nothing damaged, but we had to keep pumping regularly as nothing we tried stuffing around it stayed. We called it a squall but were left with a tear in the bottom of the main, shredded genoa, confused seas, and cold wind from the NW. Underestimating that tempest was costly. Our sticky-backed sail tape was useless on wet sails and we had no sail repair kit. By the time we got the main reefed and replaced the genoa with a Yankee, clouds had gathered in war-council, darkening the entire western horizon and we hustled to replace that headsail with a storm jib. We recognized how serious our situation was when the volume of the wind far exceeded the howl in the rigging created by a 30 knot blow. Gusts came from both NW and S and barometric pressure dropped to 955. Hurricane? We had weathered a few in the Caribbean but that was in protected anchorages. Changes were happening too quickly. We slept on the bales between our shortening watches, but everything was wet and the temperature was dropping. We secured a third reef in the main and started each watch with a crawl to the foredeck to check rigging, chafe, etc. We were steering WNW but the waves were growing, pushing us more north. Shasta declared we had an ass-kicker building.

"Down to bare poles, heading east by morning. Well, my watch said it was morning, though the world was so dark I had doubts. With numb fingers I was trying to keep us riding waves, to keep us from being rolled. Yes, we all contemplated tossing the cargo but where would you start, how would you keep *Cayenne* balanced? We dared not use the radio, and had to save what little power was left in the batteries for calling The Boys when closer to the coast. Yes, this was the edge of a hurricane, and we were heading out into the North Atlantic with seas well above the mast and wind exceeding anything we had ever known. We'd passed the point where actual measurement was possible. I could hear nothing but a perpetual roar and couldn't tell if the water breaking over my head and flooding the cockpit was rain or the sea. My Caribbean wardrobe of bikini and tee-shirts didn't layer well under the worn-out rain jacket someone had donated, and after four, or was it five, days in the same soaked outfit I was unaware of parts of my body. We were down to watches of an hour or less. We never removed anything, not even our safety harnesses, and we never stepped out the companionway without hooking on to something. Sydney reached for logical optimism to deal with our worsening situation. Shasta cracked jokes and made dirty comments to bring her fear under control. I had to keep a serious guilt trip at bay so obsessively focused on each detail, each task, convinced that getting us to land, to safety, was my responsibility. I had stocked the galley with little money, limited resources in the islands, and my unrealistic plan was to sprout and bake. There was no fridge and the gas bottle that was strapped down on the aft deck had leaked, so no cooking. Everything that could grow mold did.

"So, going on watch we had Nescafe instant coffee with sugar, powdered milk and water. Going off, we replaced the coffee with Dewar's scotch. The concoctions were surprisingly warm and filling when approached with conviction." Chianti

"On that note, I think it's time for jerk chicken and beer," Geena declared.

Seychelle tucked the file into her backpack. "I'm with you. Just reading the account makes me tired and hungry."

They stepped out the front door of Brian's house onto the plank walkway and turned right, a few steps taking them into Junior's Jerk Chicken Bar. Seychelle decided all memories of Jamaica would be wrapped in the ever-present smell of jerk spices, of cinnamon & peppers & thyme, accompanied by reggae from scattered Rasta boxes. It seemed everybody had one, but they weren't competing, rather crossing and combining, a maze of reggae tunes wafting from every direction, echoing the pace of life, the attitude.

She sat down on a shaky folding chair at a stable but scarred wooden table that faced the door. Beauregard settled at her feet, though his gaze stayed riveted on the back door leading out to where birds were sizzling over charcoal.

Geena grabbed a couple of cold Red Stripes from the noisy ancient fridge in the corner. "You will soon meet your chicken," she declared. "Lord, this table's seen a lot more of life than have we. Where is our tacky pink and green flowered plastic tablecloth?"

"Relax and drink, you spoiled Yank," Seychelle ordered and they clinked bottles. The beer was good in the midday heat. "What do you think of Brian?"

"Nice ass," Geena quipped, giving a crooked smile. "I don't know what Seagull told him but I like the warmth of our reception. We're not going to make much of a dent in your inheritance if folks keep taking such good care of us."

"Yeah, a charming house in the center of Port Antonio. Hot and rough but the fan works, and it's ours. He said he's staying with his family. Think that's wife and kids or parents?"

Geena stretched, "I don't think it matters much. This is the West Indies, not the sanctimonious South with its pristine Protestants of hypocritical purity."

"Goodness gracious me, y'all are so right," Seychelle drawled. They were still laughing when Junior came in to cover their table with a plastic cloth and chicken and roasted breadfruit. He even presented a cooked but naked and boneless morsel to Beauregard whose tail beat the floor furiously.

"I've died and gone to heaven," Geena declared as she wiped sauce off her chin with the back of her hand.

"Don't get too full," Brian ordered from the doorway. They both looked up, mouths full and chicken in hand. The sun highlighted his two gold incisors when he laughed. "Me like seein' women enjoy their food."

Geena motioned with her drumstick for him to join them. Junior automatically handed him a Red Stripe as he sat down.

"I hope you brought some fancy rags 'cause tonight we're Hans's guests at the Trident." His deep rich voice dropped an octave when he confided, "Finest place in all Jamaica, is where the Queen stays when she comes to visit."

"Why are we getting the special treatment?" Seychelle asked. "Did he know Chianti?"

"All he says is that he met her. But I tell him you fine American ladies and you like my ganja plenty and that Seagull sent you. 'Well, we'll do it right,' he say." Brian's perpetual smile widened. "Be a good night, yeah."

The sun was beginning to slip away when they arrived at the stately white-columned Trident.

Geena sighed. "I hadn't realized the ostentatious mansions left scattered around the South by gentlemen of the Confederacy had been inspired by the colonizing English. Tacky but appealing, pretentious but graceful."

Seychelle laughed. "And Leroy's limo is just perfect for the occasion."

Leroy's taxi was an ancient Ford that seemed like a demolition derby reject. Seychelle reckoned he'd recently done the green, gold and black paint job without his glasses. The back seat was a low-rider, through use not design, so her eyes were even with the bottom of a window that wouldn't close in a door that wouldn't open. She smiled. How West would have appreciated the scene.

The liveried doorman was unruffled when the door wouldn't respond to his white-gloved hand and moved smoothly around to Geena's side. She emerged in a minimalist black dress and rainbow gossamer shawl; her sleek cornrows dotted with tiny golden butterflies. Brian unfolded from the passenger seat; his pink shirt only slightly creased. A heavy gold chain and one dangling crystal earring combined with his elbow-length dreads to create an exotic aura. Seychelle felt rather wholesome next to them with her loose brown curls and jade cotton halter dress. She undid a few more pearl buttons to reveal a bit of cleavage before climbing out after Geena.

They were led through a formal entry hall out French doors to a lushly foliaged patio. Smooth low boulders served to hold the Caribbean's perpetual motion at bay. They walked across soft plush grass toward a delicate white gazebo. It's fine latticework framed the tall blonde German who stood watching dark clouds consume the tangerine horizon. He turned to face them as they stepped up into the gazebo.

Seychelle extended her hand. "Hello Hans, I'm Seychelle." Waves gave a soft swoosh as they caressed rather than broke on the rocks below them.

He took her hand, raised it to his lips as he stared into her eyes. She willed herself to neither blink nor look away from those cool blue-green eyes, but unease quickened her breathing.

"This is my friend, Geena," she said and was relieved when he released her hand and shifted his intensity.

Composed and in control, Seychelle surmised as she watched him repeat the procedure. He was going for effect in his deck shoes, tight jeans, and black tux jacket with ruffle-front white shirt left open at the neck. She thought his oversized turquoise belt buckle accentuated his vanity, though it was possibly a gift from an adoring female. He looked like a collector.

Geena's melodious laughter broke the impact of that initial encounter. "Well now," she mocked, "if that's the way y'all greet ladies in Germany, I may just have to visit!"

Though his lips were thin, his smile was pleasant, the teeth so very white, and Seychelle thought of an ad for men's cologne.

"I didn't know they produced such foxy ladies in the South. I was speechless," he teased and gave a hint of a bow.

"I'm gonna try those moves sometime," Brian said and they all laughed.

A waiter appeared and opened champagne. They toasted and talked of the sunset and Jamaica and the hurricane that had just entered the Caribbean. Seychelle was enthralled by the humorous Jamaican rhythm of Brian compared to the clipped precision of Hans's accent and Geena's warm drawl.

After finishing the first bottle, they meandered into the restaurant. They were seated at the central table beneath a crystal chandelier. Gold flatware, gold edged bone China and fine crystal were before them. White-gloved Jamaican waiters surrounded them.

"What do you think?" Hans asked Seychelle.

"In honesty, it reminds me of the old South and I feel a bit ill at ease."

Geena's laugh was affectionate. "Dear Seychelle has a guilty conscience about her cotton-farming slave-keeping ancestors and the ignorant prejudice that lingers on."

Hans shrugged. "If it hadn't been for them you might not have your beautiful friend Geena here with you now." He reached over and stroked Geena's hand. "And that would be a terrible loss."

Brian chuckled, "Yeah, you're gonna have to teach me some of those moves!"

They laughed and toasted and the evening proceeded, relaxed and congenial. Seychelle knew she didn't trust Hans but that didn't really matter as long as he answered her questions. There was a sarcastic feel to his demeanor, or was it cynical? His blatant flirtations with Geena were like a game and she simply laughed at him.

"I am not a sailor," Geena was declaring as she made short order of a fresh grilled lobster in its rich, tender perfection. "I do believe there could be no worse death than in the teeth of a shark and I've no intention of proving the point."

"There are some who propound that they've an unjust reputation. I know I'd prefer death at sea than in a prison," Hans stated.

"Ah prison, that's another matter. Those of a spiritual inclination are inclined to put themselves in prison-like situations for purification, self-knowledge. After that they reckon death is just a transition. So, prison can mean peace and total contentment," Geena said.

"I don't take you to be a romantic nor an acceptant of religious dogma. I hold that peace and contentment are so individualized that one could find them while tripping on mushrooms as likely as another in the act of sex or smoking Brian's herb or reading a book or sitting in a subway. Embracing death with a smile does not necessarily follow." He was looking around the table at each of them as he spoke.

Seychelle shrugged, "Hard to imagine any state other than debilitating terror while watching a shark give that final arch of its body before attack."

"I been there," Brian chuckled, "an' you gotta be sick to find peace in that!"

"Show the ladies," Hans said with a smile.

Brian shrugged, undid two buttons of his shirt to reveal a thick slash across his shoulder. Then he slid back his left sleeve. Seychelle's stomach clinched at his mangled lower arm. She realized for the first time that his four fingers had to move as one so only his thumb had independent movement.

"How did it happen?" Geena asked, eyes large behind her thick lashes.

"Him wanted the snapper me speared," he stated. "Was a kid."

"But you still spear fish," Hans said.

"Of course," his white and gold smile flashed. "We both got a right to the fish."

Geena cleared her throat. "I've never tried magic mushrooms. Do they grow here?"

Hans threw Brian a side eye and both gave naughty-boy grins.

"I suggest that tomorrow we take you to one of the natural wonders of the island, Reach Falls," Hans said. "It's a short drive and walk. Brian can supply the mushroom brownies to enhance your experience." He did not wait for a reply but spoke softly to the waiter who had appeared at his side.

Geena gave Seychelle her amused-quizzical crooked smile with one lifted eyebrow.

"So, Brian, you're a brownie baker and you learned from your mother, right?" Seychelle asked.

"Make you smile when you eat them, 'cause they taste good, and make you keep smilin', 'cause you have a nice trip," he beamed.

Their cognacs were warmed with ceremony and caramelized bananas were even more of a production. Then they moved out to the rough stone terrace where three locals did some Bob Marley tunes and rapped about how 'you can't get rum and coconut water in America.'

Seychelle could wait no longer. She leaned over to Hans, touched his arm. "Could we talk?" she asked and nodded toward a low stone wall with a backdrop of massive bougainvillea bushes. He gave a small nod, stood and followed her.

"Stars get closer as one gets further south, have you noticed?" he asked.

She glanced up at the cluttered sky, nodded. "Gorgeous. I don't know how much of the story Brian has told you, but I'm trying to track down Chianti, a woman whose life raft I found on the Alabama coast, close to my home."

Hans stopped her. "I met the woman, that's all. Why did you think I might be able to help you?" His casual tone seemed an effort.

Seychelle raised both hands in denial. "I'm not trying to do anything or get any information about anything but tracking down Chianti, Hans. I've given Seagull the whole story, he contacted friends around Sint Maarten and the consensus was that she couldn't get work there so came here. Seagull sent me to Brian and said that perhaps you could point me in the right direction. He wasn't sure you were still on the island. If you want the whole story, well, tomorrow we'll have time."

"Yes, I think I would enjoy hearing your story. Tomorrow." He turned and walked back to their friends.

Seychelle watched him retreat and reminded herself to move with care. This one could be dangerous. She studied the stars as if expecting them to tell her something. Finally, she shrugged and rejoined the group.

Six

Fiction. "I climbed out the companionway, slammed the slider back into place, though it seemed a futile effort as the cockpit was flooded. My first task in relieving Sydney was to manually pump the bilge. Though only 6 ft. away, I could not see his face. Behind him was a wall of water, topless waves that I had almost convinced myself to ignore since they were always there, never ending, a force of nature that can't be imagined. I attached myself to a cleat and stepped aft through butt-deep water to press my ear to his lips. Hoping I had not understood, but knowing I had, I patted my pouch pocket where I had stashed several short lines in prep for just this sort of task, for we were perpetually securing gear, trying to minimize losses. Turning, I crawled forward, finding handholds and reattaching my harness clip every couple of feet until I reached the mast and wrapped my lanyard around it. With care I grabbed the wildly flapping mainsail tack, hooked it over the gooseneck, and secured it. Hugging the mast with arms and knees, I stood but could see only rain and white foam, until I looked down into…nothing. *Cayenne's* bow was unsupported. Well, actually, her entire front half was airborne, held aloft on the crest of a bottomless wave. I was mesmerized. Only after I slithered aft on my belly and took the helm from Sydney did I register how close to the edge was our existence. That watch may have been the longest hour of my life as I felt each wave lift us, try to discard us. One small jerk of my hand, an inattentive moment, would have delivered us to the violent, hungry North Atlantic.

"After three days that seemed three lifetimes, we were able to turn and head to the West with our damaged main reefed to handkerchief size and the storm jib. When we got close enough to the coast for radio contact Sydney reached The Boys on first try. They cheered, were so relieved and we were ecstatic that they were waiting, hovering over the radio. They told us Hurricane Gretchen wreaked havoc all along the coast and several ships had gone down.

43

We were lucky. Then they asked what we would like to eat upon arrival. We'd already voted. Pizza!

"Sydney said, 'Oh, and someone must take care of my horny crew.' Shasta's chapped face reddened even further when from the radio came, 'With pleasure!'

"In celebration, and since we were starving, we opened an unlabeled can we found in the bilge. Tasteless black pitted olives, yuck. They didn't want to hear another apology for lack of food. So, heavy with guilt, I mixed our drinks. Dewars was running low. We were so very cold, hungry, and tired. But spirits were high. We and our boat and our cargo had survived!" Chianti.

Seychelle closed down, looking up at the powerful waterfall. "I don't suppose the waves looked anything like that. They would have been curling up above, as if in preparation for attack."

Hans nodded. He had refused to have brownies with them, claiming the need for one clear head in their group. Seychelle was now reconsidering her mistrust of him, thought perhaps she was paranoid. He felt solid, protective, and she wanted to share everything about Chianti with him. She was sure Sydney was quite different from cool, distant Hans. Sydney was intelligent but warm and sensitive, and he and Chianti were very much in love. She couldn't imagine Hans really in love with anyone. "That doesn't mean he's a bad person," West would have responded.

"She certainly makes the experience sound real," Hans was saying.

"I'm sure it was," Seychelle declared.

She tore her gaze from the radiant colors of the waterfall, and looked at Hans. "Won't you tell me what you know?"

He gave her a slow smile. "I'm asking around, give me a few days."

"But, what if she did survive, is in trouble somewhere. What about Sydney, sitting in prison in England, worrying, waiting? Can you imagine being in his position?"

Seychelle began pacing, felt the rush of the brownies, perspiring though it was cool there in shade under waterfall spray. She stopped at the mouth of a shallow cave, wondering if there were bats. Everything was covered with growth of some kind, even rocks were clothed in moss, nurtured by perpetual mist and slivers of sunlight that filtered through and defused in all directions. A section of blue sky was directly above them but cluttered earth rose high with thick foliage seeming intent on closing it out. Hidden was the narrow winding path they had gingerly followed down that morning. They were inside a great nest. Water reflected a multitude of greens as it tumbled down and became tranquil. Geena and Brian were seated on submerged boulders midstream, providing an audience for nature's grand display.

Hans touched her arm. "Have you seen the hummingbird?" He turned her gently, directed her toward a boulder that lay between the cave and water's edge.

"Oh my," Seychelle breathed and knelt beside a flat-topped rock. In loving detail someone had etched a hummingbird in flight. It seemed alive, hovering. She felt Hans behind her. He stroked her hair, lifted and gently pressed her loose curls. She took long deep breaths, wanted to take in the whole of the scene to keep, to store and re-enter later. All senses were engaged, stimulated. She jerked upright.

"Camera!" she yelled, and charged over to where their backpacks lay.

Hans was right behind her, took the Nikon from her hand as soon as she removed it from the bag. To her shocked face he said firmly, "I don't like photos of me. I'll do the work. Go over to the waterfall."

She started to argue, to declare her credentials, but stopped herself. He's a smuggler, she told herself, so of course he'd get nervous. Chill. She watched him, he was comfortable with it, and was getting the hummingbird from a good angle.

Seychelle joined Geena and Brian in the water and became quite uninhibited in front of the waterfall. Hans used up an entire roll of film on them frolicking naked in the cold water. They became dolphins, then statues, then frogs, a pyramid, monsters, all the while shrieking and laughing. Beauregard, totally wrapped up in investigating the area, charged back to bark and dance around with them.

They all seemed to become chilled at the same moment. They charged out of the water into a patch of sunlight to dry and dress. They were subdued.

"I wish Chianti and Sydney were here," Seychelle said wistfully as she rubbed and shook her wet hair.

"I wish I had a hot chocolate," Geena said as she stretched.

"Well, I wish someone would share my spliff," Brian said through a cloud of smoke. He immediately became the center of attention. Hans stowed the Nikon and joined in the sharing. There followed enthusiastic, inspired dialogue about the magic, the grandeur and the spirituality of Reach Falls.

45

Seven

Fiction. "There was just a whisper of dawn when we arrived at the mouth of the river. We tensed when a small wooden skiff approached, but the two guys were relaxed, their welcome warm. They handed over a small radio, which was to be kept on, they said, in case we needed directing or warning. We followed them, barely breathing, with all senses alert, the incoming tide our ally. After a few quick tacks and some very tense moments we managed to make it to the assigned cove without need of a tow or radio. A wholesome blonde in an open fishing boat pulled alongside as we dropped both sails. He maneuvered our bow toward a fog-cloaked bank where we dropped anchor. Without wind or engine, we couldn't set it properly, but we trusted our guide. He gave Sasha a smile, a wink and a bulging plastic bag, and then disappeared around the bend. Without hesitation we charged into the cockpit, ripped it open, stripped and donned warm, dry jogging pants and sweatshirts. What a difference! There were doughnuts (without doubt the best I've ever eaten in my entire life), as well as thermoses of coffee and hot chocolate. Blessings be upon all of you!

"The sky had taken on a hazy glow by the time an old powerboat approached through thinning fog. The bearded captain motioned us into his boat and in silence took us half a mile further up-river.

"It all felt quite clandestine but never at any point did I feel I was doing anything wrong. Getting away with something, yes, and that gave a sort of mischievous satisfaction. Sydney and I had discussed the possible ramifications of a bust, but we both were doing exactly what we wanted to do, had set out to do, and we were quite high from our success that morning. When we stepped out onto the grassy, solid, bank, Bradford was waiting. His familiar face convinced me we really had arrived. Whew!

"He drove us to a traditional New England house in the hills, seemingly without neighbors. Three enormous, hot pizzas were waiting for us. I found the smell and the look of them intoxicating. Someone must have been really connected to score fresh deli pizza at sun-up on a Sunday! But they were barely touched. I managed one piece, pepperoni and all, but I had trouble keeping it down. My stomach was not ready for spices, oil, and meat. A fire was blazing, there were lines on the table and Steely Dan added perfect harmony. A clear acrylic pepper grinder and two white rocks were placed before me and I was assigned line production. That felt about the limit of my capabilities, to be honest. There was a family feel to the gathering of ten, which included Wolfman and Reliable Rachel from the Caribbean. Bradford, carrying a bottle of Dom Perignon and two glasses, led Shasta away to a bubble bath, ignoring the howls and cheers. We looked rough, but our bodies were fit after the extreme workout. I was down to the size I had been in my teens and was hungry for a good feel of Sydney's fit trim body. In fact, we dubbed that run The Diet Cruz, and may market it. Only scammers may apply. We survived Gretchen and delivered the shipment intact, hopefully dry, so we three had improved standings in the eyes of our peers. And, we felt pretty damned good about ourselves.

"It seemed Bradford was the conductor for that section of the symphony. Nevertheless, as in the Caribbean, there was no boss feel. Everyone was working together, so the lines blurred between job descriptions. We spent the day at the house, relaxing and telling of our voyage. That first hot shower was positively orgasmic! Amazing how quickly discomforts and dangers took a back seat. Of course, the quality coke and being in the spotlight may have enhanced the thrill of survival and heady flush of success. We were even beginning to plan for our next sail.

"What drives sailors after such abuse? Is it a search for the ultimate adversary? Or, the desire for the high of nature's unleashed power? Or, is there an in-born need for life on the edge? Whatever, I could have readily set sail immediately. However, we needed to off-load the cargo, *Cayenne* needed cleaning and an overhaul, and we needed some rest. Oh, and to be paid.

"They took us back to the boat just after sunset. The dark quiet of the river was eerie as we waited for offload. Bradford assured us that *Cayenne* was closely watched throughout the day and all was well, that the entire area remained clean. Though we trusted his control, we were exhausted so uneasiness crept in as midnight approached.

"They came in silence. The three were in black, baklavas to boots, even their open powerboat was black, and their rowing was precise. Their appearance beside *Cayenne* startled us. It took whispered reassurance from the one who had ferried us earlier to spur us into action. No longer the rank amateurs who had stumbled through loading, we tied them alongside, got into position and began the relay of bails. The first few are wet and heavy, my movements uncoordinated, but a low urgent, 'Hurry!' from the companionway got my adrenaline pumping. We had rhythm, we had energy, and before long we had an empty boat. The guys gave us quick hugs and whispered, 'Congratulations!' Kneeling on bails, they put oars in the water and were absorbed by the night.

"They left with us a generator for charging our batteries and a shop-vac for the big cleanup. We filled garbage bags with plastic sheets, tape and the layers of clothes we wore throughout the voyage. We scrubbed her out and washed the deck, and had barely finished when two guys in an inflatable pulled alongside and handed us a couple of heavy garbage bags. We gave them the shop-vac, generator, and all our rubbish. Quick hugs, though in fact we hadn't met, and they were gone.

"We took the bags below, excited and curious. In the first we found bread and cheese, cereal and milk, bagels and cream cheese, fruit and yogurt, as well as a thermos of hot coffee. Solid food was so welcome. They had made the run up from the Caribbean at some point so understood our needs, though we were the first accompanied by a hurricane. We were being cared for as friends, and it felt so very good. Ravenous, we attacked without cocaine to hamper appetite. The sun was making a determined effort by the time we turned to the second bag. Reliable Rachel had taken our slimmed-down measurements and gone shopping for us in the afternoon. We looked and felt different in yachting attire, were clean and prepared for inspection. Sydney cleared in by radio and explained that our engine was down. The officer told him to stop by the immigration office before sunset tomorrow to show them our papers and get Shasta's passport stamped. 'No problem,' Sydney agreed. We were so relieved we would not need to withstand close scrutiny, so radioed Bradford. Within minutes a small fishing boat slowed as it passed and handed us another heavy garbage bag. We took it below and opened it in silence. I lifted out a cold bottle of Dom Perignon and Shasta pulled out its closed box. What a picture our faces must have been when she lifted the lid and we beheld neatly banded stacks of hundred-dollar bills! With trembling fingers, in silence, we each took a few bundles. We felt it, fanned it, sniffed it. They were old, soft, well-used bills.

We counted them. Three boxes. Ninety thousand dollars. Shasta giggled. Sydney just kept smiling. They would give us the rest later, after weigh-in. 'We've done it!' I whispered, and we went mad. We laughed, cried, hugged, danced, howled, and drank champagne from the bottle. We were kids, we were fools, we were delirious. It was an incomparable experience!

"Since then I've asked others about their first run, but no one seems to have been as intensely affected by the moment. Of course, we had survived a hurricane. Sydney was as giddy as Shasta and I. He had grown up without a father and his mother died when he was young. He said, 'I was pushed further, had to give more of myself, than ever in my life. I loved the challenge. All my life I'd dreamt of facing a storm at sea. We survived and got paid for it! The bonus is that our group of scammers is virtually an extended family.' Shasta grew up in a poor farming family so that cash salute to our success was a major landmark in her life. Her plan was to go home and buy a farm. And for me, well, I guess rainbows became reality." Chianti.

Seychelle stretched out, rested her head on Beauregard's smooth brown and auburn back. He groaned, his tail thumped the teak deck a couple of times and he went back to sleep.

"That did not come from anyone's imagination," she said with conviction. "They took that shipment into the States. The entire file is full of similar stories though this first run is my favorite. I've gotten to know Chianti and I must find out what has happened. If she survived, she may need help. If not, well, Sydney needs to be found and told."

She sat up, stared at Hans. "Did she take a load for you?" she demanded.

He was sitting on a sail-bag under the awning. He wore a colorful batik sarong around his hips, designer sunglasses, and a thin smile. He took a sip of his mineral water. "Let's just say."

"This is not a game!" Seychelle burst out. "Let's just say I wish she had been working with the same group she did on that first run. They would care what was happening with her. They would have followed up. It wouldn't take some stranger who'd found her empty life raft to get the search going. You're so busy covering your own ass you don't care!"

Geena, who was still in Hans's bunk in the aft cabin, poked her head up through the open hatch. "Now, Seychelle, I do think y'all are a bit out of line. Hans has known us for less than three days. Maybe he doesn't trust us yet." She turned her large dark eyes on Hans in a most soulful gaze.

He sighed, shrugged, "I only supply. This island is my area of operations. She had only her reputation and *Cayenne*, not even a crew since her partner was inside. I am not as bad as you think, Seychelle. I fronted her 100 kilos of grass on top of the hundred she purchased, even though normally I only deal in payment up front in cash or bearer bonds. I told her to get the money to me before the end of the year."

"And you've not heard from her? Where was she going?" Seychelle asked.

"I asked no questions. She said she had a buyer lined up."

"Think it was anyone from the Sint Maarten group?"

He shrugged. "Bradford's Maine group went down a few years ago. In one place too long. Big Bad John has relocated to somewhere in Asia. Bandaid was sampling the goods too much after he got into the coke trade. He will be in prison for quite a while."

She sat up, went down the list she had compiled. Hans had only heard about some, and hadn't known about others. Seychelle was frustrated, felt no closer to unraveling the web.

Hans volunteered, "I heard she was connected to Dolphin Dave, but he has a wide base of operations." He cleared his throat. "I was a touch piqued when I heard later that she was trying to score from someone else as well."

"Who?" Seychelle brightened.

"A local albino called Yellowman. I don't know if he gave her any. The drums aren't always accurate."

"Where can I find him?"

"Ask Brian."

"Doesn't she mention family?" Geena asked. "I mean, surely she gives some indication of life before drug running on the high seas."

"They didn't run drugs," Seychelle snapped.

"Alright already, grass smuggling, but surely she had family somewhere."

Seychelle frowned. "It was like she purposely blanked it. Protecting them. I think she wanted her story told, but no path. When in prison she said she was happy they had no children to be responsible for, but did wish they'd been able to set up off-shore trust funds for their godchildren."

"Godchildren?" Geena asked.

Seychelle laughed, "Yeah. The stories are good. Shasta went on quite a rampage after their run, feeling invincible it would seem. The result was a baby girl, their goddaughter. She took her home to Australia. And there was an

American couple they met who were going through the South Pacific on their boat. They became friends after Chianti helped deliver their baby on board their boat in the Marquesas Islands. She had some experience helping deliver animals, and luckily there were no complications."

Hans scoffed, "Not much difference, and neither belong on a boat." He stroked the well-maintained cockpit teak. "I had *Regina* built to my specifications, she is perfect. I would never degrade her by having children or animals aboard."

He raised a hand to stop protests before they could begin. "Beauregard is a special guest. Seriously, on a long-term basis it doesn't work. I bet the couple moved ashore soon afterwards."

Seychelle and Geena exchanged looks. Geena had slept with him but his declaration insured it would be kept strictly sex. She was seriously family-oriented and Seychelle knew she'd not waste time on a man who was not.

"Well, yes, shortly following the birth they sailed to Tahiti and sold their boat. They moved back to work in his folk's boat building business near Pensacola, Florida." She stopped. "Geena, that's just down the coast from home!"

Geena's smile was smug. "I knew it. You just have to keep chewing on the evidence in a case, usually related to family, or extended family in this case, and things just start falling into place. Names, she must have mentioned their names. Or, if she made them up, there'll be some link."

Hans stood. "You must forgive me, but I have an appointment and must move *Regina* to her safe mooring. Hurricane season, you know. Port Antonio is not protected enough for my liking. If you will all climb into the dinghy, I will run you ashore. How long are you staying?"

Geena climbed out the hatch, stretched like a cat. "Me, I'm into playing islander and watching sunsets. This one's been hanging around with her hound too long. She's got the scent and nothing's going to pull her away from trailing Chianti."

"There's absolutely nothing more you can tell me or do to help?" Seychelle asked Hans.

"As I said, I have put out feelers but nothing yet. It is important to me as well, albeit for more cold-hearted reasons than your romantic quest. I will let you know as soon as I have any information at all."

Geena put her arm around Seychelle. "Time to visit Junior. Beauregard and I are hungry. Tell you what, you go through her journal, see if you can find a name, anything. I'll go find the local phone and try to get a call through to the college library. They'll research it for me." She sighed. "Breaking my vow. I'll never be a successful lawyer if I'm this soft."

Eight

Fiction. "Hanamenu is a secluded bay on the NW coast of the island of Hiva Oa in the Marquesas. In your dreams of an idyllic life on a lush South Pacific island you'll find it, but I have doubts even the most dynamic of imaginations can conjure its true magnificence. One must approach from the open ocean with an entourage of dolphins, under perfect blue skies, with a scattering of soft clouds and a steady breeze. Even under sail we seemed loud and clumsy, the dropping of anchor near to breaking a sacred seal. From the 4000 ft. peak of Temetiu draped dense jungle, cloaking high cliffs that descended into a narrow valley and grudgingly gave way to a thin strip of beach and the surrounding bay. Filtered sunset gave a ghostly aura to palms and shadows suggested an abundance of secrets. Our lovemaking on deck had an exhibitionist feel though there were no other boats and we'd been told the valley was uninhabited. Our passion was intense, our surroundings an added stimulant. I can close my eyes and hear the night music but can't identify individuals in nature's ensemble.

"We slept soundly and awoke to the neighing of horses. In disbelief we charged up into the cockpit. Morning light was soft, the rising sun masked by densely cloaked hills and cliffs. On the narrow beach two young horses, one chestnut and the other a white-faced bay, ran and played, seeming to celebrate life and freedom and beauty. Standing above them in the palms was a larger bay with black mane and tail and white stockings. We were mesmerized. The two followed when the lone bay turned and disappeared into thick greenery. Without words we sprang into action, inflated our dinghy and slid it into the water. I grabbed my camera and we headed for the beach with the enthusiasm of kids, anxious to catch up, afraid they would disappear. We followed their tracks up the well-worn sand and shell path between palms into an enclave of bougainvillea gone wild, pinks and purples gently shocking amidst cool greens. The path slanted upward, dissolving into a wall of tropical growth, making a womb of the Valley of Hanamenu. We rounded a curve, stepped between lime trees and red cluttered hibiscus bushes onto a lawn where the three horses faced us. A white-socked colt lay beside the bay mare, so new, still wet from birth. The horses' ears were back, their muscles tensed in mistrust. Babe, trembling, got up on its long skinny legs to nuzzle into the security of the mare's teat. Tears sprang to my eyes, the beauty of the moment overwhelming. We stood staring at them as they contemplated us. We were the aliens. Mare made her decision, turned from us and walked away with her colt in awkward attendance and the others closing ranks. Only then did we realize there were a few chickens foraging around and a small frame house with thatched roof and closed shutters. The house needed paint and general maintenance, but the horses had kept the grass in neat trim and a plethora of hibiscus and guava trees prevented any impression of abandonment. We followed the horses across the yard into thick growth through which they had a well-defined walkway. Limbs of bushes flapped back after their passage, hiding and protecting them. After a short walk we found the undergrowth too punishing on our naked legs and arms so we retraced our steps. Close examination disclosed flattened stones, the remains of a road that had led up the valley. Who had laid the stones? When? Ah, the stories!

"We both felt like intruders as we passed the house so didn't stop to investigate. Once out of the yard I spotted a small waterfall. A border of ferns and vines followed its progress down through rocks from a protruding stone lip. Moss formed the background for clear water as it tumbled into a sand and rock-bottomed pool. Without hesitation I stripped, threw my clothes over one of the large smooth rocks, and waded in. Ah, the sensation of cool pure water! Aboard *Cayenne* my baths consisted of little more than a bucket of the Pacific dumped over my head and a buff-down with bath cloth, so this was total pleasure, every sense engaged. The place became deeply etched into my being, though only waist deep and perhaps 10 feet wide. I submerged, then floated, staring up at the kind of scene Gauguin had tried to capture on canvas. I slurped from cascading water, laughing and choking. 'Sydney, what are you waiting for? It's magic, the elixir of life, you'll live forever after one dip!' I splashed at him, but he stood, frowning. 'What's wrong?' I demanded. He was quiet, looking up and around. 'We shouldn't be here. I feel it, like someone is watching. I'm going back to the boat.' I was annoyed. Whether he spooked me or we were, in truth, being watched, I was no longer relaxed. As I dressed, I felt uncomfortable and was almost relieved to see an American flagged ketch sailing into the bay. We rowed back to *Cayenne*, grabbed a bottle of wine and some grass and headed over in our dinghy.

"I declared, 'Welcome to paradise!' as we pulled alongside. The tall unsmiling man with red hair and freckles stared at us. 'We were going to Tahiti to have the baby but we had to pull in. She's in labor!' He turned and knelt beside the very pregnant woman who was lying on a blanket in the cockpit. No need for details. I grew up on my grandparent's farm and had helped deliver animals, so I aided gentle, lovely Sky in giving birth to a squalling redhead, luckily without complications. I doubt the colt had been so ugly and loud when first introduced to the world. They gave her my middle name, Sierra, Hana for the bay, and their last name, Murphy. As soon as the birthing was complete, the mess cleaned up and Sierra nursing contentedly, Barry explained they had not wanted to stop here. Locals had told them that this valley was cursed, that all born here die young. He declared they were going home to the safety of his folk's boatyard near Pensacola to raise her. That birthing was one of the high points in my life, without doubt." Chianti.

Seychelle gave a sigh. "Protected by superstition. Is that why we're destroying our planet, because we just don't believe and accept? Because we have to question and test, destroying as we go?"

"It's called evolution," Geena drawled. "I vote for it. All superstition does is get organized into religions and cause wars. We can only save this place through understanding and intelligent planning."

"Or, if nature strikes back and saves itself."

"I rather doubt that whatever might evolve if we bipeds are wiped out will show great promise," Geena ventured and took a sip of her beer.

Seychelle threw her head back and began laughing. "Murphy boatyard near Pensacola with a son named Barry. Surely, they keep in touch. Maybe that's where she was heading!"

Geena smiled. "Hope she didn't invent it."

Seychelle shrugged. "I just bet it's a real place with real people."

"Brian said the public phone is in the house by the post office. It'll be open this afternoon so I'll go hang and try to get through." She shook her head. "Can't believe I'm doing this."

Beauregard barked and charged outside, tail in serious action.

Seychelle laughed, "He's either on the scent of jerk chicken or a human he likes." She reflected that it must not be Hans. For whatever reason, Beauregard didn't seem to care for him. That was unusual so she filed it as a character reference that reinforced her own vibes.

They both were quite surprised when Beauregard returned with Seagull in tow. With a shy smile he nodded at Beauregard. "Wouldn't take no for an answer, insisted I come buy you a beer." He kissed each on the forehead and went out back to find Junior. Returning with three Red Stripes, he pulled up a chair at their table.

"Missed us that much, eh?" Seychelle asked with a smile.

"You know it," he said and met her eyes. She felt her face warm.

"Something tells me it is business," Geena said. "Or have those gendarmes gotten too close?"

He leaned down to scratch Beauregard's ears. "So, you like it here?"

Seychelle gave Geena a look and said, "Beautiful, and thanks for introducing us to Brian. Charming and a great host, and he gave us his house just around the corner. Geena and Beauregard have become jerk chicken junkies so I may have trouble getting them off this island."

As if on cue, Brian walked in the door. "Got the word," he said with a smile. "I owe you big time for sending me these fine ladies." Junior appeared and placed a beer before him as he sat down. "Thinkin' of stashin' them up in the mountains, keepin' 'em."

Geena smiled. "Well, if that's where you grow that righteous reefer, I'll go willingly."

"Look out," Seagull said with a laugh, "his stuff will have you believin'."

Brian's smile widened. "Jah's gift. Geena, phone's open now. Best you beat everybody there. I be leaving the typewriter in the house for you," he said to Seychelle.

He looked at Seagull, nodded and stood up. "We catch you ladies later," he said and headed out the back door.

Seagull brushed Seychelle's cheek with his full soft lips as he stood. "Later," he whispered and followed Brian. The girls stared after him. Beauregard whined.

"Now that was what Mamma would call 'reeking of suspiciousness'," Geena remarked.

Seychelle frowned. "Didn't feel good, did it? Must be trouble. Were they afraid to go out the front door?"

"Well, I know cousin Yolande was wound up about Charlie." She lowered her voice automatically, almost whispering the names. "If she started stirring, it would be trouble-for-true for Seagull as well." She shook her head. "Grassin' just isn't done."

"I do understand where she's coming from, but she wouldn't have put Seagull in it, she's just not like that," Seychelle said with conviction.

"No. But one domino."

In silence they ate the chicken Junior had prepared while Beauregard was invited out back for his feast. Seychelle's gaze followed him but the boys had obviously departed out the back gate or through Junior's house.

When they had finished the bird and downed the last drop of beer, Geena announced, "Let's go, there are some Murphy's to be found!"

Nine

"To realize one's destiny is a person's only real obligation."
Paul Coelho, 'The Alchemist'

"Yes, mahn, she cum to me," Yellowman said, his voice soft, in tune with surroundings. He took a long deep drag on the cigar-sized spliff. Beauregard sprawled close to him; belly pressed to the cool hard-pressed earth floor. He slept contentedly, an occasional grunt or thump of his tail contributed to the background rhythm of rain on the low corrugated roof.

Seychelle watched the slender fingers with their covering of faded freckles on chalk white skin. Fragile, artistic, but the nails were those of a farmer. With both hands she received the righteous weed he had perfected.

"Best seeds from de best plants in de best dirt with God sun and God rain." He chuckled. "Like Tina says, 'Simply the Best'."

Seychelle smiled after a gentle, long inhalation. She was surprised at how soft the smoke felt, a caress. Almost sweet in taste and musty green in scent, it was seductive. She took another tentative toke and passed it on to Brian who sat next to her on the smooth log. Reverently he cradled it in his hands, passed it under his nose slowly with eyes closed. "Ummmm…" he groaned. "Don't get no better."

Yellowman gave a lazy nod and Seychelle leaned back against rough boards that formed the back of the lean-to. She stretched out her legs on the dirt, sighed, slowly let her eyes cruise the surrounding landscape. Rain formed a delicate veil around the three open sides of their low shelter. Sunlight glittered and colored as it filtered through rain's prism. Did Chianti sit right where I am, she wondered. Did she sample the same crop I'm sampling?

Yellowman accepted the joint from Brian. "Her ol' man locked up in England. She out first." He shook his head sadly. "Plenty Jamaicans there. Most fo' carryin' shit. Fools."

"Have Chianti and Sydney taken your grass before?" Seychelle asked.

"Been long time since took a load o' commercial up fo' Dolphin Dave. Then dem cum see me fo' some Best fo' demselves. Gonna sail 'round de world, dem say." With a contented smile, he held his chipped brown mug out under the dripping eves. Leaning back, he sipped, nodded. "Did, too."

"But she came to you alone this time and she had no money, right?"

"Not a problem," he said expansively. "She tol' me where she goin'. I know her, I know Dolphin pay her good. No problem."

She sat up. "Will you call him? Find out if she arrived, if she's okay?"

Gracefully, with complete concentration, he filled his lungs. Seychelle realized the rain had stopped, that there was minor dripping from the eves and birds seemed positively joyous in their varied chorus. Crickets and frogs joined in, or was she just beginning to hear them? Were his eyes closed behind the wrap-around sunglasses?

"Don't you care that she may need help?" she blurted out. She felt her eyes water.

Slowly the tall skinny Jamaican turned toward her. He reached up with his free hand and removed his glasses. She was transfixed by his stare, the pink irises highlighted by enlarged dark pupils and long white lashes.

"'Course I care," he breathed softly. "Word done gone out." He handed her the joint, replaced the glasses and resumed his relaxed demeanor, gently stroking Beauregard's long ears.

Seychelle felt foolish. She felt Brian's eyes on her, and wouldn't look at him. He smiled with understanding, then handed her a lighter. Taking a deep breath, she lit up and abandoned herself to the mood of the place.

After a while they crawled out from under the lean-to, stretched and breathed in the fresh green earth aroma. A forest of ganja, some plants taller than Brian, stretched in all directions. They were in a valley of gentle hills, with mountains as backdrop to the East and the North. Thick trees dotted the fields and outer edges and everywhere there was green, so many shades of green. Laughing, she began dancing around. She buried her face in one wet plant, then another.

"The Garden of Eden," she declared. "Peace and love in a perfect, tranquil ecosystem." She plucked a crimson tomato from one of the bushes that were randomly scattered amongst cannabis giants. Looking around she spotted eggplant, peppers, okra and chilies. Granny's garden had certainly not looked like this.

"Why you so interested?" Yellowman asked.

She looked up at him, unsure of what to say. Brian chuckled, "Him always ask de questions got no easy answer, make you think."

Seychelle studied the tomato in her hand, took a big bite and wiped the juice from her chin. "People don't believe these are fruit, but they would if they could taste how sweet they can be." She shrugged. "I don't know. It just feels like I don't have a choice, like I'm meant to look for her."

The albino gave a piping, melodic laugh and put his arm around her shoulders. "Good 'nough, Girl, good e-nough."

Seychelle, Brian and Beauregard followed him across the field toward the stream where a small beat-up wooden rowboat would take them back to the village. From time to time Yellowman would give a low laugh, murmur, "Jus' meant to be."

Ten

"Believe me! The secret of reaping the greatest fruitfulness and the greatest enjoyment from life is to live dangerously!"
Friedrich Nietzche (1882)

"Why on earth do you want to go home?" Seychelle asked and collapsed into the flowered corner chair, her bare feet scattering old foam stuffing that littered the floor. She slipped her vest off, unbuttoned her sweat-soaked white cotton shirt, tossed her visor Frisbee-style at Geena and leaned forward to shake out her wet curls. "Great day in the ganja fields, you should have come."

"Well y'all just gotta understand I simply could not drag my little ol' self out of Hans's naughty den of ill repute," Geena said, batting her eyes and stroking her hip. "Sun was up long 'fore we went down."

"I doubt that," Seychelle said with a sneer and ducked when Geena threw a pillow at her. Leaping from the chair, she tackled Geena onto the bed and began pounding her head with the pillow. "Talk, you hussy, tell all!"

Geena threw her off, trapped her and began tickling, the ultimate weapon. Weak from laughter, tears streaming down her cheeks, Seychelle finally begged for mercy.

"Bitch!" she gasped, drying her eyes with the tail of her shirt. "Brought you a gift but you are not getting it until you tell me what's going on."

Geena got up, shrugged, and looked out the window. "Just want to go home for a bit. I'll come back after I see the family, make sure everyone is okay."

"So, call them."

Geena retrieved the bag they had knocked off the bed and began refolding. "Look what you've done. Hans is picking me up in fifteen minutes."

"Why Hans?"

"Why not? He's taking me to the airfield. Better than hoping Leroy's taxi doesn't break down. I want to get to Montego Bay in time for the late flight. Connect to New Orleans, home early in the morning."

"Why, Geena? Talk to me. I know you can't afford it. What's wrong? Is Mamma okay? Look at me!"

She glanced over as if to speak, but turned away to get something from the closet. "This way I can track down your Murphy family. Never could get through on that damned phone," Geena said into the closet.

"You're going to play mule for him," Seychelle stated in a flat voice.

Geena said nothing, closed her bag and began checking her make-up in the discolored vanity mirror.

"Geena, this is madness! I don't trust him. It's coke, isn't it?"

"Chill, Seychelle. My life, my decision," she said into the mirror.

"Your ruined life if you're busted."

"I won't be."

"Listen, you're getting the scholarship and I hatched a plan while getting totally wasted in Nirvana today with Brian and Yellowman. After I find Chianti, or even if I don't, I'm going to stay in the Caribbean for a while. I want to write about the people, their cultures, and the sub-culture that's grown up around the ganja business. Bless West, my inheritance means I can do it. But I don't want to just leave the house closed up. You can find someone to rent it, sort of keep an eye on things, and then anything above the land tax, which is very low, is yours. Good for both of us!"

Geena looked at her. "What a woman, what a friend. I'll take you up on it. It will help support me and I'll make sure it is well taken care of. I love that old house." She paused, memories softening her resolute features.

She took Seychelle's hand. "This little trip will take the pressure off Mamma. And, assuming I get the scholarship, it will lessen the burden of law school. So, even if I don't get the scholarship, well, we won't go there—"

She was interrupted by a car horn. She went to the front door, returned with an apologetic smile. "Gotta go."

Seychelle jumped up, threw her arms around her. "Oh Geena, please don't do this!" She put her hand on Geena's smooth dark-chocolate cheek. "Bad karma, Chianti said. Damned stupid, I say."

Geena pulled away. "Just wish me luck and give me the keys to the house. I'll check on it while I'm up there."

Seychelle stared into her dark eyes, seeing the iron will she knew so well. She retrieved her vest, fished the keys out of an inner pocket and gave them to her. "Start West's truck when you go to Gulf Haven. Better yet, use it while you're there since you don't have a car. And, go see West's lawyer, Mr. Johnson, tell him the plan. I'll write to him confirming."

Geena stuffed the rest of her things in the bag, gave Seychelle a quick kiss on the cheek. "Don't worry! Love you," she whispered and charged outside.

Seychelle followed her to the door, glared at Hans and did not return his wave. She watched as the yellow Jeep pulled away.

"Lookin' awful sad," Brian said.

She turned a blank gaze on him.

"Where she off to?"

Seychelle hesitated, shook her head, "Oh, see her family. Back soon."

He studied her closely as she turned to stare in the direction her friend had gone.

"Well, Beauregard came in without you so thought I best check. He be in the back with Junior. I just ordered an' Junior don' like his food gettin' cold." He took her arm and walked her around the corner to the table that had become theirs. He got a couple of Red Stripes and started on his chicken. Minutes later Junior brought a plate for Seychelle, but she just sat staring out the door at the slow increase of Port Antonio activity as shadows cooled, the sun allowing the next, more animated chapter in Jamaican life to proceed.

Seychelle accepted the beer and chicken without looking up. Snap out of it, she told herself. She's neither dead nor busted. She'll be fine. It would break Mamma's heart if she knew. She shuddered at the thought of Geena in jail. She took a long swig of beer, slammed the bottle down. "Damn it to hell!"

Brian sucked his teeth. "She be fine. Nothin' you can do."

"What do you know about this? About Hans's operation?" she snapped.

"Nothin'. Just guessin' from the way you actin'. Hans been in business a long time. Professional. Eat yo chicken."

"Why was Seagull here?" Seychelle asked.

"His business, not mine." He raised an eyebrow at her. "Not yours," he stated with finality and amply doused his rice & beans with hot chili sauce.

"Where is he?"

"He gone."

"Are they after him?"

Brian got up, went to the back door and asked for more beers. He was smiling when he sat back down. "Ought to change yo name to Question."

Junior appeared with Red Stripes in hand and Beauregard in boisterous attendance.

Leaping into her lap without invitation, Beauregard greeted Seychelle as if it had been weeks of separation. Laughing, she hugged him. "You glutinous mongrel! You stink of chicken. Will you ever be satisfied with mere dog food again?" He leapt to the floor to follow Junior outback, priorities firmly established.

"Might refuse to leave Jamaica," Brian observed.

"So, might I," she smiled, with a last glance outside, so fresh and clean after the day's rain had settled dust on the packed earth street. A gold tinge with shadow highlights was moving in, softening wooden structures.

"Will you rent me your place for a while, Brian? For a few months perhaps?"

"Done got in yo blood, eh?" he said with a smile. "Yeah, sure, but you might have to put me up from time to time."

"Deal," Seychelle said and extended her hand.

He looked at it, wiped his on a disintegrating paper napkin with exaggerated care, and reached to shake with her. "You Yanks start this custom?"

She shrugged, "Never thought about it. Is cannabis indigenous, or did someone bring it in and start farming it? Is it a long-standing custom?"

He threw his head back and laughed, really laughed, one of those uninhibited bursts of real pleasure. Seychelle tried to remember if she had ever laughed like that.

Gleefully he mimicked her, "Never thought about it." Wiping his eyes, he called out to Junior.

In charged Beauregard with Junior close behind, sweating and wiping his hands on his once-white apron. Tall, grey haired Junior had the 'been there, done it all, got nothing to prove' demeanor.

"Junior, she ask how long Jamaica have ganja," Brian said with a show of effort at keeping a straight face.

Junior's dark eyes twinkled. "Better you ask, how long ganja have Jamaica?"

Eleven

Seychelle devoured two plump ruby mangoes, unashamedly letting the juice drip down her chin and breasts. She sat naked on a towel in the sun that streamed through her bedroom window. Leaning over a steaming mug of Blue Mountain coffee on the floor beside her, enjoying its full rich scent, she gave a satisfied sigh and lifted it to her lips. She sipped, smiled. Her file of Fiction copies lay open before her, Chianti's poem on the top.

ODE TO JA RED
So, I went to see the farmer, "Hey man, what you growin' here?"
"Sensi," he said with Jamaican cheer.
Through the village into forest, his daily walk a trek for me,
To behold his crop of magic ganja trees.
A few samples in the lean-to as afternoon rains come down.
"Hey man, pass that sample 'round!"
Raftin' home down the river, "Is it good, will it sell?"
"Can he deliver? How much a bail?"
On price, amount and packing we agree and set
midnight tomorrow out in the Bay for delivery.
They're gonna love us Stateside, cabby up front, a grand a pound.
And again we will be empty and with full sails southbound.

Seychelle laughed. "You'll not get published, Chianti, but we've shared something special." She jumped and grabbed an oversized Sunsplash tee-shirt when she heard Beauregard bark and the front door open.

"You're not still in bed, are you?" Geena demanded as she charged into the bedroom.

Seychelle threw her arms around her friend, tears coming with the laughter. "You cow! Why didn't you call? It's been a week! I've been worried sick!

What happened? Where have you been?" She pushed Geena away. "I'm angry!" she declared.

But Geena was laughing. She handed Seychelle a small, expensively wrapped present and sat down on the unmade bed. "Okay, I'm sorry. But I must tell you honestly that I was advised against calling anyone I knew, and Junior's Jerk Chicken wasn't listed with directory assistance. Each morning I thought I'd head back. But things happened. A cup of coffee and I'll fill you in. God, I didn't know how good coffee could taste 'til Blue Mountain graced my taste buds. I'm going to take all I can carry home the next time I go."

Seychelle held her peace, biting her tongue as she got dressed. She went to the kitchen and made more coffee while Geena wrestled with Beauregard on the floor. She had brought him a new flea collar as well as a scarf in the Jamaican flag colors of black, green and gold. He liked the changeover game and was energetically making replacement of his old garb difficult.

"How's Mamma?" Seychelle asked when they finally sat facing each other across the unsteady kitchen table.

"She's fine, sends you big hugs and says, 'Bless your heart!' She is thrilled about the house. I, uh, told her that was why I had come home, to get it squared away for you." She glanced away then rushed on. "And I did, I went to see your Mr. Johnson. He did not blink when he saw my black face enter his office, which won him points, but he even knew me! And about some of my awards and the possibility (he said probability) that I'd be the first black female to receive a scholarship for law school in Alabama. And he knows that I'm your best friend."

They stared at each other, emotions only barely under control. When she was young, and West was away, Mamma would bring Geena with her to fix food for Granddaddy and Seychelle at Gulf Haven. After Granddaddy died Seychelle was sent to boarding school, but she stayed with Geena's family when she was home if the Navy demanded West's time. Attitudes and prejudices came in all ages, colors, denominations, but they were bonded, their friendship unshakable.

Geena cleared her throat, sipped her coffee. "He said to tell you hello, thought it was a good idea to rent it instead of just letting it sit, and gave me a paper for you to sign giving me limited management. This makes it legal, and makes me responsible. Better, eh?"

"Yes, and you can get him to do leases, anything." Seychelle said. She took a deep breath and said, "Okay Geena, what happened?"

"Piece of cake! Waltzed right in, sweating buckets but they didn't notice. A man met me in the New Orleans airport, hugged like old friends. I gave him the bag of duty-free coffee I'd purchased in Mo Bay airport. He thanked me profusely and left a McDonalds bag on the floor by the table when he said goodbye."

"But, how did you carry it?"

"Stuffed in sanitary napkins," she said and giggled. "Switched it to the coffee in the toilet on the plane. Hans showed me how." She reached across and took Seychelle's hand. "Get that The Bastard look off your face. He didn't persuade me, I wanted to do it, and not just for the money. I've been the conservative one, the one who kept us out of trouble as kids, but your dreams and Chianti's stories must have infected me."

Seychelle shook her head, "But..."

Geena touched her finger to her friend's lips. "Listen, it's done. What you should know is that your DEA friend, Jerken Jr., has been hanging around asking about you. Even showed up at the airport when I was leaving. Just happened to be there. Right," she drawled and rolled her eyes.

Seychelle sat upright. "Why me? Who's he been asking? What did he ask you?"

Geena gave a sarcastic sigh. "All you did was pocket some evidence. You didn't conspire with President Nixon or commit bank fraud." She laughed, sobered. "Jerken Jr. wanted to know where you had gone and why and when you'd return. He had gone to see Mamma the day after we left, though he didn't tell her how he knew we'd gone. When he walked up to me in the airport I nearly choked on my Coke. First thought was that he knew about the cash I'd put in my safety deposit box. Didn't lessen my tension when I realized his interest was only in you, since I'm your accomplice."

"What did you tell him?"

"Same story we gave Mamma. Told him I came up to get school stuff sorted since we want to keep traveling, seeing all my relatives, until school starts. Ignorant red-neck said, 'Oh, a roots thing, eh?' I wanted to spit on him. But I smiled."

Seychelle saw her jaw tighten, her delicate hand close into a fist. "He's not worth your energy," she said softly.

Geena swallowed hard. "Cain't fools like him see the hatred that pours from our black eyes above our white-toothed smiles?"

"Their simple minds don't probe and wonder, don't try to see and understand. They just blank out or condemn what they don't comprehend."

Geena shook her head, sighed. "Got a joint?"

Seychelle gave her a quick hug then grabbed her vest from the closet. From an inside pocket she took a rolled plastic bag. "The present I brought you from Yellowman's farm. Sister, you have never tasted ganja that is this good! When he says The Best, he is not just whistlin' Dixie!" She handed Geena rolling papers and a lighter, then got a couple of cold Red Stripes from the refrigerator and they transferred to the living room daybed.

With a joint in one hand, cold beer in the other, Geena settled back, stretched her legs out on the bed. "What I did get from him is that they've learned nothing else from the raft, or so he said. I told him you never talked about it, we were having such a good time partying and laying in the sun that you seemed to have forgotten about it."

Seychelle scowled, "Well I just really don't like it."

Geena had a mischievous smile when she passed over the joint. "Don't y'all want to know what I learned about boats?"

Seychelle was in mid-drag, choked on the smoke, murmured, "Bitch."

Geena, thoroughly enjoying herself, rescued the joint and waited for her coughing to subside.

"I made a small sign: 'Looking for a boatyard in the Pensacola area. Want to sail around the world and need the right yard to build the right boat for me.' I drove West's truck around and posted it in a few marinas, boat stores, and libraries. I must admit I was so wrapped up in my scam that I almost forgot until yesterday." She gave slow, deliberate care to lighting the joint.

"And?" Seychelle demanded, sitting forward.

"And I went to the yellow pages," she beamed, unable to remain cool and aloof, "Murphy's Boatyard was there. Address, phone number and all! I couldn't believe it. It was like all of a sudden, for the first time, I believed that Chianti existed. My hands were even shaking when I dialed the number," she said with a giggle.

Seychelle sat dead still, barely breathing.

Geena drained her beer. "Well, I thought it out before I called. I mean, Mamma had told me Jerken Jr. was snooping around. And, in case Chianti was hiding out there, I didn't want to go spooking folks. So, I told the woman who answered that a friend of mine had met an American couple 8 or 9 years ago when he was in the South Pacific. He had really liked their small wooden boat, was impressed by the workmanship, and they told him they had built it in their parent's boatyard in Pensacola. I thought that, since I live in Mobile and don't really know what I'm doing but do have a dream, well, it would be a good place to start."

Seychelle laughed, "Wow, remind me to enlist your help the next time I need to formulate a lie."

Geena looked embarrassed. "Kurt Vonnegut would have called it a foma, a little untruth that hurts no one," she said. "I just hope we don't have to build on it. Anyway, the woman said, 'Oh, that would have been Barry & Sky.' Well, I just about dropped the receiver! She said they were away but she expects them back on Friday." She looked steadily into her friend's eyes. "I made an appointment to meet with them Saturday morning at the yard."

"But that's four days away!"

"Listen, Seychelle, if you're right about all this then they must be away in connection with Chianti. If you go charging in before they're back, well, maybe the family knows nothing and then where would you be?" She held up the half-smoked joint and smiled. "Another puff of this and I'll be totally dysfunctional. I need to eat."

Seychelle quickly ripped open the fancy box she'd been cradling in her lap.

"Oh, Geena," she breathed and fumbled to get the silver dolphin off its velvet bed. Smooth and solid, the dolphin seemed to have energy. She could see it gracefully leaping out of the sea. With trembling fingers, she undid the clasp at its belly, opened the locket, and burst into tears. The picture within was of West looking proud and confident in his dress-white uniform as he cradled her in his right arm. She was only a few days old, naked, bald and smug, secure in her contented sleep.

Geena cleared her throat. "I, um, went to the house to lock your stuff away and realized you hadn't touched West's room. Understandable. Anyway, everything is in labeled boxes locked away in the attic." She fumbled in her bag for the keys and handed them over. "The picture was stuck in the corner of your mother's portrait on his night table. It was so tiny. That's what made me think of getting you a locket. You okay?"

Seychelle couldn't speak, nodded and dropped the silver chain over her head, felt the dolphin settle at her cleavage, felt her heart beating beneath it.

Geena stood up. "Get dressed. My nose tells me Junior is ready for us next door. You know how good Mamma's home cooking is, but I'm going through serious withdrawal. I need a jerk chicken fix!"

On cue, Beauregard began barking and dancing around the door. Seychelle gave Geena a quick hug, pulled on a pair of shorts and followed them out into harsh midday reality.

The next day they taxied to Ocho Rios, took an island flight to Montego Bay, and checked in for a couple of nights at the Rose Hall Great House. Eating, drinking and shopping passed the time but Seychelle was focused so did not take full advantage of the adventure. She alternated between silent contemplation and babbling on the early morning flight to Pensacola.

"I do feel like I know her," Seychelle said as Geena led the way into Murphy's Boatyard and through a wide variety of boats in stasis. The closer they got, the more intense was her excitement.

"They look lonely, waiting for action, uncomfortable on land," she said. Most of the boats were covered with tarps that had been decorated by seagulls, and some still roosted as if in residence. The smells of fish and wood and salt water and oil, both fresh and stale, filled her nose. She felt a certain comfort, and could imagine them as a full-time part of her world.

Geena smiled. "Hopefully you'll meet the elusive Chianti in the flesh soon. Pity we left Beauregard with Brian; he would be in heaven here. So many places to sniff and mark. Luckily his legs are so short he'd not be able to discolor any nice white topsides."

As they rounded the corner Seychelle's laughter was cut short by the scene at the water's edge. "It's them," she whispered.

Beside a huge weathered old building that looked more like a barn than a warehouse, extended a rough but sturdy wooden pier over rock-strewn beach and gentle surf. Long, lean, red headed Barry leaned against the first, tallest bollard. Sky and Sierra worked on an upturned rowboat, paintbrushes in hand. Sky's straight black hair was lustrous and thick whereas Sierra's loose auburn curls glowed in the midday sun.

"Well, it's your show," Geena drawled. "I declare I'm as tickled as you and almost as anxious."

Seychelle advanced with a smile and a mixture of feelings. Well, West always said that if you were up front and open you would rarely go wrong. She noted a slight reserve during introductions but was encouraged by the unwavering eye contact of all three.

"I found a life raft on a beach beside my house," she began, and laid out the whole tale, well, most of it. The paintbrushes were left unattended and Barry studied her face closely, his body taut. There was tension but not hostility.

"So, that's why we're here. Please tell me you've seen Chianti, or at least heard from her. I've become quite obsessed and don't feel like I can get on with my life until I know she's okay."

Barry and Sky exchanged looks.

"Listen, if you don't feel like you can talk to me, fine, I do understand. I'll give you her book and be on my way if you'll just assure me she's safe."

Sky stepped forward and took her hand. "Are you sure that the DEA man didn't follow you?" Her dark eyes were troubled, moist.

"We don't know he's DEA, but yes I'm sure. From Jamaica we flew to New Orleans, then Pensacola and rented a car yesterday. We've probably seen too many movies, but we did everything with cash. You are out in the boonies here. Anyone trying to follow us on that little dirt road would have been obvious."

"We are worried about her," Sky said. She glanced over at Barry. "Chianti was coming here. When she was late, we got in touch with our mutual friend. He promised to check out the logical route, and said he would get a chopper if it came to that. We've heard nothing and have only a phone number for him. I've tried repeatedly but no one answers. We know him as Dolphin and we think he works for Charlie, who seems a tough character, but that's all we know."

Seychelle bit her lip. "What about Sydney?"

Barry shook his head and his solemn green eyes softened. "We write to him regularly but he's not allowed to receive calls. No good getting him upset since there's nothing he can do. Chianti didn't tell him about the run as he wouldn't have approved and would have just worried. Bad situation. Frustrating for us, as there seems to be nothing we can do either. We didn't check the Coast Guard for obvious reasons. With the current flow and wind pattern she should have landed west of here so we've spent the last eight days searching the coast. We've kept our radio with us all the time and stopped at every public phone, checking in here since she has this number." He shrugged. "Nothing."

Geena spoke up for the first time. "What were y'all supposed to do with, uh," she glanced at the little girl, "the cargo?"

Sierra gave an exaggerated sigh. "I know Chianti was bringing grass. You can talk around me."

Sky put an arm around her shoulders. "We're a close family, we discuss everything. It was just a matter of Dolphin arranging the offload. We were to get a cut for the holding time that was promised to be less than a week. The yard's had trouble, the money would have helped us."

"Doesn't she have family or friends, anyone she keeps in touch with?" Seychelle asked.

"She said one time that they had friends all over the world, but that we were the only ones they kept in touch with in the States. She never talked about her past or family with me, seemed to avoid it," Sky explained.

"Chianti grew up on a farm with her grandparents," Sierra said firmly. Everyone turned toward her. "She told me all about it, she was really happy there. Her parents died in a car crash before she started school."

Seychelle studied the girl's tawny face, clear green eyes and sprinkle of freckles across her well-defined nose. "Well, she didn't say anything about it in her book. Can you remember the names of any people she talked about or where the farm was located?"

Sierra looked smug and very grown-up. "It was north of Mobile, but I don't know exactly where. She called them Granny and Granddaddy Lee."

Seychelle beamed. "You are a star! She didn't say the name of her school, did she?"

Her smooth brow furrowed, the praise stimulating real concentration. "I'm sorry, Miss Seychelle, but I don't remember." Seychelle smiled. At least she hadn't addressed her as ma'am. Ah, that Southern upbringing.

"Don't you worry, you've helped a lot." She said and turned to Barry. "Perhaps I can use your phone while y'all check out Chianti's book. Maybe a name will ring a bell." She pulled the heavy notebook out of her backpack, opened it to the first mention of Sint Maarten. "Other than you, she only named the business associates in Sint Maarten, people she had worked with."

Sky led her through the barn, where only one commercial fishing boat was being worked on in the massive space, to a small tidy office.

"Business has been bad?"

Sky nodded, "A big group opened a yard not far from here. High tech, low prices, fast work. We can't compete. Barry's dad left the yard to him, including lots of bills." She opened a cupboard that was crammed with phone directories. "You can use this phone. You should stay for dinner. Barry's mom feeds everyone at noon. I'll go tell her you'll be with us. Chianti is known only as a friend of ours, Sierra's Godmother, who visits occasionally, okay?"

Seychelle nodded.

Sky stopped at the door. "We are trusting you, all three of us." She closed the door gently.

Seychelle felt a chill. Was that a threat, or was Sky just a protective mother? Understandable. They had just waltzed in with quite a story. Sierra was an adult child, probably much as she herself had been at that age. West had talked straight with her; said she was the only person who would listen to him pontificate for hours. He reckoned that was because he used to do the same thing when she was in the womb. When her mom went to sleep, he would lay his head close to her belly and talk softly of his plans and dreams. She shook herself, picked up the phone.

When they all gathered for dinner Seychelle selected a seat next to Sierra.

"Chianti doesn't eat meat," Sierra said as she heaped her plate with peas and sweet potatoes and sliced tomatoes. "And neither do I. It isn't right."

Seychelle looked at the meatloaf she had on her fork. "Well, we each have to do what feels right to us," she said. "I've said I was giving it up many times but just never seem to have the gumption."

Sierra nodded sagely. "It isn't easy for everyone." Her voice dropped to a whisper. "Chianti didn't sink, you know, she's too good a sailor for that."

"I hope you're right," Seychelle whispered, and changed the subject.

After eating they helped clear the table but Mrs. Murphy wouldn't let them wash dishes. They joined Geena and Barry outside under the shade of a giant old oak.

Seychelle stretched out on the grass. "Nice people. Your mom always feeds everyone?"

Barry nodded. "It's like a big family. Some of them are working for commissions now but I don't know how long they'll stay." He looked away. "I grew up in this yard."

"And his daddy before him," Sierra chimed in and jumped on his back. His gloom lifted immediately as he flipped her to the ground and began tickling until she screamed for mercy.

"Well, I spoke to Chianti's granddaddy," Seychelle said. "They live outside a small town about 60 miles north of Mobile. I know the area so I'm driving up this afternoon. He sounded really old, a bit out of it. He said, 'Oh, we ain't seen her for a while.' I told him I'd see him around sunset. I'll probably learn nothing new, but I've got to go."

"Okay if I don't join you?" Geena asked. She turned to Barry. "I'd really like to just hang out here, if you don't mind."

"Can I go, please?" Sierra piped up, grabbing Barry's hand.

"Please?" Seychelle seconded.

Barry's eyes sparkled as he studied the three faces. "As if I could say no to any of you," he laughed. "But you go get Sky's permission first," he directed and slapped his daughter on the behind. She danced a circle and charged off toward the office, her giggles filling the hot humid yard.

"I'll drive carefully and take care of her," Seychelle promised. "We'll be back before midnight. Or, we can stop for the night at a hotel if it seems too late."

"You may tire of all the questions and opinions," he laughed. "Seriously, she is a great traveling companion, and can even help navigate."

"And you can put me to work. I'm a painter at heart," Geena volunteered.

Seychelle was just getting up when Sky came out. Her face was solemn. "Sierra is packing a small bag in case it's an overnighter. I won't pretend I'm enthusiastic, we have just met after all, but she was too excited for me to refuse. You must take my telephone number with you and call as often as possible." She handed over the notebook. "We only know Dolphin Dave casually but we trust him. Charlie, we don't know well and don't feel particularly good about him."

Sierra came running out with a big smile and a dolphin backpack. "Ready!" she announced. She handed Seychelle a framed photo.

Taking a deep breath, Seychelle studied the woman she felt she knew so well. It was taken from the center of a sailboat, she assumed by Sydney. Chianti was standing at the tiller, smiling confidently with orange sunset as backdrop and no land to intrude on the smooth ocean patterns. She was bundled up in foul weather gear, only her face and short, ash blonde hair uncovered.

"That was when she and Sydney were sailing to Holland but the stupid English busted them before they got there," Sierra explained.

Seychelle's heart quickened. This was from their last scam, their last sail together. Heading in from the North Atlantic. She asked, "When will Sydney be released?"

Sky said, "In two weeks. We must find her before then. I think we should keep the photo here, Sierra, since it's the only one we have."

Crossing her arms, she took a deep breath and glared at her mother. "We'll take loads when she gets here."

Barry stepped in, picked her up and threw her over his shoulder. "You two had better get going. Old folks on farms go to bed with the sun, they'll not wait for the likes of you." He walked briskly toward the front gate with his now giggling bundle bouncing awkwardly, her head hidden by her long auburn mane.

Seychelle handed Sky the picture and gave her a quick, awkward, hug. "I know it's very hard for you, everything at the same time. But Sierra is safe with me, please don't worry."

Seychelle was shocked to realize there were tears on Sky's cheeks. "I do trust you. My concern is that she is going to be devastated by the loss of Chianti. And Sydney, what about him? They've been so good together, shared such love and adventures."

"Come on, Miss Seychelle!" Sierra yelled.

Geena took Seychelle's arm. "Enjoy the trip," she instructed. "As Mamma says, 'Worry don't get you nothin' but wrinkles'."

Twelve

Fiction. "Sydney woke me with one of his wonderful soups just after midnight. Lots of garlic and hot chili, we're addicted to both. My watch is so quiet and tranquil, no ships to be seen out here in the Pacific, over 500 miles from the nearest island. And now the dolphins have joined us. Their dance around *Cayenne's* bow is magic, their grace and energy incomparable. I watch and hunger to join them, find I can't vanquish the smile and good feelings they inspire. I'm sitting on the bow, watching a babe between two adults. Teachers or honor guard or parents, they dive and glide and leap over and over in perfect harmony. The peace they embody reminds me of the birthing of Sierra in Hanamenu. What an experience! I'm tied to her for life. As Godmother, yes, but more. She's part of me. Perhaps some of it is the curse that hangs over the bay. Protecting and uniting. I approached it with, 'I've delivered animals before, no problem.' But it was spiritual, more intimate than just the physical act. I have never wanted to reproduce, but wondered if I would miss the actual birthing experience. Sky and Sierra have given me that, I thank them. Ah, the sun is about to make its appearance, that slight pink glow to the East excites me, always will. Listen to me gush. I Love This Life!' Chianti.

Sierra closed the book, sighed. "Can I make a copy of this when we get back, Miss Seychelle?"

Seychelle laughed, "Actually, I think I should make a copy and give you Chianti's book." She caught herself. "Unless she wants it back, of course." She leaned forward to tune the radio. "Should have rented a car with a cassette player."

Sierra studied her closely. "You don't believe she's coming back, do you?"

Seychelle looked at her. "I wish I had your faith. I did until we talked with her grandfather. I believe she loves you and him so much that had there been any way possible at all she would have been in touch with one of you."

The little girl was silent for so long that Seychelle felt a bit of panic. What do I say, how to cheer you, bring you out, help you not hurt?

"Hey, I've got an idea! Why don't we go to my house for the night? It's too late to drive all the way to your place and we're only half an hour from mine. We'll stop and get pizza on the way."

"Yeah!" Sierra sat upright, beamed.

"The place may have been taken over by ghosts by now, but they're friendly and will let us in," she said with a laugh. "Do me a favor and find something on the radio. And think about what kind of dessert you want so we can grab something before the stores close."

Seychelle watched her concentrated tuning. They had left the farm with heavy hearts. His wife had died, so the old man now rented out his farmhouse and fields to a family who seemed to have sort of adopted him. One wall of the 'guest house' that he occupied was covered with postcards and pictures from all over the world that 'our Chianti' had sent. He just smiled and nodded when Sierra told him the story of her birth. From time to time he would chuckle and say, 'Haven't heard from her in a long while, must be at sea.'

By the time Seychelle turned her key in the front door she was regretting her decision. In truth she was too tired to drive further safely, but perhaps a hotel would have been better. Without West, or even Beauregard, the place seemed almost morbid. But Sierra went charging in, excited and curious.

"Wow, great house! How old is it? Did you grow up here? Is there an attic? Are there really ghosts?" It all seemed to come in one breath and Seychelle began laughing. They were so much alike.

"Help me get the rest of the stuff out of the car and I'll take you on a tour." She had left the house phone connected, so was able to call Sky. She seemed reserved but did not object to the change in plans. Seychelle promised to call her before they headed out the next morning. Sky was the no-nonsense, logical half of the couple and a good counsel to seek in serious matters. She was a good person to have on their side in such a precarious situation. Was Sierra the only one holding onto hope for Chianti's survival?

After a giggling candle-lit tour throughout the place, they ate pizza and settled into Seychelle's bedroom for a short pajama party and crashed early. Sunlight was filling the room by the time Seychelle opened her eyes. Realizing she was alone in bed, with a surge of panic she shouted, "Sierra!"

From the kitchen Sierra shouted, "Get up sleepy-head, breakfast is ready!"

Seychelle quickly dressed and scurried downstairs. She was suitably impressed by the spread on the table. "Well I'll be. You are something else!" she drawled.

Leftover pizza and doughnuts shared space with apples and peaches Sierra had gathered from beneath the trees in the yard. She'd even made coffee. They tucked in with enthusiasm and Seychelle fielded questions about her youth.

When they began clearing up Sierra asked, "Can we go see Chianti's raft?"

Seychelle hesitated. She'd not thought about that. "Sure, but we'll call Sky first and then we'll go." She told herself to stay positive, keep it light and short.

On the way they stopped by her dilapidated treehouse and swing. "West built this from an old sugar cane press," she said and opened her dolphin locket to show Sierra his picture.

"Is that tiny ugly baby you?" Sierra asked, laughing.

They walked on and when the raft was in sight Seychelle could see the little girl's body stiffen. "Race you to it!" she challenged and they both broke into a run. She slowed a touch but there was no need as Sierra easily beat her.

It looked the same, perhaps a bit more sun-bleached. She held up the canopy as Sierra clambered around, seeming to play out what might have happened, much as Seychelle had that first day. That seemed so long ago now. She heard car tires on the loose gravel, heard the car stop and a door close. She turned and could hardly believe her eyes.

Sonny Jerken Jr. gave a good-old-boy smile and wave as he stepped around the trees and bushes that blocked the area from view. Her stomach churned. Stupid, you stupid girl! She waved, tried to smile, leaned down.

"Sierra, don't tell this man you know Chianti. You're just the daughter of friends of mine," she whispered. A subtle thumbs-up from the girl reassured her and she forced herself to think clearly.

"Well, I sure wasn't expectin' to see you 'round here," he said, stepping around the last smooth boulders. His Ray-Bans hid the scrutinizing gaze but she could feel it.

"I'd prefer to hang out in the Caribbean, but Daddy's papers weren't sorted. I'm having a friend rent it out for me."

Sierra emerged from the raft, smiled sweetly, and extended her hand. "Hello Sir, my name is Sierra. Pleased to meet you." Honey almost dripped off her.

His face broke into an unnatural smile and Jerken Jr. took her hand. "Now aren't you a pretty little thing, Sierra. You just call me Officer Jerken, that's what all the kids call me. I'm with the, uh, Coast Guard. I help rescue people who have trouble in their boats."

"Have you heard anything else?" Seychelle asked, cursing herself. It was silly to pretend she hadn't spoken with Geena about him. Would he be suspicious? More suspicious, she corrected herself.

"Not a doggone thing. I was just passin' by when I saw you and thought I'd just come on over and ask you the exact same question."

She shrugged, "The Coast Guard would be the first to know if I had. I do hope they didn't go down with their ship. Maybe some fisherman picked them up. Can't you trace the raft or the RDF?"

"That's why I'm wonderin' if they weren't up to no-good. Both had their serial numbers scraped off." He chuckled, "W-e-l-l, probably couldn't have tracked them down anyway, being old equipment and all, but sure makes you wonder what they were tryin' to hide."

Sierra took Seychelle's hand. "Pardon me, Miss Seychelle, but I need to be excused."

"Huh? Oh, yes, we'll have to go back to the house. Good luck, Mr. Jerken. I'm not sure when I'll be back, but I sure hope you find them."

"Y'all want a ride? Be quicker."

"Thank you, but we'll just take a short-cut I know." She led Sierra up the beach across a narrow path and into woods. When they heard his door slam and the car start up behind them, Sierra stopped.

Seychelle said, "I'm afraid you'll just have to use the bushes if you can't wait, but I just couldn't face more time with him."

Sierra began laughing and dancing around. "I am a great actress! Even you were fooled. I always get the lead in our school plays. I may be famous one day."

Seychelle was distracted. She frowned at the little girl. "What?"

"He was lying and you were nervous, so I had to help. Geena is right, he is in the drug squad."

Seychelle was amazed. She began to laugh, stopped. "We'd better run. If he is spying and we don't show up at the house it won't look good."

As soon as they were back Seychelle began getting ready for departure while chastising herself. Can't believe I brought us here, gave him more

79

ammunition. Must think like a scammer. The plot seems to be thickening and I can cause real problems for good people if I'm not careful.

She jumped when Sierra asked, "Shall I telephone Sky?"

"Yeah, tell her we're taking the scenic route. Tell her it will be late when we arrive. Don't y'all stay on the phone too long, okay?" In movies they could trace almost any call.

"Okay!" Sierra beamed.

And with a determined smile Seychelle began planning their convoluted return trip. She had to stop by the post office first to pick up mail they were holding for her, and she had to make sure she couldn't be followed. I must think like a scammer, as if I've brought in a load of grass from Jamaica. With that mind frame came a bit of guilt as well as a high from theoretically getting away with something. One is still vulnerable, even after the act, she coached herself, so there is the need for cunning in reading and anticipating the moves of the enemy.

She glanced upward, gave an embarrassed laugh. Were Chianti and West in attendance? "Well, give me some guidance and common sense if you are. I stumble a lot."

Thirteen

"How could you possibly live your life looking at a door and not go open it?"

Robert D. Ballad, Institute for Exploration.

"You can't be serious!" Seychelle exploded.

"He wouldn't listen to me," Sky said, hurt and anger resonant in her voice. "We always discuss everything, but he's been too worried for too long, his reasoning is clouded."

"I could wring Geena's neck. It was bad enough to do it once, but again! And taking Barry along!" She shook her head. "It was just too damn easy the first time."

Sky touched her arm. "You'd better sit down, there's more bad news." She glanced toward the shed. "The surprise I sent Sierra off to see is a new litter of kittens but I don't know how long it'll keep her occupied. We tell her absolutely everything, but she must not learn that her father is bringing in coke, no matter what the circumstances. Lying and hard drugs are virtually the only taboos we've set for her."

Seychelle had turned in the rental car, taken a taxi to the Dauphin Island ferry, crossed to Fort Morgan and grabbed a taxi to the Gulf Shores airstrip. From there the final cab brought them to Murphy's and she had dismissed him at the gate. Each leg she paid in cash, small bills, as would a good scammer. Sky, who had obviously been awaiting their return, met them at the old oak with its heavy overhang of moss. Now Seychelle pressed her hands against the rough trunk. Give me some of your strength and tranquil energy. How many bubbling cauldrons have you watched in your two or three hundred years? Oh, for your fortitude!

"Barry finally got Dolphin last night. He said that they would continue to search but he didn't hold out much hope," Sky said. She swallowed, inhaled slowly. "I'm trying to accept that we've lost Chianti."

Her dark troubled eyes moistened, she shook her head firmly, cleared her throat. "I'm pretty sure that was the deciding moment for Barry. Within an hour he and Geena headed for the airport."

Seychelle felt the early evening breeze, realized her tee-shirt was wet with sweat. She loosened her hair, dropped barrettes into a vest pocket and lay back against the oak. "I assume they told you nothing except that they were heading for Jamaica."

"Right. Better for all concerned and all that shit."

Sierra's return with a mewing newborn clasped to her breast ended further discussion, to Seychelle's relief. She needed to think. They returned the kitten to its worried mother and then went in to supper. Sierra gave Sky a detailed account of their two days, barely touching her food. Sky was distant, perhaps too rung out emotionally to react. After a walk on the beach her excited recount wound down and she was willing to turn in early, exhausted by adventures.

Evening was cool, with crickets and frogs in full voice when they finally strolled down to the pier. Seychelle topped up their glasses with locally grown Perdido red and leaned back on a weather-beaten piling. "It was stupid to go to my house but Sierra was so down after seeing Chianti's grandfather."

Sky shook her head. "Don't worry. I am of firm belief that there are flows of energy over which we have no control. Even a gentle trickle can have unimaginable consequences. If you look at all of this as a result of Chianti delivering my baby, well did it actually begin when Barry and I first met at school, or when his grandparents moved here from Ireland, or, well, you get my drift." She smiled and lifted her glass. "And we won't venture down the path of my Cherokee spirit wanderings. I toast your creative return trip. Sierra loved the ferry ride and it would certainly have thrown anyone off your trail."

Seychelle lifted her glass and chuckled. "My head is finally in the right place as I come to better understand this subculture. However, this new twist sure enough endangers everyone." They tensed when they heard a car approaching on the dirt road. When it stopped, they both stood.

"People come see us without phoning ahead," Sky said with a hint of a smile, though it was obvious she was far from relaxed. "Don't forget that we're in the country and we do have a business. Let's go see who it is."

"Don't you worry about thieves with all these boats?" Seychelle asked. "I mean, there's nothing but a wooden fence and open gate."

"Nothing's ever happened, so I guess when it does, we will. It's one reason this place means so much to us. Barry's making a desperate move, but we'll lose everything if we don't come up with some money before month's end."

They walked without talking through boats toward the open gate, each wrapped in dark premonitions. Seychelle gasped when she saw the tall slim figure standing before them.

"Seagull?" she asked in disbelief.

He gave a deep chuckle, stepped forward to where she stood in shock, and gave her a gentle kiss on the lips. "Missed you. Wasn't sure I had the right place."

"What, what are you…" she stopped, her stomach knotted. "Sky, this is Seagull from Sint Maarten, Charlie's friend."

Seagull extended his hand but Sky stood looking at him. "Who sent you and why?" Her smooth voice was hard, controlled.

Seychelle put her arm around Sky. "Let's go sit on the pier and talk."

As they walked in silence Seychelle's list of questions took form but the pleasure she felt at his presence disturbed her. As soon as they were seated, she asked, "Is this about Chianti?"

Seagull nodded. "Dolphin had a helicopter cover the area for several days and he's had fishing boats out, but no trace of *Cayenne*. He has a connection with the Coast Guard, but other than unsubstantiated calls, they've only come up with an unclaimed life raft, which must be the one you found, and two unmarked dinghies."

Sky said, "Her dinghy is an old Avon inflatable with the exterior and interior bottom painted orange for easy spotting."

Seagull shook his head, "Neither was an Avon. I'm sorry, Sky. Geena told me how close you were."

"Geena?" Seychelle asked.

"That's the other reason I'm here. I was in Jamaica when they arrived early this morning. I'm to let you know that all's well and I'll meet them when they get here."

Sky said, "Aren't you working for Dolphin? Chianti thought he only handled cannabis."

"No," Seagull looked away, seeming embarrassed, "not Dolphin."

"Not Hans!" Seychelle demanded, not trying to hide her disappointment. When he began to shake his head, she sighed. "You're Charlie's coordinator, aren't you? No need to be coy, Sky and Barry were to have held Chianti's load for Dolphin. But you must know that."

In the dark his expression was impossible to read but she could feel his apology. He was caught up in one of those flows, more powerful than individuals, just sort of sweeping folks along. Was she making excuses for him? For them?

"That had nothing to do with Charlie. But he has tried to help. It was his chopper that searched."

"When are Barry and Geena coming back?" Sky's voice was still tense. Seychelle felt guilty for entering their lives, for bringing Geena with her.

"Both should be here having dinner with you the day after tomorrow."

"I'll fill you in on the latest developments," Seychelle said. She carefully delineated facts and perceptions, though she didn't complicate the story with the West saga. She was acutely aware of Seagull's foot pressed against hers.

They sat in silence after she finished. Waves gently broke beneath them and her body was keenly sensitive to water movements around the pier's supportive pilings. Clouds obscured the moon and a few stars escaped. Night felt heavy and humid, the earlier breeze stilled.

"Feels like a storm is brewing," Sky commented.

"Mostly just tropical depressions so far. They've already named some but no damage yet, all fizzled out," Seagull observed, distracted.

"They aren't coming back into Mobile, are they?" Seychelle asked, attempting a casual tone.

"That's left to Geena and Barry," Seagull said. "They were given product and a cash advance. After they clear in, they'll ring a number, then I'll receive their message. I call our central phone every hour."

"Neat little business. Just round up the mules," Sky quipped. She stood. "You should go now."

"I, uh, I'll walk you out," Seychelle offered as she and Seagull scrambled to their feet.

Sky turned without a word and walked toward her house. Sadness washed over Seychelle, almost overpowering her. I've not had a chance to mourn for Chianti, but do I believe she's gone? So how must Sky feel?

Seagull stood staring after Sky.

"She's got everything to lose if Barry's irrational action fails," Seychelle said. "It was a desperate move to save this yard."

They walked in silence. At the gate Seagull turned and put his hands on her shoulders. "Don't shoot the messenger. Please," he whispered. He gave her a quick hug, kissed her forehead, and was gone.

Fourteen

"Tacking!" Seychelle chanted as she pushed the mahogany tiller to port with her knee and released both sheets. She watched Sierra move like a dancer, crouching to slide beneath boom to windward, balancing the small dinghy as they worked their way in against a 15 knot westerly. As the day warmed the wind was dropping and shifting. The incoming tide was their ally, the process of tacking their pleasure.

Seychelle flashed on Chianti's 'I Love this life!' declaration. When she laughed Sierra gave her a quizzical look.

"I'm happy, I'm just so happy!" she shrugged.

"I am too. Barry's back! I just saw him in the yard!"

Seychelle's heart quickened. She had been tense and worried but had been able to relax on this early morning sail. Had she really forgotten for a while? Now there was an urgency to get to shore. Why were Barry and Geena two days late? He had called, but had only said not to worry, that he was fine but delayed. She looked at Sierra's wide smile. Sky had only told her that he had gone to see Geena's friends to arrange financing for their boatyard. But Sierra was so attuned to everyone and everything around her. Only now did Seychelle realize how difficult the time had been for her. She's a child, Seychelle reminded herself, and her relationship with her dad is much like mine with West.

Both girls were tired by the time they finally leapt out of the boat onto firm sand. They were hurriedly furling and securing the red Dacron mainsail when Barry ran up, grabbed Sierra and hurled her, screaming and kicking, into the water. She regained her footing quickly and tripped him, then charged up the beach to hide behind Seychelle. The laughter was infectious and a tension release that all three needed.

Sky came out and interrupted their play. "Telephone, Seychelle."

"Where's Geena?" she asked, regaining her breath as she followed Sky into their office.

"Ask Seagull," Sky said, her soft voice just above a whisper as she closed the office door.

Seychelle studied Sky's face and her hand began to tremble as she lifted the receiver to her ear. "What happened?" she asked, barely able to articulate the question.

"Seychelle, they stopped her coming into Miami. I've sent in an excellent lawyer. This kind of case is his specialty. He says she's doing fine, very calm and together."

Seychelle felt cold all over, automatically began taking long deep breaths. Seagull kept talking but she wasn't absorbing his words. She cleared her throat. "Um, sorry Seagull, y'all need to tell me again."

She sat down and listened, holding the phone with one hand, Sky's hand with the other. After a minute she motioned for a pen and wrote down the numbers he gave her.

She cradled the receiver, turned unfocused eyes on Sky. "Guess I'd better head on down to Miami and see her. Or, should I go break the news to Mamma? Geena's the youngest, the star, the pride of the family, whose future promised success. Stupid, such an unnecessary, stupid thing to do." Her words were slow and deliberate, her hot angry tears uncontrolled.

"Talk to Geena before you do anything," Sky said, her voice firm. "Is one of these numbers a lawyer? Call him first. I'm sure Seagull told him to expect to hear from you. He'll tell you how to arrange a visit. I can go down with you if you need."

"No," Seychelle said and hugged her. "But thanks." She wiped her eyes with her sleeve. "You shouldn't get involved, stay away from all of this. I need to talk with Barry, get details before I do anything else. Think I can get him away from Sierra for a bit?"

"I'll tell him there's a call. Stay here."

Her thoughts were fragmented. From imagining Mamma's face when she receives the news, to a flash on Geena falling out of her tree house when they were younger than Sierra, to Chianti in a life raft. She was relieved when Barry walked in and closed the door.

Avoiding her eyes, head down, he stood with slouched shoulders. "I'm sorry, Seychelle. It's my fault. When Geena told me about her run, the easy money, I jumped on it. She tried to talk me out of it but I pushed. She was just going to introduce me to Hans but once we were there," he shrugged, "temptation was too much for her."

Seychelle shook her head. "No blame to be handed out. Geena is an adult. She knew exactly what she was doing, the risks, how it would affect her family."

She studied his face. He looked much older, with bags under his eyes and his whole being sagged.

"It could have been me. I risked my family's happiness. Can you imagine what it would have done to Sierra?" He shook his head. "Kids her age do coke. Don't like myself much."

Seychelle didn't feel inclined to try to ease his pain. It was something he would have to live with. It was done, and perhaps he had saved Murphy's Boatyard.

"What happened with you?"

"I came in through New Orleans. We had talked about it, decided she shouldn't enter through there again and that we should come in separately. I don't know what went wrong for her in Miami. We were to have arrived at the Pensacola airport, gotten together at the nearest McDonalds and called the assigned number so Seagull could pick us up. When she didn't show, and they were preparing to close, I called Seagull. He picked me up and we went to a beach house near Gulf Breeze, made some calls. He paid me half, and then left with the gear. He admitted he was worried but said they were checking on Geena. He brought the rest of the money the next morning and asked if I'd mind staying that day to receive messages. He knew then that Geena had been arrested and suggested I call Sky but asked I not tell her. A lawyer had been sent in, the best, he said. Bail was refused, Seychelle."

She was unable to maintain eye contact while he spoke, sat staring at the numbers Seagull had given her. Scholarship withdrawn; family disgraced. Would it make the headlines of the Mobile papers? She dialed Zachariah J. Carter. The best, a specialist in this kind of case, Seagull had said. Well, he should know, or anyway Charlie should.

The secretary connected her immediately.

"Hello Ms. Austin, Zachariah J. Carter here," came the deep voice. "I was expecting your call. Geena asks that I tell you that she's fine and declares her stupidity before you have a chance to and begs that you not contact her mother." She was relieved he sounded older and Southern, but educated, a bit like West, whose years in the Navy had minimized his drawl. Being addressed as Ms. was also reassuring.

"May I visit?"

"Yes, tomorrow afternoon. You will come by to see me first, won't you? Be sure you have your license with you. Oh, and no guns," he chuckled.

She wrote down directions, hung up and turned to Barry. "Would you mind running me to the airport? I'll catch the next flight to Miami and stay at a hotel tonight. I'm to see this lawyer in the morning, Geena in the afternoon. He sounds okay."

"Do you want me to go with you?"

Seychelle shook her head. "You've got plenty to do here from the sound of it. Is there a plan? I mean, just paying off some debts isn't enough, is it?"

He motioned toward the shed. "Now we can get the material to finish the catamaran we're building for a charter company in Biloxi. If they're happy, and we're under the contract time and budget, they want two more exactly the same." He gave a weak smile. "That will be the turning point for us. At one time this yard employed over forty, now it can barely support four. But I know I can get it back up. There are people out there who want quality and personal service and attention to detail. The art of boat building isn't dead."

His passion touched her. "Well, if I were having a boat built this is where I'd come," she said with a smile. Both brightened but the moment's pleasure was overridden by guilt. Geena's situation was a dark cloud that ruled.

Fifteen

Fiction. "Cannot believe Sydney is still inside. The island nation of England remains wrapped in the past. Charming but for the fact they are not updating their legal system or thinking in many areas. But I won't get off on that. America is behind as well. We've both written many articles, research papers and letters about the situation. Some were even published. The following I penned on my flight home after release.

"Call it the worst experience of my life, our lives, that night, the night of our bust. The 46 ft. steel German-built cruiser they gave us was not our kind of boat but right for such a large load of hash. *Isis* was comfortable, luxurious even with hot shower, teak interior, etc. But a racer she wasn't. Anyway, we hung off the Moroccan coast one hot summer night at assigned latitude & longitude for a couple of hours, nervously watching fishing boat lights that dotted the horizon. We could hear the low hum of a diesel, but were startled when an unlit trawler pulled up next to us. Dolf jumped aboard with radio in hand. He guided us closer to the coast. Though we were only five miles off, no lights were discernible on that sparsely populated stretch of land. Within half an hour a fishing boat about half our length came alongside. Two uniformed men jumped aboard and my heart stopped, however Dolf greeted them warmly and our loading process began. We had been told that military assistance in cannabis and drug trade was normal in many developing countries, but this was our first actual encounter. Each kilo brick was sealed in plastic, foil and wax, and then securely duct-taped into bundles of 12. They were wet, heavy and dirty so loading was messy, hard work.

"A slight paling of dark night told our well-adjusted eyes that dawn was approaching when the trawler pulled away. Sydney and I stared at the 1,000 kilos of hash that filled our salon. Quite amazing. Adrenaline displaced exhaustion and we motor-sailed due west, keenly aware of everything, suspicious of every blip on the radar screen.

"I spent the first two days and nights of our voyage north packing bricks away, out of sight, while Sydney navigated, nurtured the temperamental autopilot so we stayed on course, and kept watch. His hot spicy noodle soups kept us awake and alert, no sleep possible 'til all was hidden in bilge, lockers and every discreet location I could uncover. We stayed 200 miles away from Portugal and gave that infamous Bay of Biscay even wider birth during our 13 day beat north. We encountered only one force nine gale that made our last North Atlantic night a long one. The following day we headed into the English Channel, being careful to avoid the territorial waters of France and England.

"At this point I must say Sydney and I had a hot, quick session on the foredeck at sunset. Tension, exhaustion and intensity of watches meant passion hadn't been part of our partnership during that sail. But sex just doesn't get any better than when you're living on the edge. We had survived the unrestrained energy of a storm at sea, were going against the unjustified laws of society, and besides all that, we were just about to run the gauntlet. Yes, that was an awesome session!

"So, finally we entered the English Channel, heading for Holland. *Isis* was tiny between two lanes of freighters, container ships and tankers that were going to and from the North Sea. And there were ferries crossing between France and England, just to add interest to heavy traffic. Our open-ocean watches of six-hour duration were cut to one hour. You need that kind of freshness for total attentiveness in such conditions. At midnight we shared hot chocolate in the cockpit before I went below to stretch out. I'd just pulled the duvet over my head when Sydney's urgent call jolted me to full alert. I charged out the companionway into the cockpit and was blinded by two huge spotlights that were trained on us from astern. One was to port, the other to starboard, and they were drawing closer.

"Sydney said, 'Well, my Love, I believe this is it.' A disembodied bullhorn bellowed out, 'All hands on deck and arms in the air immediately! You are being boarded!' We moved closer together, raised our hands. They kept repeating their demand, obviously not believing it was just us two, a couple, in what they considered to be a major drug bust. I can tell the story coolly now, but do believe my head and emotions did a defensive shutdown at that time. Two large inflatables pulled up, one on either side of us, and fourteen men scrambled aboard, guns in hand. They were fully decked out in black, from knit caps to bulletproof vests to boots. Looking very professional. It was a bit like being on the set of a movie about terrorists. I wondered how long they'd been rehearsing for this scene.

"They knew we were heading for Holland and that we had hash aboard, were even armed with screwdrivers for taking the place apart in their search, but no Miranda Rights were read. The commander (I didn't catch his name or rank) ordered Sydney and I to sit in the pilothouse with him. One of his men took the wheel for the fourteen-mile trip from international waters to the nearest English port while the rest of the guys began digging out carefully stashed bricks. Irony was that they were importing highly illegal cannabis into their country, not us. Much like in olden days, when lanterns were hung to guide booty-laden square-riggers into those dark rocky southern bays, the Brits were breaking their own laws.

"We had agreed to carry the large shipment because cannabis is legal in Holland and the illegal act of importing such a quantity would have been punishable by less than two years' incarceration. It seemed an acceptable risk for $400,000. However, primitive laws of the island to which we were taken meant we were handed eleven-year sentences, commuted to nine because we pleaded guilty, as advised by our court-appointed solicitor. We hadn't figured that possibility into the prospectus since we were staying in the international lane, not intruding into English territorial waters. It hadn't occurred to us that English Customs and Immigration would be so hungry for headlines and atta-boys for a big bust that they would stretch the Geneva Conventions.

"What followed was a sad farewell to the sea as we were led away in handcuffs. Humiliating strip-searches, filthy public jails, intimidating interrogations, white-wigged court scenes, farcical inaccurate media coverage, blatant lying by Her Majesty's Customs officials, transport in urine-permeated meat wagons, and the trauma of our separation are amongst the experiences I shall pen someday. I'll need time and distance before I re-enter that chapter. What we did learn was that we were just unlucky, that we drew short straw that year. Seems the Moroccan government notifies the EEU of a few smugglers each year in exchange for protection of their fishing rights. The main national income is from tourism, cannabis & fishing. Otherwise big European fishing fleets rape their coastal waters. Sad truth is that they have already depleted that area to such an extent that fish stocks may never recover. Anyway, farmers and military had been paid up front for our cargo, so they lost nothing by handing over info on our boat. Those who had financed the entire excursion felt the loss, without doubt, but we remained discreet, shared no names, no info.

"Our first six months were the hardest, and then we settled into prison life. We each studied and developed. Zen and the Art of Making Incarceration Work for You. As deportees and well-behaved inmates, we received early parole. They've released me now. After only four years I'm on a 747 heading for Atlanta, but not Sydney. No matter how much I argued and declared equal responsibility, they're making him serve an extra six months because his name was on a Liechtenstein bank account. Sydney's godfather had set up an account for him at birth but it had never been used until a recent deposit. They have confiscated the money, but insist Sydney serve the time as well.

"They removed the cuffs when they put me on this plane for deportation. I'll be free and clear upon setting foot in the States since they don't recognize foreign convictions. But, leaving Sydney is more than painful. My partner in life should be with me. He should be free. I'm really working on the 'everything happens for a reason' concept, but it doesn't wash at this point in time.

"Both Sydney and I have developed our inner freedom and peace, things that cannot be touched by those with keys. However, there's a lot to be said for physical freedom. I'll get back to our boat, go for a sail and clear my head, then devise a plan of action." Chianti.

Seychelle returned the pages to her daypack and stared out at surrounding clouds in faded blue stratosphere. It was beautiful, but more so when looking up from a boat. She reflected on her morning sail with Sierra. How incredible Chianti's first sail must have been after those years in prison! And food. Sky had laughed about the amount of okra, tomatoes, corn-on-the-cob, watermelon and peaches Chianti had eaten at their place, her first stop after Atlanta. Stepping into the sea must have been positively soul-stirring! Freedom, what do I understand of the value of it? Oh, Geena, what have you done?

Seychelle rented a car and checked into a hotel right away. She'd travelled to large cities many times with West, but always felt a bit intimidated. The madness of city traffic the next morning had her quite tense when she walked into Zachariah J. Carter's plush office. Her first thought was that defending drug offenders must pay well. Her second was that he must be good at it.

"Well hello, Ms. Austin," said the tall gray-haired gentleman with a warm smile. He stood and stepped from behind his large teak desk. "It is good of you to come. I haven't seen you for so many years!"

Confused, Seychelle extended her hand, stared into his large brown eyes. His impeccable chestnut double-breasted suit seemed to match their color, the silver rim of his glasses to match his hair and brows. "You know me?" she managed.

"Oh, you know, Geena talked so much about you and your father did bring you with him a couple of times. The cute little girl has become a lovely woman."

She frowned, "My father?"

"I know his death has been difficult for you. Of course, you were so small, you wouldn't remember coming here," he said, motioning her to a soft leather chair. "Surely, he told you about me, about us."

He studied her blank stare, cleared his throat. "I took the liberty of ordering some coffee and pastries for us since it is so early. I trust you will join me."

There was a tap at the door and the woman who had shown her in entered carrying a tray laden with silver service. She served them coffee, uncovered the bakery goods and departed. Seychelle used the time to steady herself.

"No Sir, my father told me nothing. What in heaven's name are you talking about? Why would he come see you?" she asked, her last word given enough inflection to indicate he was probably an alien or at least despicable.

The lawyer frowned. "He called me shortly before his death to, um, say goodbye. He said he put everything into a safe deposit box for you."

Seychelle was vexed. "Our lawyer gave me the key to the box when he read the will but I wasn't ready emotionally for exploring memorabilia. What is supposed to be in it?"

He was watching her very closely and she thought she wouldn't like to be on the stand under his interrogation. He sighed and gave a curt shake of the head. "You must go examine the things your father left for you before we can discuss the matter any further. You may not even wish to see me again. But that would be a shame," he said with a sad smile.

She was glaring at him, but caught herself, lowered her eyes and sipped her coffee. "What about Geena, Sir? How much will it cost to defend her and what kind of sentence will she get?"

"The costs are covered," he said while spreading soft butter generously across a cinnamon roll. "Sentence, well, I don't know who the judge will be. I figure we'll go guilty, trying to pay for school, honors student, valedictorian, poor one parent family, first offense, all that. Could be anywhere from a suspended sentence to eight years, to be brutally frank."

Brutal is right, Seychelle thought. "Her mother is just about the finest person I know. Do you have to depict her in such a bad light? Geena got herself into this mess and it has nothing to do with Mamma or her upbringing. Between the scholarship and income from renting out my house she probably wouldn't have needed to work. She is so intelligent, but this was downright stupid!" she declared.

"We all need to test ourselves at times," he said, his deep voice soft, consoling. "Then there's the thrill of it, of living on the edge. No excuse, just plain ol' human weakness. I'll run the defense arguments by her before we go to court, but the poor single parent angle wins big points. That was a really nice gesture on your part, the house arrangement. She is very upset about letting you down."

"I'm fine, it's Mamma I'm concerned about."

"She doesn't want her told until afterwards, is of the naive hope that she will be able to keep her in the dark if she doesn't get a long sentence."

Seychelle sighed. "I'll talk to Geena. Without doubt it'll be me who has to tell Mamma. I'm feeling guilty, illogical as that is." She downed her coffee like a shot of whiskey, replaced her cup and stood.

"I feel anger right now, Mr. Zachariah J. Carter. Mostly at Geena, but some at West, even some at you. After I see Geena I'm going right back to Mobile. I'll go to the bank on Monday. If there are questions, well, I'll call and make an appointment with you, Sir."

"I understand your frustration and confusion. However, your father was a very good man, I respected him immensely. Once you understand the whole situation, I'm sure you will appreciate his actions as the best for all concerned."

With his words consuming her thoughts, Seychelle got lost twice though his secretary's directions had been clear. She stopped for lunch but drank iced tea distractedly, hardly touched her fried shrimp and hushpuppies. West, what had been going on? Her full attention did not turn to Geena until she was sitting across from her friend.

"Are you okay?" Geena asked with concern.

Seychelle gave a short laugh. "Now wait, I came to ask you. Of course, I'm fine."

"You look like you did when you told me West had cancer. Listen you, I'm okay, more embarrassed than anything. Don't go worrying yourself sick about yours truly. I got myself into this and I'm a fool and I'm paying for it. My concern is for Mamma." Her eyes clouded; she cleared her throat. "And that we're still friends."

"Fat chance of that changing," Seychelle said. "Take more 'n doin' somethin' stupid tah git rid o' me!"

They both smiled, tried unsuccessfully to laugh, but both were reassured that their bond was still strong. Seychelle studied Geena's face. Worry lines between her brows and darkening under her eyes betrayed real strain. "How are they treating you?"

Geena shrugged. "They're just folks doing their jobs, some with attitudes, but nobody's been hateful. I'll admit I'm glad this isn't Alabama. Food's not as bad as I feared but the cell and bunk are straight out of an old black and white movie. Hey, wait 'til you meet Zachariah, the quintessential lawyer. Whoever is the top dog is paying big time. If anyone can get me off, he can."

Though Seychelle knew the bravado was a defense, she wanted to shake Geena, demanding she be realistic. "I went by his office on my way here. He's big time for sure," she said and forced a smile. She wanted Geena's solid reasoning, wanted to tell her all Zachariah had said, wanted her friend to go to the bank with her to open West's box.

"What about Mamma?"

Geena looked away, and wouldn't meet Seychelle's eyes when she said, "We've gotta keep this from her. It's not big enough to make the Mobile papers. I can just be naughty, not keeping in touch for a while 'cause I found a boyfriend in Jamaica. I'll get Brian to send Zachariah some postcards, then I'll write notes to Mamma on them during legal visits and Zachariah will return them in a package to Brian to be mailed. So, she'll get postcards with Jamaican postmarks. Just don't go see her, okay? I know you're no good at lying, so I won't ask it of you."

Seychelle nodded. For distraction and to ease tension she told Geena about Chianti and Sydney's bust. She tried to convey the spirit and positive thought she'd picked up from Chianti's account. She promised to get a copy to Geena. Kindred spirits, shared misadventure, not as bad as it seems, etc.

Their allotted 45 minutes was over too quickly. Their good-byes were too cheerful, smiles forced.

Seychelle's feet felt heavy, the air thick, and the sun harsh. Identifying her rental car took real concentration. Yelled insults from a pot-bellied dog-walker she almost creamed when pulling out of the parking lot pulled her attention to present matters. With care she negotiated her way to a service station and got organized for her drive to Mobile.

Sixteen

Seychelle drove north through the Florida countryside, such a contrast to the city. Surprisingly, folks seemed even lazier than Alabamians. Down-home friendliness was there, but they'd experienced tourist business and sincerity was dubious. She found that she got better service when she exaggerated her drawl. One of us.

When she got close to Mobile, she pulled off Interstate I-10 and hit a large mall where a couple of up-market shops supplied pieces she needed for her disguise. She used her credit card, figuring there was nothing suspicious about buying clothes, and then drove into old Mobile, down oak-lined Government Street where she checked into an old colonial mansion that now served as the Old Magnolia Hotel with sincere Southern charm. Columns, wrought-iron balconies, ceiling fans, canopied beds with embroidered spreads. Her heritage, she supposed. She called Sky and filled her in on Geena, careful to avoid names, then ate her fill of crayfish in the hotel restaurant. A bottle of Perdido wine, soft and slightly fruity, complimented delicate crustaceans and helped quiet her myriad questions. Afterward she fell into a deep, exhausted sleep.

At precisely 8:00 the next morning Seychelle parked in front of her bank and quickly stepped inside. Feeling rather silly, she removed Costa sunglasses and tucked them into her leather shoulder bag with which she was decidedly uncomfortable since she was a travel vest and backpack kind of girl. She knew she looked older in the Ralph Lauren suit with low heels and her brown curls tucked under Navy fedora, so tried to walk with a more refined gait. She hadn't been in very often, had done few transactions other than ordering new checks, so figured there was no reason for anyone who worked there to remember her. She approached one open window, told the teller her name and asked to get into her box, though it might be in the name of her father.

After a few minutes a nondescript middle-aged woman came out, her ring of keys rattling. She smiled and led the way to a small room in the back.

"The safe deposit box is in your name as well as Mr. Austin's. I'm sorry to hear about his death. Such a nice man, a true gentleman. It must be really hard for you; I just know he was a good daddy."

"Yes, thank you," she said, trying to relax. An everyday activity, she told herself, and handed over her smooth featureless key. She watched the woman insert it and her own key into one of the largest doors and remove a long metal box. She placed it in Seychelle's arms and led her to another small room where there was a table and one chair.

"I will be outside when you finish," she said.

Seychelle found she was reluctant to open it. As when entering their attic alone as a kid, excitement and fear quickened her breathing.

"Hope there's some money, West. I sure have been spending freely of late and could make a habit of it," she whispered. Though they hadn't had any money problems, that I knew of, she reminded herself, he'd taught her to always be aware of exactly how much she had, not to plan on having more until it was in her hand, and to splurge occasionally. He was against credit cards, and had chastised her for getting one, but she'd been prudent and it had often come in handy.

She could almost hear her heart pounding, and kept telling herself to relax. What dark secrets were you hiding, West? What were you doing that needed a Miami lawyer?

She lifted the top and looked down upon one chubby green velvet pouch and two large brown envelopes. One looked innocently thin, but the other bulged and was rather heavy. She stuffed everything into her large leather purse with jerky furtive motions. Were they watching, were there cameras? Seychelle glanced around, stood and started for the door, sure she was radiating guilt. Calm down, she told herself, this is a normal procedure, every little ol' thing is just fine. She returned the box to its compartment and retrieved the key. My key, she thought, to my box, to West's secrets. Back in the rental car she looked around, expecting Jerken to appear, but there was no Jerken.

Breathing a bit easier, she returned to her room and rang for room service. She ordered a big breakfast with bacon, ham, biscuit, grits, fried eggs, coffee, the works. She also asked that they get her suit done for her. Be prepared. She stripped off her sweaty suit and stepped into an oversized tub, though what she wanted was a cold shower. She sighed. Big bathtubs are for hot baths in cold weather or to share with a man. Over six months since anyone. Geena says I'm too picky. Maybe she's right. Wonder where Seagull is, what he's doing. Bet he's a great lover.

Relatively refreshed, she grabbed a thick terry cloth hotel robe and opened the net-curtained French doors. Her shaded balcony overlooked a charming courtyard with a weeping willow, thickly stuffed planters, bird chorus and central fountain, segregated from a hot, humid outside world.

Turning, she darted to the large canopied bed, grabbed her new expensive bag and slung out its contents. With a sweep of her hand the fat envelope was ripped open and a pyramid of tidy bundles of cash formed before her eyes. Fifties and hundreds, that's what Seychelle was staring at, and she stood frozen, unthinking. A knock at the door made her jump and sent her into a minor panic.

"Just a minute, just a minute!" she called, as she shoved it all into a drawer. She was clumsy, her hands sweating. With heart pounding, she charged over and opened the door. A smiling, rotund, coal-colored woman bustled right in with her heavily laden tray.

"Now I'm bettin' y'all got a hangover, what with gittin' up at this hour for breakfast. I just came to work myself but it's not often I serve the mornin' meal so late." She gave a warm chuckle. "Reckon I'd be sleepin' late myself if I didn't have four young uns ta look after and feed. Gotta work, but I don' mind." She chatted on as she arranged breakfast on the round white balcony table. A pleated linen napkin matched the pink azaleas she centered and their print was repeated on the China.

Try though she did, Seychelle could think of nothing to say, and she could not help repeatedly glancing at the drawer.

"Now, where is that suit y'all want me to freshen up?"

Seychelle rushed to pick it up from the floor and hand it to her lest she begin to search.

"Nice suit. Ah can tell the quality right away. Now don't y'all worry, ah'll have it just like new for you before sun goes down. Y'all want anythin' else?"

Seychelle closed and double-lock the door behind her, then sank onto a chair. You're not a very good smuggler, even in make-believe. Chill out. Whatever West did, he certainly never got in such a state of nerves.

She opened the drawer and, refusing to focus on the money, took out the thin envelope and carried it out to read with breakfast. With deliberate attention she placed the napkin in her lap, drank her juice, poured some coffee, and then opened it. Her father's orderly compact script hit her physically, almost taking her breath.

"Okay West, you're here. This is no hoax. That money is real. My life is being turned upside down and nothing, not even my memories of you, will ever be the same. Was my life a lie, was I living in a bubble, created and controlled by you before you died and I found Chianti's raft? Or was it just secure and normal and balanced, the way life should be? Where's the line, what was real?" she asked, her voice barely above a whisper, her throat tight.

She put the loaded letter aside, picked up utensils and attacked her breakfast. She was cutting into a thick slice of smoked ham when Sierra's words interfered with her first bite. Or were they Chianti's? Well, right or not, I like my ham. It didn't taste right. Annoyed, she doused it with tomato gravy and proceeded to eat every bite, grits and all, before refilling her coffee and retrieving West's manuscript.

"How's my Seychelle? You've probably got that quizzical frown with your right brow arched above serious green eyes and are tugging at a curl with your left hand."

Realizing he was exactly right, she shifted position.

"I know my death will be/is/was difficult for you, but you're a tough cookie and it's time to get on with your life. Hopefully you can appreciate my story, not resent me for keeping secrets from you, and use the gifts I have left to enrich your life. Am sure you ripped into the fat envelope before you opened this one to get answers to questions that were choking you. Ah, you and your questions! I didn't always have the answers, did I?

"In the beginning… I joined the Navy to make Dad proud and to get out from under his control. Do you remember how domineering he was, Seychelle? Anyway, I progressed through the ranks. It was logical that Kathy and I would marry since we were sweethearts through high school and hers was an old Navy family as well. Her fear of flying meant that what little overseas duty I had was served solo. I'm pretty sure her old man pulled strings to make sure his only child's husband didn't see action though there was plenty going on back then. I was in the Philippines for a few months early in my career. Charlie, one of my friends there, dared me to take some grass back with me on home leave. Couldn't resist. I've never believed there was anything wrong with grass so breaking the law was my sin and defying Navy regulations was tantalizing. After the thrill of that first heady success, I would smuggle a bit of grass for Charlie whenever possible, though I could never smoke the stuff, just ended up coughing. The developing business grew when Charlie left the Navy and set up operations in the Caribbean. You and I moved in with Dad when we lost Kathy. I was stationed in Pensacola then and the Navy let me stay there until I had to retire. I became the off-load planner for Charlie's shipments that he sent up by boat. When there were problems I would liaison with his lawyer in Miami, Zachariah J. Carter. He's a good man, I even took you with me a few times when you were little."

Seychelle laid the papers down, poured herself some warm coffee. One sip and she headed to the closet refrigerator for a brandy. They had only one conversation about grass, and that was when she told him she wanted to try it. He pointed out that it was illegal and that she should be sure the experience was worth the risk. Discretion and safety were the watchwords. The next day she'd found a shoe box containing a peanut butter jar of grass, some rolling papers, a lighter and a spray can of air-freshener on her dressing table. It had been very similar to their short talk about sex. After that one he'd left a box of condoms on her nightstand. She laughed. Geena adored West and it became virtual worship after such cool moves. What will you think when/if I tell you the rest of the story? What do I think/feel now?

She poured both tiny bottles of brandy into a cheap snifter and went to her money drawer. She fanned through a bundle. All hundreds. Replacing it, she lifted the green pouch, touched the soft velvet to her face, and with slow careful fingers she untied the cord. Confusion furrowed her brow as rough stones fell out onto the bed. Rough greenish rocks, none larger than her thumbnail, lay before her. Confused, she bagged them, and returned the bag to the drawer with all that money.

"I'm emptying the closet, Seychelle, so brace yourself. Kathy had a problem with heroin. One reason I kept working with Charlie was that he could keep her supplied with good quality stuff, and he was discreet, of course. She tried to quit many times, Seychelle, but an addiction is like a disease. Try to understand. She managed to stay clean while she carried you, but after your birth she started back. It is very possible that her car crash wasn't an accident. She hated her weakness and more than once had said that she feared only death would free her from it.

"Dad's addiction was gambling. You know that, you've heard stories and jokes. But only I knew that he lost the house and property just after we moved in with him. With Charlie's help we managed to recover everything."

Seychelle took a long drink, felt brandy warmth in her chest. She stroked her dolphin locket. I didn't know her. Am I lucky I wasn't born deformed? Charlie couldn't have known who I was. Could he? She shivered.

"Seychelle, I was an outlaw. Our problems were more easily handled as a result, but I can't in honesty use that as justification. I loved the challenge, the danger, the thrill of successfully out-thinking opposition. I loved living a double life, secrecy. Keeping my other life hidden from you was the painful part, difficult but necessary. I can't say I've ever felt I was doing anything wrong, though as I pen this synopsis to my favorite person in the world, I wonder if I'm hurting you, disappointing you. However, I won't know your reaction. I had planned to charter a boat and take you sailing in the Bahamas for the week of your 23rd birthday and reveal all. Doesn't look like I'll make it and I'm afraid I'll not find the right words while doped up, laying in a hospital bed before departure. So, I'm attempting clear organized thought, honest revelations, and I'll either get this into our safe deposit box or mail it to Zachariah, who's become my friend, lawyer and confidant. Please contact him and he will explain details of an offshore account from which you'll receive a monthly income. It's clean in that it came from grass and investments, no drugs, but I must admit that a few laws have been trampled upon. You can pester him with your questions. I settled accounts with Charlie and have not worked with him for a few years. Zachariah can contact him if your curiosity burns, but he is better left as part of the past, Seychelle. Your determination to understand everything is one of your many strong points, but go with care, study those you encounter before extending trust.

"Those rocks are rough emeralds from Colombia. You can have them polished into pure, exquisite pieces. When you are ready. Their story I take with me, their beauty I leave you to discover. As with life, sometimes it takes a bit of determined effort to reveal true beauty.

"Perhaps you and Geena can take a Bahamian cruise. The cash is for splurging. Please don't be practical! Had I splurged in my youth, I wonder if I would have needed to become an outlaw. Outlaw, Seychelle, not criminal. You know, or will quickly learn, the difference.

"Identifying your needs and dreams is vital. Just remember: The World is Yours!"

Seychelle gently put his missive aside and downed in one throw the remaining brandy. Oh West, if only I'd gone to get this stuff before taking Geena to Jamaica! She stopped. That line of thought would accomplish nothing. Two bees were exploring the azaleas on her table, searching for their golden hidden treasure. There was more buzzing and ferreting to her right where a honeysuckle vine had climbed a stone and stucco wall to her second-floor balcony and merged with its tortured iron rail. She plucked a white flower and carefully nipped its base. Laying it on her tongue, she slowly withdrew the stamen for that one tantalizing drop of nectar. So sweet, but not satisfying.

Seychelle stood and gave a long stretch, reached toward the cloudless blue sky, felt her muscles strain, then relax as she dropped her arms and began to laugh. She untied her robe and dropped it, picked up West's letter and returned it to the drawer.

Her laughter subsided into giggles as she threw herself spread-eagle on the bed and stared up at an ornate, slowly spinning fan. Hugging herself, she rolled around and laughed 'til her stomach ached. Finally tears came. Long sobs and moans shook her before she felt purged, sorrow and guilt and loneliness dealt with for now. Eventually she lay exhausted and let the mesmerizing overhead rhythm lull her into a deep, deep sleep.

Seychelle jerked upright, frantically scanned the room. Shivering, she wrapped her arms around her clammy naked body, trying to orient herself. Her head ached. Slowly she moved her feet over the side, nearly fell, the floor was so far down! She stopped. Think, where are you? Leaning, she held onto bed, nightstand, chastised herself for drinking all that brandy, for falling asleep under the fan and getting a chill. She looked around, remembered, made her way into the bathroom, got the water running to warm. Dry heaves. Damned brandy. The room spun. Under the steaming shower she finally stopped shivering, checked her watch, and swore. Grabbing a towel, still dripping, she ran to the phone and called the front desk.

"No, ma'am, your suit's not back yet, I'm really sorry."

"Yes, ma'am, banks are still open, 'bout 15 minutes more."

"Yes, ma'am, I'll sho nuff have a taxi out front waitin' for you."

With determined concentration she pulled on jeans, shirt and vest. She avoided the mirror, moved everything from the money drawer to backpack and made her way downstairs to the taxi. Collapsing into the back seat, Seychelle told the driver where they were going, and congratulated herself for thinking clearly. She had to get everything back into her bank box and was in no condition to drive.

The burley straw-haired driver got out and opened her door after pulling up in front of her bank. "Missy, my name's Tom. I'm gonna wait right here for y'all. Don't get me wrong, but ya ain't lookin' too good. I'll just make sure ya get back to your room okay."

Attempting a smile, Seychelle said, "You're alright, Tom. Thanks." Her clothes were soaked through with sweat and she was freezing. "Caught a chill."

By the time a manager showed her into the small room everything was hazy and transferring her stuff from backpack to box took real effort. She started to close it, sighed. Just one, see how it feels. She took a bundle of 100's, shrugged and grabbed one of 50's, removed a rough emerald from the pouch, and zipped everything into a hidden inside vest pocket.

Tom helped her into his taxi and kept glancing in his mirror at her as he drove. He pulled up in front of the hotel, got out and opened her door. Last thing Seychelle would remember was his rough, red, full-jowled face above her.

She smelled disinfectant and knew she was in a hospital even before opening her eyes.

"Well, we were sure enough worried about you."

I'm dreaming, a nightmare, she told herself. But Sonny Jerken Jr. sure sounded and looked real standing there beside her white-sheeted hospital bed. Her frown deepened when she licked dry, chapped lips.

He stepped up alongside, held towards her a glass of water and directed its straw to her mouth. That straw was real. She lifted her hand, touched his and looked into his eyes. "You're real, aren't you?" she croaked.

He chuckled, "Last time I checked. Nurse said you couldn't have but a sip at first." He took it away.

She looked at the needle in her arm, up at a bottle of clear liquid that dripped down a tube into her. "What's going on?" she asked.

Before he could answer the door was thrown open by a bustling pole of a woman, all wrinkles and white uniform and seriousness. "Excellent, you are back." She almost smiled, turned on Jerken Jr. "You were to have buzzed as soon as she awoke. Get out."

He stared at her. "Nurse, I'm sorry, but she just woke up. I was just about to call you."

She had her back to him, checking Seychelle's drip. "Yeah, right. Out."

He turned, stopped at the door. "I'll wait outside until you're through. I need to talk with Seychelle." Receiving no reply, he left.

Seychelle let out a long breath. "Thanks," she whispered.

"How do you feel?" Nurse Dora asked and gave her another sip of water.

"Unbelievably tired, weak, dry, and I have a headache. What happened?"

"Food poisoning. Ham." She was making notes on the clipboard, studying her, glancing between her and the beeping monitor.

"Damn. The Magnolia."

"Yeah, they're worried. Kitchen was closed down for a couple of days. But it was traced to their distributor."

She frowned. "How long have I been here?"

"A week."

Shocked, Seychelle was quiet while Nurse Dora reset the monitor above her bed. Her thoughts seemed to be slow forming. Was my brain damaged? Geena!

She tried to sit up, but collapsed back. "There is a friend I have just got to call, really. No, wait, why is he here?" She glanced toward the closed door.

"We needed to find a family member and his card was in your vest pocket. Since he's a family friend," she hesitated, watching Seychelle's eyes, "we asked him to get in touch with your family. He told us you lost your father recently, that he had been your only close family."

Think, she told herself frantically. Her hand went to her breast. "My dolphin!"

"All your valuables are locked away. Your locket is there, as well as everything you left at the hotel. I can bring whatever you need."

"My vest?"

"In this closet, the contents of the pockets are in our safe."

Seychelle looked at her, picked up on no real reaction, and there most certainly would be if they'd found the bundles of money. She was so tired. "Must I see him? He's not really a friend." She stopped; afraid she had said too much.

106

"No, of course not. Rest is what you need. But he will probably come back later. Is there anyone you want me to contact? The doctor will be here in a little while."

"I must call a real friend now," she said emphatically, though it was barely above a whisper. "I need to use the phone. And my locket, I must have it!"

Nurse Dora frowned. "Dial 'O', she'll give you an outside line. The hotel's paying for that too." She gave a curt nod and left.

A week! Geena would feel deserted. What state must her head be in? Sky and Barry would be worried. What's Sierra thinking? Is Beauregard okay? She fell into an exhausted sleep, her unresolved concerns stimulating some very strange dreams.

"Seychelle, Seychelle." A familiar voice. Waking up was a drag, she just wanted to sleep. "Seychelle." Slowly, she opened her eyes.

"Mamma!" she croaked, eyes flying wide.

Her round, concerned face broke into a relieved smile. "Honey, you are hard on this old woman. They let me come in 'cause they said you were awake. Here, drink some of this."

As with each time she had been awakened, a straw was placed between her lips. This time it was apple juice. Nice. She drank slowly, trying to organize thoughts.

"Thank goodness you had that nice Mr. Jerken's card or they wouldn't have known who to get in touch with. Well, I suppose police would have tracked down your no-account relatives but I know you don't think much of them. Doctor says you're fine, just need to rebuild your strength now."

Seychelle asked her standard question.

"Why Honey, it's been 10 days. You have lost too much weight. Soon as you're able I'm taking you home with me. I know how to fatten up a child who's been sick." She chuckled and started listing some things she would fix.

It barely filtered into Seychelle's troubled thoughts until she heard Geena's name.

Mamma went on, "I did have a note from Geena yesterday but not a word about how to contact her. Only know she's in Jamaica. With some boy, no doubt. Have you been able to call her yet? Now I'm sure there's a US embassy there and if you want, I will get them to hunt her down."

"No! Uh, I'm okay, please don't call them. I'm fine. I can't call her, but there really is no need." During one of her lucid periods she had called

Zachariah. He'd sent flowers and candy and started action to sue the ham distributor. She'd argued but he insisted it was necessary to ensure they cleaned up their act. They could have killed her after all. He'd said that Geena was okay and sent her love and her trial was probably a month away. Seychelle had asked him to ring Sky and Barry, but tell them not to visit since Jerken Jr. was hanging around. They too had sent flowers. She'd made sure all cards were removed.

"Loves you like a sister, Geena does. She would be here in a minute if she knew. Sowing her oats before settling back into school, I guess, but I don't want her having so much fun she forgets to come back and finish up and graduate." She stopped, straightened her ample figure to full imposing height and looked disapprovingly at Seychelle. "What were you doin' staying at a hotel anyway? Especially one that was low-down enough to give you bad meat?"

Seychelle managed a smile. "Oh Mamma, honestly it was a nice hotel. I've always wanted to stay there. I just had to come up for some stuff West left unfinished. It was supposed to be overnight. Don't you worry about me. Or Geena."

Though Mamma exuded a warm love that was a healing force in its own right, Seychelle was immensely relieved when Nurse Dora came and hustled her out. She'd have to slip away. Though Mamma's TLC and good food would be welcome, she couldn't lie to her about Geena. And she couldn't face Jerken Jr. She fell asleep hatching a plan.

She awoke with a start.

Nurse Dora gave a soothing, "Everything is fine, I just removed your drip. You look better but for these junkie tracks." Seychelle had become comfortable with her wrinkles and starch and dry humor now. After two weeks of tests and drips she was fairly marked up.

"Good thing that hotel's paying for this private room or we'd not have been able to block calls and visitors to give you the rest you needed. And, you would have disturbed neighbors that first week." She laughed, "You mumbled about everything from dogs to seagulls to prison to storms. Entertained us." She smiled, nodded. "We'll get you up later for a bath and you can go for a garden stroll tomorrow morning."

As soon as Nurse Dora closed her door she sat up and stretched. She did a few practice walks around her little room and actually felt pretty good, just weak and tired. The garden stroll would be her chance. She had convinced them to let her wear her locket and watch. Money and emerald had remained hidden in her vest, which was now hanging in the little closet along with her suit and everything she'd had in her hotel room. She could see from her window that there were always a couple of taxis out front.

She tired quickly, and had just placed her butt on the bed's edge when the door opened.

"Don't you know to knock?" she demanded angrily and turned her naked back away from Jerken Jr. Damned hospital gowns! Damn you! She swung her feet onto the bed and jerked the sheets up.

"I, I'm sorry. I didn't want to disturb you in case you were asleep."

"Sure. Well what do you want?" She was truly vexed and flustered. "I'm really tired, I need to rest."

"It's important that I talk to you. I get the feeling you don't like me, but I want to be your friend. That string-bean of a nurse will probably throw me out any minute so I'm going to be blunt."

Seychelle's skin crawled when he approached her bed and stared into her eyes. "I know what your father was up to. We were hoping he'd lead us to the head honcho, but reckon he retired from that business even earlier than he did from the Navy. I couldn't figure out where you were coming from when you called about that raft. Thought maybe you wanted to tell me something." He hesitated. She kept her face passive with great effort, and did not shift her eyes from his.

He cleared his throat. "Your trip to Sint Maarten got my attention. But I really sat up and started tryin' to piece the puzzle together when your friend, Geena, got busted in Miami. You went to see her, naturally."

She felt her face go hot. Her palms were wet. She concentrated on her breathing.

He gave a half smile just as her door opened. "You have my number if you decide to share some secrets with me." He gave her a cocky nod and pushed past Nurse Dora who stood glowering after him, her hands on her hips.

Seychelle felt as if she were caught up in a Stephen King film. Could all that had passed be part of ham-induced hallucinations? She listened to water running as Nurse Dora prepared her bath. No, it was all too horribly real. West would not be waking her from a bad dream with loving laughter and a hug. This was her life now and she had to take control of it.

Seventeen

"I don't know, maybe it'll make him more suspicious that I ran away, but I couldn't face another session with that creep and I couldn't have woven some web of lies for Geena's mother." She leaned back against the oak. Strength through osmosis, she hoped.

She felt safe now. Old Magnolia Hotel absorbed all hospital and hotel expenses so all she'd needed to do was pack. That was easy since everything fit into her travel vest and daypack. She left in the early morning, just after shift change and asked a taxi driver to take her to Walmart. She had enough small bills to pay him, knew she couldn't hand a driver a hundred or she would be remembered for sure. She broke a couple of hundreds buying stuff for Sierra. Then she got another taxi to a different shopping center where she purchased kitchen stuff for Mother Murphy and got more change for a taxi to the bus station and another to Murphy's Boatyard. Barry and Sky had warmly welcomed her. They felt like old friends, family.

"What a story!" Barry said. "Imagine finding out your father was a grass smuggler! You've no idea how much is in your off-shore account?"

Seychelle shook her head, laughed. "My off-shore account. Wow. No, not until I go see Zachariah. Now I'm nervous about that, and even about going to see Geena, though I must of course." She frowned. "I know you don't keep secrets from Sierra, but I'd rather she not know all this about West. Not yet."

Sky shrugged, "That's totally up to you, but there is no reason she should be told. She knows you were in the hospital so expect some lecturing about your negative carnivorous habit."

Seychelle smiled. "I brought her a book of sailing stories, where is she?"

"She went to see Chianti's granddad with Sydney."

She gasped, sat up, "Of course, he's back! Oh Sky, is he okay? How did he take it?"

"Seagull picked him up in Atlanta and they spent a few days with Charlie at one of his places. He's in pain and he's angry but he seems to accept that all was done that could have been. He only stayed here overnight, and said he had to go tell her grandfather. He seemed relieved when Sierra asked to go with him. They are mourning together, but I think each feels the other needs their strength. I had been worried about Sierra closing it up inside. Helping him is her way of coming to terms with reality, of accepting that Chianti is gone."

Their contemplative silence was filled by birds rustling in the tree above them and gulls squawking as they congregated. A tribute to Chianti, Seychelle thought. The smell of the place made her comfortable but she felt sort of hollow. Like an empty place was left where Chianti had been. West was still with her, always would be, though she needed a better understanding of his other life, of the West she hadn't known. Perhaps that was part of the emptiness. And now Geena. At least I have a real direction now, she thought, 'cause I must unravel this subculture, the grass smugglers, though that just might lead into the dark side, if I'm to truly understand. 'Go with care, study those you encounter before extending trust.' Okay, West, I shall, but you better stick with me.

"Did you give Chianti's book to Sydney?"

Barry nodded. "I felt a bit guilty that we had read it, had entered her private thoughts before him. But he said he was relieved only friends had read it, that you had kept it from the man. He wants to meet you. Seagull told him about your passion for Chianti." Barry was sitting on one of the rounded, exposed roots with his long legs folded Buddha-like. He took Seychelle's hand. "You're staying with us until you've fully recovered. My mother will insist on fattening you up, so be prepared."

She was exhausted and so grateful. There were some nightmares but Seychelle went down for a long, deep sleep. She awoke sweaty and in a bit of a panic, unsure of where she was, but settled when she remembered. In the hot shower she began to revive and realized she was desperately hungry. She put on the jeans and shirt Sky had left for her and was shocked that they fit. Well, some pay big money to lose weight quickly. Me, I just used up one of my lives.

She rang Zachariah before going down but he was in court so she asked his secretary for the earliest appointment possible. Three days. Perfect. She could sleep and eat and maybe even meet Sydney. After seeing the lawyer, she needed to head to Jamaica to get Beauregard, perhaps stay there for a while. No better place to get my head together.

Ah, she smelled coffee! Her stomach was growling when she stepped into their dining room. Bright sunlight streamed in an open window as did birdsong and woodworking sounds, like drilling and sawing. There was a giggle and Sierra was on her, laughing and hugging. Unable to fight off the exuberant child, or even catch her breath, Seychelle just collapsed in a chair and accepted her love.

"Great book, thanks! I'm going to read every story over and over and know them by heart!" she fervently declared. Then she released Seychelle and went quite solemn. "Sky made me promise not to scold you right away for poisoning yourself with meat, at least not until after you have eaten. I knew smelling coffee would wake you since it always works on Barry. Now, I won't watch you, but Granny says you must eat a little of everything. She heard you showering, so fixed delicious breakfast stuff for you. I must go to dance class but Sydney is going to take you walking. You have slept for over 14 hours and need exercise."

She kissed Seychelle's cheek. "I'm glad I didn't lose you too," she whispered and walked out, shoulders squared.

Seychelle watched after her until breakfast smells captured her attention. With enthusiasm she slathered butter over pancakes, hot grits and biscuits. Cane syrup and fig preserves topped the feast and rich red watermelon finished it off. Has food ever tasted better? She was licking her fingers, remembered her manners and picked up her napkin.

Mrs. Murphy was smiling when she came in from the kitchen. "Sierra would be proud of you. Now, go find Sydney, he's needing a friend."

Seychelle raved about the breakfast, gave her a quick hug and went through the noisy boatshed to the office.

Sky said, "Now you're looking like yourself. You made me worry when you arrived."

"I didn't realize how bad I felt until I'm feeling good again," Seychelle beamed. "That great breakfast helped! Lots of activity around here, looks like you're rolling."

Sky pointed to a stack of papers on her desk. "We are. I'd forgotten what it was like to really work. Parts to order, estimates to draw up, old connections to renew. When business lags, enthusiasm drops and you get behind with everything. No matter how I might feel about Barry's run, that money sure breathed new life back into our business. And us," she said with a hint of a smile.

Seychelle smiled. "Y'all deserve a break. Where is Sydney?"

"Said he'd be out around the pier. You'll like him, Seychelle."

She walked out into a brisk morning breeze. Clouds were shifting position quickly and she imagined Sydney was planning sail changes as he sat so very still at the pier's end. West said that sailors were always navigating or trimming sails even if metaphorically.

Her enthusiasm waned as she approached. What should I say? How does he really feel about this stranger who read Chianti's private thoughts, their shared intimate experiences? She was hesitant to disturb him, her steps tentative. She studied his relaxed posture, broad shoulders slightly curved, his head tilted to one side. Was his short-cropped Afro fashionable in England, or just what you got in prison and kept as a matter of convenience?

"Sydney?"

He turned to her slowly, his distant look softening into a smile. "Hello Seychelle. Won't you join me?" His deep, smooth voice was cultured, warm.

She sat down beside him, but was at a loss for words. There was quite a lot of gray in his neat black beard and mustache but his ebony skin looked baby soft and smooth. His dark eyes were large, and had that far-seeing look with wrinkles from squinting into the sun. She could picture him at the helm in a storm. Missing nothing, total concentration.

"Fish love junk food." He tore off a small piece of bread and dropped it at their feet. They watched as a multitude of tiny mouths attacked, sending ripples in all directions, though the sun's reflection meant it wasn't possible to see individual perpetrators. "Chianti loves taking spaghetti down and creating a riot amongst reef dwellers. I'm afraid all her negatives were on *Cayenne*, but her granddad has some prints. He loves taking out his albums and regaling you with stories. He and Sierra sat for quite a while, but it was a bit too much for me. Later."

"How did he take it?"

"Better than I did. He just nodded slowly and said, 'Well, my girl was doing what she loved.' He didn't go through the questioning, ranting and self-flagellation, just accepted and was sad."

He shifted his gaze to her face. "I can't tell you how much I appreciate your sensitivity. You didn't just keep Chianti's memoirs, you protected them, and reached out to try to help someone you'd never met. But, can you tell me why? I mean, from what Seagull has told me, you are not in the business."

Seychelle looked into those deep intelligent eyes and knew she could tell him anything. She began with finding their raft, even gave details of thoughts and emotions she hadn't shared with Geena.

She was dry and thirsty by the time her narrative was complete. She felt naked and drained, had surprised herself by revealing her mother's drug needs and grandfather's gambling addiction. Details she'd not told Sky and Barry, had planned to tell no one.

His response was, "Let's go sit under the oak and I'll make some iced tea for us."

So, what next, she asked herself, thankful for shade and a moment's solitude. Well, I won't know that until I talk with Zachariah. Why did I bare my soul to Sydney? I don't really know him. Not the behavior of a good smuggler.

"Seychelle?"

She opened her eyes, frowned.

Sydney smiled, "I was going to apologize for taking so long but you took a nap so it must have been a good thing. I should have moved you into shade sooner but was enthralled with your story. Here, this will renew your spirit."

She was so thirsty, took a long drink. The tea was cold and sweet with freshly squeezed lemon and an edge. "Did you put whiskey in my tea?"

"Only a bit. An old Southern remedy, I'm told. To your good health," he said, lifting his tall amber glass to her. Ice chinked softly as they toasted. "This is the way tea was meant to be. Brits use milk instead of lemon and drink it hot. Absolutely vile. But then, their taste in food is bland, heavy and unimaginative."

"They really drink warm beer?"

Sydney nodded, laughing. "And for breakfast they fry everything, including slices of white bread. Grease drips down your chin when you bite into a piece."

Seychelle shivered. "And prison food must have been horrid."

"Not as bad as you would think." He leaned back, sighed. "Things happen for a reason. Separation from Chianti and the open ocean was very difficult."

Seychelle quietly sipped her tea, giving him time, though she wanted to bombard him with questions. Wanted to know all about it, details, attitudes, schedules, fights, what other prisoners were like, were there murderers, everything.

"We met West."

She sat bolt upright, nearly spilling her drink. "You did? Where? When?" she demanded.

"Years ago, at an off-load party in Biloxi. Charlie used to put on a big bash for all participants after an operation was complete. That was when it was only a grass thing, when we were all sailing bails up from Caribbean. For Gulf Coast business your dad did what Bradley did in Chianti's account of our first run up to Maine. Those parties were special, a touch outrageous. Charlie would reserve the top floor of a club or a whole restaurant. Food and champagne, waited on like royalty, with plenty of pre-rolled joints and lines of coke. West was sitting next to us at that Biloxi affair. He wouldn't smoke or do lines, but was as high as any of us. It was raw oysters and crayfish and shrimp gumbo that night, so tempting that even Chianti indulged."

He touched her hand. "Can't believe I'm sitting here talking to his daughter." He gave an embarrassed laugh. "I was a little jealous because Chianti talked and danced with him more than with me."

Seychelle was still, nearly uncomprehending. West? Chianti had found him attractive, flirted with him? My father. What a scandal if he'd been busted! She shrugged. "I'm a hybrid. Mamma was a heroin addict and Daddy was a cannabis smuggler. Did you know he was in the Navy for 28 years?"

Sydney laughed, shaking his head. "He did seem rather straight and respectable, but I didn't analyze it since he and Charlie were the oldest of our associates. Umm, would have sent shock waves through the solid military foundation of our country had his secret life been uncovered. Liked living on the edge, did he?"

"Yes, it seems he did, but I had no idea until I read his letter."

"He's right about Zachariah. Too bad we didn't have someone like him defending us in England. He and West tried to talk Charlie out of moving into hard drugs. Charlie had always done a bit on the side for friends, but as America's Drug War intensified and surveillance technology became more efficient, smuggling bails became more risky. Busts increased and profits went down. To Charlie it was just a logical transition. However, last week he admitted to me that he misses good old grass days, that it's a much lower caliber of folks involved in every sector of the business."

"I assume that's why West pulled out."

He nodded. "Charlie lost most of his best people. We had commenced our voyage by then, but had seen it coming. Changes were immense by the time we returned. As you know, that was why we took that Moroccan run."

Seychelle watched his features alter as memories and loneliness edged in. She desperately wanted to lessen his suffering. Without thinking she said, "Why don't you go to Miami with me? I'm sure Zachariah would like to see you and…" She started to say, 'It would give you something to do,' but caught herself.

"Well, it would be good to have company," she told him. "I'm still coming to terms with all these surprises West has laid on me and with Geena's situation. I've got to head to Jamaica afterwards to get Beauregard. You can go with me, go spend time with Yellowman on his farm. He is growing some quality weed you will not believe!"

Sydney sat tranquilly contemplating her. "I can't stay around here. Love them though I do, I feel her absence too strongly. I need to do something."

Seychelle started laughing. "My birthday is in a couple of days and West left me cash for splurging, ordered that I not use it for anything practical. I would have taken Geena to Disney World or the Bahamas or somewhere to party and spend money. Oh, Sydney, say you'll go with me! I've been dreading spending my twenty-third alone."

His smile was warm. "I could refuse such an offer?"

She jumped up, kissed his cheek and ran in to tell Sky about their plan.

Eighteen

"What we perceive as hard matter is mostly empty space with a pattern of energy running through it. This includes us." Einstein.

"Nervous?" Sydney asked.

"Me? You forget I'm a hybrid. Piece of cake." She stepped out of the car, telling herself not to tug at her skirt or adjust her jacket, and mounted steps with a confident swagger. I own this bank. The world is mine. Right.

Seychelle's imagination was in full swing as she followed the manager. Everyone was staring at her suspiciously. That teller was probably calling Jerken Jr. or the police.

No hesitancy this time when she opened her box. She added a bundle of 100s and three bundles of 50s to unspent cash inside her purse. In a flash she was zipped and tidy, had returned and locked away her box, and was stepping out of the bank. She wanted to take more, and was not planning to return for quite a while. However, Sydney had warned her away from wandering around with a lot of cash. People were wary of cash transactions with large bills, especially in Florida.

"Mission accomplished?" Sydney asked, pulling away from the curb and into traffic as soon as she closed her door.

Seychelle leaned back, gave a long exhalation of relief. "Ridiculous to get so paranoid. In reality I've done nothing."

"In fact, you're right. However, I've seen these drug chasers. They become quite obsessed and relentless. They believe even the most minor of leads may point toward a cartel head honcho. Saving America's youth is their justification, and we won't get into real human motivations. Of course, the black market they've created since the late '40s is an extension of that nurtured by Prohibition. Man's not very good at learning from past mistakes."

"You're sure you don't want to go by and see your raft?" she asked.

117

"No, that would be an unjustifiable risk. This Jerken Jr. is keeping watch, from all you've told me. I most definitely do not want to be seen around our raft, fresh out of English prison for hash smuggling. Besides, if he can find any scraps from the past, he just might start tying bits together. Also, associating with me wouldn't be good for you in his eyes."

"I hope I never see him again," she grimaced. "Do you think Chianti was going to contact West? That she intended to navigate toward our vicinity?"

"No, only Charlie had any contact with him. We only knew him as West, though few people use their real names, and had no idea where he lived. We did know he was no longer in the business. I've gone over charts, currents and wind patterns with Charlie, Dolphin Dave and Seagull. There is no navigating with a life raft but it would have naturally been taken there. It was just lucky that it made it in past outer islands and cays. Lucky because it meant you were able to save her memoirs. We believe Chianti prepped the raft, but didn't make it to it, so she went down with *Cayenne*."

Seychelle heard his voice thicken, saw his jaw go taut, his grip on the wheel tighten. She turned to gaze out her window.

They were approaching open country before she asked, "Does Charlie know who I am?"

"Zachariah rang Charlie while I was there. You had called him from your hospital bed and he thought Charlie should know about West's death and your situation. He was surprised, well as surprised as a person who's been through as much as he has can be. He made Zachariah promise to keep him posted and said he'd cover any expenses the hotel didn't. He proceeded to get quite drunk and really got into reminiscing. What stories! His opinion of your dad is very high. He considered him honorable and a friend."

Seychelle sank into assorting puzzle pieces that made up her life. Alice at the Mad Scammer's Grass Party. Sydney settled into driving and she dozed off before they had progressed far down Florida's west coast. She sat up from time to time with a question, and then withdrew into thoughtful silence or sleep.

"Good Cider Ahead," she groggily read aloud from a haphazardly painted sign that was nailed to a passing pine tree.

Sydney saluted and pulled off the two-lane paved road over a narrow-rutted culvert cover into a grassless yard. He sought shade under a pecan tree and chickens scattered in all directions. Barking mongrels converged from beneath a ramshackle house that had at some time been white with a full front porch.

"They look to have had a hound dog mama who visited all the neighbors," Seychelle said with a laugh. "Would you mind going in? I am not brave enough to face what they may offer as facilities but really need to get out of these city clothes."

With a dog entourage Sydney headed inside. Seychelle made the transition from her suit, which she still considered as her disguise, to jeans and vest. She was jotting notes in her journal by the time he returned.

Sydney handed her a bottle and two paper cups. "Quite a place. They also sell sugar cane, army fatigues, cigarettes, rubbers and guns." He smiled ruefully. "But I got the definite feeling that the old redneck wouldn't have sold yours truly a gun. And from the way he was staring out his window at you and glancing back at me, I don't think he would have sold me any rubbers either."

Seychelle felt herself flush as his skin color and the type of area they were in surfaced in her head. "I'm sorry."

He laughed aloud. "Apologizing for history and ignorance amongst some people who share your skin color? Ambitious, aren't you?" He backed up and again headed south. "Come on, pour me a drink, Wench! I braved those natives to score and I'm thirsty."

She unscrewed a beat-up top from the plastic bottle and poured them some foamy, tangy-sweet cider. She toasted him, "To the antibodies we're developing."

After a sip she asked, "Did you and Chianti run into much prejudice?"

"No, nothing obvious. Funny, all the way around the world but only in an English prison and with that fool back there have I been confronted with blatant prejudice, though you can most certainly interpret or misinterpret looks and reactions if you're of that mindset."

After a few miles the bottle was empty and Seychelle returned attention to her journal, which she had christened Quandary. "I've an idea, Sydney. Be totally honest, okay?"

His lips twitched and eyes danced but he gave a solemn nod. "Promise."

"Well, I'm dying to pick your brain. I mean, you've done so much, seen so much. You're intelligent and educated and sensitive to the world around you. If I combined your adventures and perceptions with Chianti's file it would make a great book!"

She had slid forward in her seat, was facing him in her excitement. "It could be a collection of short stories or a novel or a biography! Just your circumnavigation could make an exciting adventure book. And honestly, I can write. I mean, I've not tried to get published but have taken creative writing and journalism courses and my teachers said I had the 'write stuff'."

He smiled, glanced at her, and gave the road full attention. Seychelle sat back. A slightly uncomfortable silence ensued.

"It must have been wretched when they put you in handcuffs," she ventured.

"It was worse when you were handcuffed to one of the guards. But at least they didn't have waist and ankles like they do here." He cleared his throat. "I think the most painful part was when I saw them put cuffs on Chianti."

Seychelle's eyes watered. She fumbled sunglasses out of her vest pocket and quickly slipped them on.

"It will have to be a novel," he said firmly. "More notoriety I don't want. Our names show up nowhere. Agreed?"

"Yes, yes! Anything you say. And any questions you don't want to answer, well fine. And tell me if I'm a nuisance. And, don't take this wrong, but I should pay you for interviews, for research assistance. I mean, West left cash for just this kind of thing! He used to say that he thought I should be a writer. I wrote stories when I was a kid and he would edit them for me." She pulled herself from her reverie. "It would be business so you should be paid."

Sydney shook his head. "Between Dolphin and Charlie, I'm okay. If it is a big seller you can pay me a commission." He extended his hand.

She gave it a firm shake and beamed. "I was going to hang around in the Caribbean, look for something to study and write about. I was sort of adrift. That's one reason I liked Chianti. She was so comfortable with herself and with life. It was almost like identity wasn't a big, looming unknown, but a comfortable sure thing that she embraced. I really admire her." She stopped. "I'm sorry."

Sydney stated flatly, "Saying I'm sorry can become a negative habit. You're not that kind of person." He turned on the radio, tuned in a classical station. "I admire Chianti as well. Most people who know her admire and like her immensely. Her belief is that souls go through graduating stages of development and select bodies that best serve each level. When its purpose is served, that body is abandoned. Interesting concept."

"What do you believe?" she asked gently.

He lightened. "That energy just keeps changing form. I suppose that means she might be right."

"You've shared such adventures, taken chances, gambled with life. And had real, complete love. You're so lucky."

"Very lucky," he whispered. After a minute he said, "Right now I'm more hungry than anything else. You're the scout."

"Aye aye, captain! Too bad this isn't a boat with all provisions aboard. I'd go below and make us some sandwiches."

"Sierra gave you a very capable on the tiller. That's a high accolade from someone who was born in a cockpit and won her first dinghy race at age four."

Seychelle was so pleased she giggled. "Didn't realize I was being assessed but sure enjoyed that morning sail with her. I hadn't been out for a couple of years, and had forgotten how much I love it. West taught me when I was small. I read Chianti's recounting of your adventures and she sure made me want to go to sea."

"Why don't you?"

"Someday I will," she said with conviction.

"What are you waiting for?"

"Nothing." She stopped, stared out at the pine trees, electric poles and road signs flashing past. "I, uh, I don't know enough to just head out. But I will. I'll get some time on boats in the Caribbean."

Sydney chuckled. "Sure, are sounding defensive to me."

"No," she responded automatically. They both laughed.

"I trust you're not awaiting The Man with the Boat. Chianti and I met several intelligent, independent women who were caught up in the doldrums of that fantasy."

He looked at her, shook his head. "No, I think you're just temporarily off course. A lot of extremes in a short time. I didn't mean to be pushy."

"I haven't asked myself why not, I've just shelved ideas. It's like I don't know what I want so I can't plan anything. I think the man I'm waiting for is Zachariah. I need answers but I'm not even sure of the questions."

He frowned. "So, we both need some therapy and we're thinking of Disney?"

"We can find a marina, charter a boat for a couple of days, if that would be better."

He sighed. "Though I've desperately missed the sea, the thought of going without Chianti holds no appeal. I am out of sync with life now, outside of mind-numbing prison security, without the solid reinforcement of Chianti's love. I can't yet call or write friends who should be told. And out there," he swallowed hard, and shook his head. "I'm not ready to face reality yet. And the ocean demands that above all else."

Nineteen

Seychelle listened as the two men reminisced. Their enthusiasm was infectious, their mutual respect obvious. Shared sailing created bonds, not just friendships. Was it because it tested people, revealed weaknesses as well as strengths? Or was it simply shared love of the ocean, sailing, freedom?

Zachariah was speaking with affection about an afternoon when Chianti took him snorkeling. Seychelle saw Sydney's eyes water and took the chance to intervene.

"How is Geena? Can I see her?"

Zachariah turned to her. "I didn't tell her you were coming but did schedule a visit for you this afternoon. She's maintaining really well, and is researching her own case. She's saving my paralegals time scanning a stack of relevant cases. I might give her a job after this is over," he said and his smile reached his eyes, giving Seychelle reassurance.

"When will it be over?"

He shook his head. "I don't venture into time frames. I will say I believe they should administer a minimal hand slap. Now," he cleared his throat and stood, "I'm taking you two to lunch. We're celebrating Chianti." He put his arm around Sydney's shoulders. "I do envy you Sydney. You're so lucky to have shared life with her. And we're toasting freedom as well as your birthday, Seychelle."

Before she could ask how he knew, he continued, "You and I will have our meeting after you see Geena. But right now, I want to hear about food poisoning and English prison."

Two hours later Seychelle was feeling guilty for her pleasant champagne buzz as she walked into the drab, barred visiting room. She had left them laughing and talking in the posh Puerto Rican restaurant. She hoped Zachariah didn't get too plastered as she needed clear-headed advice and information when she met with him later in the afternoon.

"Well, you look okay for back from the dead," Geena said, smiling across the table.

Seychelle ached. She wanted to hug her, to lead her out of there. "Zachariah told you about my misadventure then."

"Only a few highlights. I want every sleazy detail, even bedpan stories. Were any of the doctors worthy of an under-the-quilt?"

Seychelle's laugh was a little too loud. She cleared her throat and began her story. She was quite graphic, enthusiastic in acting out some bits. She had decided to edit West's section, saying only that a farewell letter and some money were in their bank box. She promised silently that she would tell her everything later, and share some of West's illegally obtained endowment with her. Her stories were rather disjointed due to the editing and her reluctance to talk about Mamma. When Seychelle did begin recounting her visit, Geena tensed.

"Damn that red neck!" Geena hissed. "Gettin' in with Mamma. Obviously, he hasn't filled her in or I'd have heard from her. Damn, damn, damn. Oh Seychelle, how am I going to tell her?"

Seychelle looked at her distraught face and realized that she'd been so wrapped up in her own situation, and Sydney's, that she hadn't contemplated the danger Jerken Jr. now posed for Geena.

"Easy way is to sit and write it all out. That's what West did. He left a letter in our safe deposit box, explaining everything he hadn't while he was here. Made it easier for both of us, actually. Time to digest it all without explosions or recriminations. He didn't have to see my hurt, I didn't have to see his guilt."

Geena almost smiled. "What on God's green Earth could West have had to confess or feel guilty about?"

Seychelle looked at her quizzical expression. "When we sit with a bottle of wine and the sea at our feet, we'll tell each other all the things we can't share now. But our immediate concern is that Mamma must be told." She took a deep breath. "I will talk to her for you, if that's what you want."

Geena shook her head, squared her shoulders. "I can't ask you to do that. I'll write to her. But I have gotta do it right now, Seychelle. You understand?" She held onto the table when she stood. Harsh light emphasized tears on her cheeks and dark circles beneath her eyes. Lapsing into Southern country was indicative of how very distraught she was.

Seychelle's heart ached. She nodded. "Tell Zachariah to call if you need me. I'm going down to pick up Beauregard but I'll be in touch with Zachariah. I love you, Geena."

Geena tried to smile, turned quickly and walked over to an officer with keys.

Seychelle watched the gray steel door close behind her. She held back tears until anonymity in the taxi's back seat let her vent deep pain. She'd read recently that the US prison population was greater than that of Alaska, North Dakota and South Dakota combined. Two thirds of that populace was in for non-violent stuff. And here was her peaceful, gentle friend joining them. She couldn't believe laws were right that made criminals of people like Geena. And West, she reminded herself.

She was composed but tired by the time she joined Sydney on a leather sofa in Zachariah's outer office. His secretary presented them with coffee and chocolates.

Sydney smiled. "I may come back as a lawyer in my next life."

"Not enough shark blood in you," Seychelle countered.

"How is Geena? No, first tell me how you are faring."

She sighed. "Geena is writing to her mother. Hopefully it will get to her before Jerken Jr. drops the bomb. Me, I just want to get to Jamaica and smoke a spliff. I feel guilty for having freedom to do exactly that."

"Zachariah wants to talk with you, then it might be a good idea to head for the airport. There's a flight to Jamaica in three hours. I'll book two seats. Your option, but time with Yellowman is exactly what I need. You won't help Geena by weighing yourself down with guilt. Besides, it is unjustified."

Seychelle shrugged. "I know, I do know. I just can't believe there is no way I can help. I should have gotten in touch with Geena as soon as I talked with that sleazy bastard at the hospital—"

The secretary interrupted. "Mr. Carter can see you now, Ms. Austin."

Seychelle caught herself straightening her hair and vest as she entered the door of his formal office, but relaxed when Zachariah stepped forward, took both her hands and kissed her cheek.

"I wish we could have carried on partying through the afternoon but I have a client in need of defense. Must pay rent you know," he said amiably.

"Would I be a good character witness for Geena?" she asked without preamble.

He led her to a chair and moved behind his desk. Establishing business mode, she mused. He opened a file that lay before him, the only clutter on his heavily varnished teak desktop.

"What do you think of these willing folks?" he asked, handing her a typed list.

She scanned his list. "Perry Mason would be impressed," she said. "All are respected, established local business people and teachers. Perfect witnesses, a jury would like them. Most have known both Geena and I all our lives."

He leaned back in his chair, and seemed to grow taller. "The best thing we can do for both of you is keep you apart." He raised his hand when she started to protest. "You said you weren't going to tell her about your father. Did you?"

"No. Zachariah, she is so distressed about Jerken Jr. getting close to her mother. She's writing now, explaining. I should have told her when she visited me at the hospital."

"If there is any should have it is that Geena should have said no to playing mule. It's history. Flogging is no better for you than it is for dead horses. Now listen to your gentleman lawyer's advice. I presume you are engaging my services?"

She had to smile at the raised charcoal eyebrow and near-cherubic look of innocent inquiry.

"Can I afford you?"

He took a large envelope from a drawer and leaned forward to hand it to her. "You'll need to sign that in front of me." Then he returned attention to his Geena file.

She shook its contents onto the desk and stared at a platinum credit card. Beside it was a stack of stapled papers with what looked like a bank statement on top. It was in Spanish but her name was often in evidence and at the bottom she stared at a dollar sign followed by one and seven zeros.

"I would have contacted you even if my client, Geena, had not issued an absolute ultimatum. You see, I am the executor of this estate. Your father had me structure a solid, conservative system that is discreet and secure. As of your birthday tomorrow you will be receiving $5000 each month and each year that amount will increase by $500 a month. The money goes into a Panamanian bank as savings. The rest is tied up in long-term investments through an offshore company. Your income is your salary for doing environmental research, and access will be through the card. Anytime you need extra money for anything, you must simply contact me and I will arrange loans at considerably lower rates than your money is earning. If, heaven forbid, anything happens to me, all is set up to work automatically through this office. On your 50th birthday you may change everything, liquidate, whatever you wish. In theory you will never need to go to, or have any transaction with, the bank. All details are there. Keep turning, you'll find the English translation." He glanced at the papers and smiled at her frown.

"I, um, I'm rich, aren't I?"

"Well, Seychelle, that is a relative term," he drawled. "However, yes you are, I suppose. It's tied up so you can't just burn it in a frivolous moment. I am rather pleased with this arrangement and have done similar set-ups for other clients."

"What about tax?" she asked, attempting intelligent adult concern.

"Covered. It is all there so I do recommend that you study the papers thoroughly. West was very patriotic, so the amounts that would have gone to taxes, had it all gone through normal channels, are allotted to charities here in our beloved country, though you will have the opportunity to select other charities, if you so desire. Now, I do apologize but I must get to court. You just read over that little ol' stack of papers and then you can write or call me with all your questions. I do advise that you skedaddle on down to Jamaica, or whatever island you may choose, and stay there until Geena's case is settled."

"But I can't just leave her! She needs my support."

"And if you are brought in by prosecution and West's escapades revealed, even if without substantiating evidence, then she will be portrayed as involved in an ongoing criminal enterprise. It would totally obliterate the defense of an intelligent law student who made a foolish, impetuous mistake and is desperately remorseful."

Seychelle stared at him, the reality of his words settling heavily. She spoke in a low, flat voice. "Please explain all this mess to Geena. I know her legal mind will understand, but I couldn't bear having her feel I've deserted her."

Zachariah stood, stepped around and took both her hands. "I will. Trust me Seychelle, this is the way it must be. Your Mr. Jerken Jr. is dangerous."

Twenty

"Beauregard!" Seychelle called as she crawled out of Leroy's taxi. She called again as she stepped up to try the door but before she could raise her hand she was attacked.

She tried to steady herself but ended up sprawled on the rough plank sidewalk and he was on her, barking, whining and licking. Seychelle was laughing and crying, half-heartedly attempting to save her face from the exuberant hound's slobbery affection.

"You stink of jerk chicken and weigh a ton. Have you been living at Juniors?" She tried to hug him but his high energy meant he could not be still. He charged around, barking and stirring up dust.

Seychelle stood, wiped her face with her yellow cotton shirtsleeve. "Time to go see Junior. I have a key but I want to make sure Brian is still willing to rent to me for a few months. And," she beamed, "I need a cold beer."

"I'll be right in," Sydney said and turned to Leroy. "Can you take me to Yellowman's tomorrow?"

Leroy was laughing. "Dat a fine dog, a little crazy. Yeah, I take you up but he probably not be there. Be gone."

Seychelle went around the corner to Junior's and was almost relieved to find the table she and Geena had made their own was taken. Beauregard led her out back where she was welcomed like a family member. They shared the latest news and she introduced Sydney when he came in.

"Something is going on," Seychelle declared as soon as she and Sydney settled at a table with their Red Stripes. "Yellowman, Hans and Brian have been off-island. Junior loves to gossip, knows everything about everyone, but he was quick to change subjects when I asked about them."

"I'm lucky Leroy remembers me. He'll try to find Brian, reckons he's back but laying low. Leroy says he's heard the whole Caribbean is getting busted." He chuckled, "Drums gossip, but I do believe they're usually fairly accurate."

128

Beauregard rejoined them when their jerk chicken arrived and contentedly settled on the floor at Seychelle's feet. "He's ruint as they say back home. I see hunger strikes in the future. Junior's jerk chicken or nothing!" she said with a laugh.

"Can't say I blame him," Sydney said, licking his fingers. "Would you believe Chianti and I didn't know about this place?"

"But she didn't eat meat."

"No, but breadfruit and callaloo are her favorites, and she loves the smell of the jerk spice. Uses it on eggplant." He stopped. "I suppose I should say 'used'."

Seychelle leaned forward. "Not until you're ready, not until it comes naturally. I often think about West in the present tense. He's here, always will be."

Sydney shook his head. "I just—" He was interrupted by Beauregard's abrupt bark. He charged out the back door as Junior leaned in and gave a slight nod of his head. They followed him.

"Brian!" Seychelle exclaimed and hugged him.

With his arm around her shoulders he turned his broad, gold-enhanced smile on Sydney. "Free at last, my Man!" He clasped Sydney's hand firmly. "We grieve with you—" They held eye contact, and seemed to say so much.

Junior interrupted with, "I close early, 'body gone. Go sit down, I bring the food."

"Tell me 'bout Geena," Brian said as soon as they sat down.

Junior brought Brian's chicken and beer while Seychelle talked. He closed shutters and doors, turned a rotating fan on them. The place softened and it was quieter with only Junior's box pumping out reggae. Seychelle felt safe, insulated. She looked at the intelligent, sensitive American, fresh out of prison, and the spirited but gentle Jamaican. It really didn't matter that Brian had not told her that he and Sydney were friends. It was evident that many years had passed since they had last met, but there was no doubt of the strong bond. And both of these special men were her friends.

She completed her update on Geena and asked, "But what's going on here, Brian? Where are Yellowman and Hans?"

"Trouble for true." His smile was sad. "They listen here to what yo guv'ment say, and take their money. Cleanin' up, they say. Hans been gone, saying he read the wind. I hear they watchin' *Regina*, gonna check that out.

Yellowman took to the mountains, nobody findin' him." He chuckled. "Me, I been gone fishin' down Kingston."

"Only here?" Sydney asked.

"Kitts 'n Maarten, for sure. Barth, B'ados, maybe Nevis."

Seychelle tensed. "What about Seagull?"

He shrugged, "Gone. Can take care of self, that one."

She frowned and said, "Yes, he can." But she was uneasy.

Sydney looked at her. "Seagull is probably the most capable survivor I know, not to worry." He turned to Brian. "Think Yellowman would mind if I just went up to his field and hung out for a while?"

"Me think him like it just fine. Didn't like leavin' it with no one overseein'. 'member how to get there?"

"Leroy will take me to Reach Falls tomorrow. I can find my way from there."

"You goin' up too?" he asked Seychelle.

"No." She was bothered that Seagull had not told her that he knew Sydney and Chianti. But, as with Brian, she hadn't asked directly, so it wasn't as if they had lied. It was just how it was in The Business, she supposed. "If you're still willing, I'd like to rent your place here for a while."

"Why, we done made that 'greement. Yours long as you want. But you know nothin' 'bout me and not seen me fo' month, when we met here las' time. Clear?"

"Clear. Thanks Brian. I'll pay you for six months and I owe you for looking after Beauregard while I was away."

Brian's locks bounced when he threw his head back and laughed. Beauregard's tail thumped the floor in accord. "Me no be paid for havin' friend stay wi' me! We had good times! Besides, him stay wi' Junior mostly. Junior got the chicken. Couldn't take 'im fishin', ya know."

As soon as they finished eating Brian went out the back way, off to visit his family and check on *Regina*. Seychelle and Sydney walked around the corner to Brian's house. She immediately opened the windows, turned on fans and made coffee.

"You can use Geena's room. Just consider it yours if you want to come down out of Nirvana." She was smiling with effort.

Sydney got a couple of mugs out of a cupboard. "You're feeling her loss but you must treat it as a chapter in her life. You are a part of it because she

130

knows she has your love and support. Accept how important that is to her. Your strength, that's what she needs, as well as your normalcy. Through you she knows the outside world is real and waiting, that she's just away temporarily. Believe me, I've been there."

"But Zachariah insists that I not contact her, not even with letters!"

"I'm sure he is right. Letters are read, calls recorded, so send your letters to him. She can read them during legal visits. You feel really alone during those first few months. She understands the legal process better than I did, but you lose track of who you are. You become a case, a villain, a criminal, a number, a prisoner, a news story…you are categorized with murderers, rapists, child abusers. Your self-worth is tested. You chastise yourself. Geena is lucky to have Zachariah since he understands all of this. He is keeping her busy researching legal stuff and has someone visit her every day."

"Must have been rough in England with no one around you knew."

"The hard part was our separation and no communication at first. We saw each other at court, while handcuffed to officers. When we were finally allowed to write we had to be so careful of the contents, but what a difference those letters made! We had been together so long, had survived storms, groundings, being penniless, shared so many things. But our relationship took on a new depth. Through writing you get to know a person better. Prison had its positive aspects."

Seychelle smiled. "Speaking of writing, are you game for a bit of interrogation?"

"Only if you're rolling."

She jumped up. "Just happen to have some of Yellowman's Best. Loosen you right up. I need enough material to keep me writing while you're up watching dew settle on cannabis plants."

And so began an all-night session.

Twenty-One

"Life sometimes seems to consist of nothing but irreconcilable opposites.
Again and again we are faced with the impossibility of uniting in a single
moment all the contradictory forces of our nature.
Masculine and feminine, head and heart, introversion and extroversion; each
psychic pole is seemingly exclusive of the other and
we are often caught by the demands of our circumstances
in the wrong polarity at the wrong time."
Subhuti.

Fiction. "Okay, time to come clean. I must tell Sydney. Someday. Perhaps if I record that event here, I will be better able to share.

"*Cayenne* was in prime condition since we had poured much work and money into her. It was ménage à tois, we had become one with our boat. Life was so good! We had joined the extended family of Caribbean cannabis smugglers and loved it, and had become so close so quickly. With most we shared the love of sailing. With all we shared the love of life on the edge. And grass, of course. Ah, good memories.

"We decided to make our third run north without a crew since it was only 300 pounds to the Florida Keys. We loaded off tiny Sombrero, a nature reserve in Anegada Passage, just before sunrise. All went smoothly and we were stowed, cleaned and cruising by sunset. Tired, and satisfied we were clear of surveillance, we commenced two-hour watches. That first sleep after loading is always deep and sweet, but too short. I awoke to Sydney's kiss. He briefed me before collapsing, totally exhausted, in the forward bunk. We had spread bales forward, aft and amidships, keeping weight balanced, presenting a slightly raised waterline, not unusual in a cruising sailboat. That did not diminish performance and allowed the luxury of a head and whole cabin for off-watch regeneration.

"What a gorgeous night! Just a sliver of moon and crowded with stars. Draco the Dragon looked down on me and we ghosted along with a light southerly. The sea was gentle, *Cayenne* waltzed along, I was happy. I logged our position, checked rigging and bilge, trimmed the spinnaker, and put Tina Turner on cockpit speakers.

"I sang and danced around the cockpit, as much to charge my senses into full function as in celebration of the experience. Still dancing, I stepped up onto the aft deck to adjust Jeeves, a mechanical self-steering unit we had mounted before departure. I turned, my naked foot slipped, and I was in the water before my groggy head registered what was happening. Shock was replaced by anger at myself and that by pure panic as my stinging eyes focused on *Cayenne* moving away from me. Away! Can't say there were clear thoughts but an adrenaline rush is the ultimate high. I dove forward, pumping with every inch of me, and reached for the windvane rudder, missed! I lunged and got it, but my fingers slipped from its Teflon surface. At that moment I do believe I walked on water. Though I hold no memory of how, my hand was on the windvane shaft, my foot on its brace and I was scrambling up *Cayenne's* stern and into her cockpit. I collapsed, trembling and panting.

"What did I feel? Embarrassed. Seriously. I could not believe I had done something so stupid! As soon as I got my trembling under control I stripped, pegged my bikini and tee-shirt on the lifeline to dry and tiptoed below to put on dry clothes. I had come too close that time. Sydney had often annoyed me with his over-cautious advice, so I couldn't tell him. Still haven't, after all these years. Someday."

Seychelle lay back on the bed. How had Sydney felt when he read that? Odd, but this one episode made Chianti more real for her. She'd studied Fiction closely, was using it to fill and complete the story that was unfolding with info she had gleaned from Sydney. She knew Chianti, loved her, respected her. Good to know you weren't perfect, she thought with a rueful smile.

"Would I be where I am had I not found your raft?" she asked with a sigh. "Would Geena be where she is?" She'd written several letters to Geena and posted them to Zachariah but had heard nothing since she'd seen her friend three weeks before. She got dressed and went down to the phone house. Only one person ahead of her so the wait was short and she got through on the first try.

Zachariah was in court but his secretary expected him back within the hour and she would have him call her. Seychelle had been pecking away daily on Brian's typewriter, sometimes late into night, and had smoked a lot of grass. Which was it that had blurred time? What was happening in the rest of the world? To her friends? She asked to make another call.

"Murphy's Boatyard."

"Sky! How are you? How are Sierra and Barry? What's happening?"

Sky laughed. "Well you haven't changed. Barry and I are putting in 14-hour days, and have hired more workers. Sierra is getting ready for the Fall Regatta. She's won the last two. But I must tell you she's annoyed with you. We've explained Geena's situation. But you..."

"I'm so sorry. I've just gotten so wrapped up in writing. When is she back? I'll call her then."

"She'll be here after six. Umm, Seychelle, this is important to her. She likes you a lot and is still tender from losing Chianti."

Seychelle felt awful. "I'll do my best to deserve her friendship and I absolutely vow I'll not let her down again."

"You've been through a lot of late. How's our friend?"

"Ah, he's camping in a friend's field. Haven't heard from him so assume he's contemplating the stars and coming to terms with his loss."

She talked with Sky a bit longer, explained the phone was in a home and open to the public, though not always at the same time, but it was the only one she had access to. She would call again in a couple of hours.

She returned to the typewriter, trying to get thoughts organized when Beauregard's excited barking drew her to the front door.

"Hot shower and dry bed still available?" Sydney asked as he stroked Beauregard's long black and russet ears.

"Absolutely!" Seychelle declared and told him about her talk with Sky while she made iced tea.

Sydney said, "I've composed a tribute to Chianti that I'm going to send to all our friends. I'll make copies and mail it to Sierra."

"Good. They have a copier at the library." She hesitated, asked, "Your time constructive?"

Sydney reached into a side pouch of his large backpack and pulled out a sketchpad. He smiled. "Very. Look at these."

134

There were several sketches of a sailboat followed by detailed drawings with dimensions and notes.

"In prison I thought it out, planned it, and made some preliminary drawings. However, with the prospect of release into poverty, my direction had to be toward rebuilding our lives gradually so I put aside our ideal boat design as a dream for the distant future. Things have changed." He looked away.

Seychelle took his drawings and studied them to give him a minute.

He cleared his throat. "Barry offered me a job in their yard. If I take it, I can begin building her, doesn't matter how long it takes, and everything, all of me as well as all I earn, will go into her. So many of Chianti's ideas are incorporated. It was the core exchange for many of our daily letters."

"Sydney, I've got an idea—" Seychelle exclaimed, but was interrupted by a knock on the door. She frowned, and opened it to a teenager.

He said without preamble, "You come now, he is waiting, say plenty important." And the boy was gone.

She hesitated, frowned. "Oh, the phone!" She ran down, barefoot, only realized that Sydney had followed, and was standing next to her when she pressed the phone to her ear.

"First call received in Jamaica," she smiled, but every inch on her was tight. "Hello?"

"You even answer the phone with a question!" Zachariah chuckled. "How's the life of decadence on that splendid tropical island?"

"Well Zachariah, not really decadent, more along the lines of a health spa. I've been hanging out, writing my first best seller, and our friend just arrived back from camping in the country. We're fine, but need a report from you."

"I'm the bearer of bad tidings, Seychelle. Dolphin Dave has been arrested. He is charged with importation and conspiracy but they are building the case on ongoing criminal activities. He was apprehended off-loading cannabis from a yacht off the NE Florida coast. There was cocaine in one of the bales. He had been under surveillance and his base had been Charlie's farm near Jacksonville. I've advised Charlie to turn himself in. Please hold for a minute, Seychelle."

She turned and whispered to Sydney, their every word and action attended closely by the teenager and his mother. Sydney said nothing but his face showed the pain.

When Zachariah came back on the line she asked about Seagull. "Dave told me that Seagull should have been on the boat, but had not shown up. He also said there should have been only cannabis in the shipment. He believes he was set up."

"By whom? Not by Seagull!"

"No, he's worried about Seagull. He's saying DEA."

"What do you think?"

"No conjectures. Seychelle, my other news is worse. Geena's mother has had a heart attack."

"No! Zachariah, is she okay?" Tears began immediately.

"She is on life support. Geena is on an escorted visit to see her now, though they may not allow her in the room. She will be brought back tonight."

"Why didn't you call me earlier?" she demanded.

"Geena was sure you would come up no matter what either of us said. We both felt that would be disastrous. Agent Jerken did secure an interview in which he asked about her associations with you and your father. I was with her and she answered 'no comment' to all his questions. He was frustrated but not deterred, worse than a coon-hound on the scent."

"Oh God," Seychelle groaned.

"Seychelle, one of Geena's sisters came to see her after they received her letter. Her mother had declared she no longer had a daughter named Geena. Seems all of the family agreed. I called last night to tell them Geena was coming up and was told that her mother had been burning all of Geena's things when she had the heart attack."

Seychelle was shaking all over. Sydney put his arm around her. She sobbed, "I should have gone, I could have told her, talked with her."

Zachariah said gently, "No, Seychelle. I'm afraid she blamed you."

Sydney took the phone when she crumpled against him. "Zachariah, how is Geena holding up?"

"She was too composed at first, so when she broke down it was bad. She's on medication. I'll go by after they bring her back tonight. If I don't call you, call my office in the morning. My secretary will have the latest report for y'all. Take care of Seychelle."

Beauregard lay on the bed next to Seychelle, as he'd done since he was a puppy. She slept under the covers with her head on one pillow, and he slept on top of the covers on his side of the bed with his head on the other pillow. Unless

136

there arose the need to alert of possible danger, he did not disturb her until she opened her eyes. Then she was fair game.

When she groaned and stretched his tail gave the mattress vigorous thumps. Sunlight was streaming in through the partially open curtains and her brown curls were stuck to her sweaty face. A whine escaped in his impatience. She pulled the sheet up to cover her head but he was on her. It was a morning ritual and no matter how wretched she felt she could not suppress a laugh.

The licking and mauling was short as it was well past Beauregard's outside time. She let him out, went to her own toilet, and then headed for the kitchen.

"Well, good morning," Sydney said. He was sitting at the table, his boat sketches spread out before him.

She squinted at him through swollen, bloodshot eyes, nodded, and attended to making coffee. She'd just accomplished a flame beneath the kettle when it hit her. "Oh my God! I didn't call Sierra!"

"I did. I called as soon as they opened the phone this morning and explained. She's okay, said to tell you she loves you and she'll write to you later. She's going to write to Geena and send her a picture she drew. When I suggested she send it to Zachariah, she said, 'Yes, of course, they probably read her mail.' She is so mature and even-headed."

Seychelle nodded and sat down. After Zachariah's call she had been a mess. Sydney had convinced her to have some ganja tea, which she followed with several shots of rum and then cried herself to sleep. She hurt all over. She grabbed a jar of cold mango juice and downed most of it before smearing peanut butter on bread. She was halfway through her sandwich and first cup of coffee before she spoke.

"My idea was that I buy your first boat." She looked up at his stunned face and managed a hint of a smile. "When I was trying to trace Sky and Barry, Geena invented the story that she wanted to build a boat, but knew nothing, so a friend recommended she talk to them. And now, well, that's where I am. Things are too discombobulated for me Stateside, and there is simply no solution. I can't take control and make everything right. West's philosophy was: turn the page and find a mountain you can climb. And, well, he provided funding so I can do just exactly that little ol' thing."

She gave Sydney a cup of coffee and tucked into a banana. Sydney was quiet, glancing from her to his drawings and back.

"So, I want to go adventuring, or on a quest, or whatever. I wasn't sure before whether it was my dream or West's. But through Chianti I have learned how smokey the boundary is between fantasy and reality. I mean, it's up to me, isn't it, and I've been unable to find a sound reason why I shouldn't get a boat."

Sydney was smiling when she stood up a bit unsteadily.

"I need a long shower, hopefully hot, and I may go back to bed. Think about it. I can pay up front if you can work out details with Sky and Barry."

She stopped on her way out of the kitchen. "That is, if you're willing to sell your creation. Sydney, thanks for last night. I'm okay, my wound is cauterized."

Hot water didn't last long but even a cold shower was not enough to stimulate Seychelle. She closed curtains, crawled into bed, and fell asleep right away. She entered a series of scenes, some distressing, others confusing, and most she'd not remember. The more realistic one would stay with her. A faceless man was flying a kite and she was following him. But the kite was dripping blood. They kept passing people she knew, and blood dripped on each.

She awoke in the fetal position, clutching her locket, heart pounding. She unfolded slowly and oriented herself. After splashing cold water into her face, she pulled on a tee-shirt and tied an oversized cotton shawl sarong-like around her hips. In the kitchen she opened a cold beer and sat down to study the drawings Sydney had left lying on the table.

To her inexperienced eye the elegant 42 ft. sloop with 12 ft. beam was a work of art. Fast but not intimidating. She would be neither a radical racer nor a practical cruiser. Seychelle smiled. "A hybrid. I will call you *Wesheena*. I know you approve, West, and Geena will be downright tickled. She needs to know she's special to someone."

She jumped when someone knocked. She opened the door to the teenager.

"You come. Little girl calling."

"Hello?"

"Miss Seychelle, yes we'll build it! When are you coming home?"

"Sierra! I'm sorry I didn't ring but—"

"It's okay," she interrupted. "Sydney explained. Poor Geena. But, well, we just received Sydney's fax and Barry and Sky said I could call you and say there is a shed Sydney can work in. Yours will be the prototype. Then Sydney's Chianti can be the first of what could be our production line. Barry says that's what he really wants anyway, just to build sailboats, to have the yard specialize, but it has to pay, and this could be the key!" She had to stop to catch her breath.

Seychelle seized the moment. "Sierra, I've missed you! This is great news. You and I will get lots of sailing when I have my own boat! You can teach me so much. Are you ready for the regatta?"

"Yeah. I plan to win again. Are you coming?"

Seychelle took a deep breath. "I can't come up for a while, Sierra. I will as soon as I can. Sydney said he would be there with you. I'll be with you in spirit."

"Are you going to go see Geena?" she asked, her voice softer, almost a whisper.

Seychelle's chest tightened. "As soon as possible. There is someone at the door," she lied. "Can I call you back later?"

"Okay. Don't worry about Sydney. I'll look after him when he's here. And don't worry about Geena, they'll see she's a nice person and let her go."

How lovely the optimism of a child, she thought, drying her tears. She walked home, got another beer and had just finished rolling a joint when Sydney and Beauregard came in.

"For you," he smiled and presented her with a packet from Junior's. "We've eaten."

The smell made her mouth water. "You're a life-saver," she said, pulling out a leg. She took a bite and asked, "Have you heard from Zachariah?"

Sydney sat down beside her, lit her joint, took a drag and waited until she had a hit before saying, "I received a fax. She died, Seychelle."

Though her eyes watered and tears spilled, she was composed. She nodded. "I guess I knew, had accepted it somehow. How is Geena?"

"They sedated her. One of Zachariah's paralegals is with her. Geena's sisters blamed her and it was an ugly scene at the hospital."

They shared the joint in silence. Seychelle took long deep inhalations, allowing the smoke to soothe and relax her. She knew her guilt and grief were there, would be there, but she could cope, she had to.

"Did you know," she drawled, "that a biologist in Israel has found that cannabinoids occur naturally in us, and many other mammals, at birth. She believes that they are important as natural painkillers and appetite regulators."

Sydney gave a long, exaggerated sigh. "But still they make this gift of nature illegal. There was a German philosopher, I can't remember his name, but he proposed that man created God in his image, then made himself dependent on his creation. I sometimes wonder if he was right."

Seychelle gave him a quizzical look, smiled. "You've been sleeping amongst Yellowman's giant ganja plants too long." She patted one of his drawings. "Y'all sure did design a peach of a boat."

He leaned forward. "I faxed one to Sky and Barry."

She raised an eyebrow, flicked her hair back. "Oh, I know."

"And?" he leaned further forward.

She broke into giggles. "Yes, yes, yes!" She related Sierra's call with childlike exuberance. "So, as soon as you get up there and give me an estimate, I'll have Zachariah get the money to you." She stopped; her eyes widened. "I can't believe I just said that, that I can just do that! I mean, it's like, hey, I want a yacht and presto, there's the cash."

Sydney laughed. "A woman of means."

"I guess I hadn't really believed it until now," she said.

"One advantage of being stuck here for a while is you can hone your sailing skills. I was out wandering this morning and that rough little Yacht Club is still here. They have a couple of small boats they rent out. You can go out for an hour or so every day, maybe even to other bays as you get more comfortable."

She jumped up. "If I sit here, I'm going to sink back down into remorse, and that is no way to show respect for a spirited woman like Mamma. Let's go out now! Catch the sunset! What do you think?"

He hesitated.

"Oh," she caught herself. "I'm sorry. You're not ready."

"No, I'm okay. It's a good idea, the time's right," he said with conviction. "It will be a good way to end my stay here. I'm going to try to catch a flight to Pensacola tomorrow. I want to get started on our boats!"

Twenty-Two

"Yolande? It's Seychelle. How goes it?" She had the phone cradled against her face, was leaning against the wall in the tiny Yacht Club office, fanning her sweaty body with a newspaper. She'd gained access by joining for a small fee and welcomed the lack of audience. She figured the whole of Port Antonio probably knew the details of each of her calls thus far since the teen and his mother had listened as if to a radio mystery. However, ventilation had been sacrificed for the sake of privacy.

"Seychelle! We've just had word that Geena's mamma died. They were so close. I know she's taking it hard. Are you with her?"

Seychelle inhaled deeply. "Uh, no, Yolande, I'm in Jamaica. Geena's in Miami."

"Why is she in Miami?" Yolande asked.

Seychelle felt sick. "She's awaiting trial. She was, um, busted." A long silence followed. She wanted to say so much but nothing seemed right. Her face flushed from the intensity of her emotions. She had called to ask Yolande if she knew anything about Seagull. You didn't think, she chastised herself.

"Well, I suppose I know why my aunt had a heart attack," came her tight reply. "I assume she was playing mule. How could Geena have done such an utterly stupid and thoughtless thing?"

"I tried to talk her out of it but she said she wanted to take financial pressure off Mamma," she said and cursed herself for the lame words.

"Hah! Now I've heard it all. And I'll just bet Seagull put her up to it! Well, I've fixed him and now I be feelin' good 'bout it. Feelin' bad before, setting them on him, but 'e's goin' down, I make sure of that!" She gave a nasty snort. "They might have he already, he and big friend Charlie." Her anger laid waste to her cultured, teacher's English.

"No, Yolande, it wasn't Seagull!"

"Well, I be sure it be Charlie's cartel. He run dis island. They all got to go. You stick with Geena 'cause she sure got no family now!"

"Go easy on her, Yolande. She made a mistake, a big mistake, but she's paying, suffering."

"Tell that to kids who get hooked. Tell that to her Mamma in da ground," she said and slammed down the receiver.

Seychelle stared at the phone, feeling sad, stupid, guilty, frustrated. She stepped outside and breathed; the fresh gentle breeze desperately needed. She paid for the call, ran home to get Beauregard. A short walk and they were at the boat. Once aboard she stood up on the foredeck, oriented to the wind. The island rose up on the east and west sides but angled enough to deceive.

"We'll take short tacks, taking whatever comes until we are out far enough for true wind, then I will set the sails, make the most of gusts," she told the dog. "Oh, never-mind, I'll just keep us off the rocks and let the wind take us where-so-ever it wishes! This is that kind of day." She retrieved lines and pushed them away from the dock.

"Beauregard, we are going to have a boat and we are going to have adventures aplenty. I sure wish West had hung around, but I do honestly feel him…he's with us, dog-of-mine." She felt the sun on her face as she stood in the cockpit and stroked the warm, worn fiberglass deck. She set the sails for a mid-channel tack out. The little seven meter sloop had only the main and genoa, both well-worn and stained, but they worked just fine for a single-handing woman with no real agenda. She sat at the tiller, her hand resting on Beauregard's back. He grunted, his tail thumped, and he acquiesced to his task. She watched gulls swooping overhead.

"Oh, so much pain. I just want to sail away. Not play ostrich. But do something. I feel like The Chosen One, showered with good things but without sight. So, I just keep blundering into things. Everyone is better off if I stay away. I mean, even after they decide Geena's fate, will association with me tarnish her future? Will Jerken Jr. track me to Murphy's and endanger them? He would certainly be suspicious of Sydney with his prison record, black skin and me as a friend. And I dare not go near Geena's family. If Mamma blamed me then they all must. West couldn't have realized what a mixed legacy he left me!"

She put a Santana cassette in her Walkman, inserted earphones, upped the volume and they spent a few hours just tacking around. A light wind pushed them in just before sunset so hooking and tying off to the mooring buoy was easy.

"We're going to be just fine, Beauregard. You can trust me as your captain," she said with a laugh. "Captain Seychelle!" Beauregard responded with a bark.

"Okay, let's go call Sydney, see what we're missing," she said and finished bagging the genoa as the tender approached.

She was seriously sweating by the time the operator got through to the yard and Sydney called back.

"Seychelle, what are you up to?"

"Sydney! Beauregard and I went out, tied up to the mooring buoy after tacking around for a little while, and I've not resorted to using the outboard even once. They're happy to let me rent it for as long as I'm here, and don't charge for picking me up in their tender. Oh, I can hardly wait to fly a spinnaker on *Wesheena*! I want a real work of art with palm trees and dolphins and rainbows."

He laughed. "Aye, Mate, and you're of the right head for seafaring. Listen, they have a break between contracts here so we've got a massive team working on her. She just might be ready by Christmas."

Seychelle beamed. "Yes! Oh, I am so ready! Hey, if it costs more to get her ready early just say the word. It's not a problem," she said with a laugh.

"Ah, the quintessential customer."

"I'm so lucky. I mean, I just hang out in the Caribbean and let my skin turn brown while my inheritance pays for construction of the ideal sailboat. And, I've got a totally trustworthy top-of-the-line designer, builder and rigger all rolled into one."

"You're making me blush," he said. "Actually, I'm learning so much from the crew here. I've never built a boat, you see, just breathed new life into old ones. Barry and Sky are enthusiastic. They want to go into production. I'm drawing up the same basic design for them in 32 ft. and 50 ft. Can't believe how much I am enjoying working in this yard, being part of the family. Sierra has taken me out sailing a couple of times. Her race is this week."

Seychelle sighed. "Wish I were there, in honesty. Geena's trial begins this week as well. I shall have everything crossed for both of them. Hey, I've got to go, they are closing. I love sailing this little sloop, hope *Wesheena* is as easy to handle."

"Oh, you'll be impressed with her ease and even more with her performance. Seychelle, use this number when you call. It's the marina's public pay phone. We'll only use this one from now on, okay? These times demand over-zealous caution I believe. Just ask whoever answers to find me or Sky."

Seychelle felt a chill pass down her spine. "Is everyone okay?"

"They're a bit nervous about Dolphin Dave's bust, but otherwise all goes well."

"I understand. Must go, hugs for all."

She paid for the call, didn't stop for a closing drink with the local guys as she usually did but walked back deep in thought. Typhoid Mary, that's me, she thought, and worked at getting her head off that track. She fed Beauregard and then took a shower, standing with face upturned and cold Red Stripe in hand until hot water became cold.

"I've read about solar panels to charge the batteries on sailboats, and that the Dutch are building little units that take salt from sea water. Perfect for *Wesheena*," she told her reflection. "So, since there is unlimited salt water for converting to fresh, I will have hot showers at sea. What a luxury!"

She slowly towel-dried her hair, thinking she might need to cut it short if she was at sea for long periods of time. In her mind she was standing at the helm in mid-ocean. She could hear wind in the sails and water rushing along *Wesheena's* hull. Beauregard began barking but she'd heard no one knock or call so assumed he'd heard dogs or people walking past. They were living in the center of Port Antonio so he had grown accustomed to nearly perpetual commotion and rarely reacted. He carried on barking so she wrapped a towel around her head and went to let him out into their small backyard.

Her first shock when she opened the bathroom door was that Beauregard charged to her, barking. Her next was that Hans was standing just inside the closed front door.

"Excuse me," he said, as if carrying on a conversation.

"You could have knocked," she snapped.

"I really do apologize, but I'm so accustomed to just walking in. I'd forgotten you were renting it from Brian."

Seychelle walked across the room with as much cool as she could muster. She was so angry she was trembling when she entered her bedroom but she knew it was only in part because she was naked. He had a key, which shouldn't surprise her, but she was most definitely adding an inside lock to front and back doors. Even if he had forgotten, which she was sure he hadn't, he should have called out when he encountered Beauregard. She picked up bad vibes from him, as had Beauregard. Taking deep breaths, she pulled on shorts and a tee-shirt.

"Geena is intelligent and she did it voluntarily," she told herself softly. "Blaming Hans is non-productive."

Beauregard was sitting by the door when she opened it, on guard, and Hans was seated at the kitchen table with a beer.

"Didn't think you'd mind if I helped myself. Shall I open one for you?" he asked.

She shook her head and opened a bottle of water. "How is *Regina*? Taken her out lately?"

His smile was almost a sneer. "You must know that, with all that is going on, my boat is being closely watched."

"No, I did not know. Brian did tell me you had foreseen problems and took a trip."

"Yes, since your friend went down many people have been taking trips."

Seychelle flared. "I would think that you could call someone you slept with by name! Wait, just what are you insinuating?"

He was unruffled. "Without doubt it was just a coincidence and cleanup had been in planning stages for a while. Geena just happened to be first down. I have learned that her trial begins this week."

His soft voice infuriated her as much as what he said. "You listen to me. Geena has not given any names or information. She would never grass!"

"I'm sure you are right. However, she is under so much pressure with her mother's death and problems with her family as well as loss of her university scholarship. I will be happy to do anything I can to help Geena. Please tell her I am thinking about her."

She studied his cool features with loathing, and wondered where he got his info. "She does not need your help but I will give her your message. Now, if you will excuse me, I have things to do."

He stood with slow, deliberate moves, finished his beer and placed the empty bottle gently on the table. "You know that many people are closely associated with me and that discretion is key to our continued success. Indeed, to our very existence. Geena's cousin in Sint Maarten has created many problems. I suppose that is why there is concern about Geena. I trust I judged wisely. I am rarely wrong about human nature and I believe she is strong as well as honorable. Will you be going up to be with her?"

"I'm not sure since Geena says she prefers to go it alone and wants no one tainted by her mistake," she lied. It seemed he did not know about West and she was relieved. Actually, she didn't believe Charlie would have let him near their inner circle, and would not have trusted him. Hans seemed to be a lone agent and ego demanded he be in charge. She couldn't tell where a dividing line was, but Charlie had leapt in, put Zachariah on Geena's case immediately. She blessed him for that. Hans was slimy, out for himself alone. Don't be naïve, she chided herself, so is Charlie.

"Yes, no use getting tarred with the same brush, as they say. No good for anyone."

"That has nothing to do with it!" she retorted. She shook her head, gentled her voice. "You do not understand the depth of our friendship, Hans. Maybe you have never known such complete love and trust."

He stared into her eyes for a long moment. There was a discernible softening when he said, "Perhaps you are right, Seychelle. I am sorry this has happened to Geena. Though I doubt you believe me, I regret it for her sake, not just for mine."

He opened the door, leaned out and looked around, then glanced back at her with an embarrassed shrug. "One never knows who might be lurking around. Tell Junior if you need me. He'll get word to Brian." And he was gone.

She closed and locked the door behind him quietly, deep in thought. She replayed their exchanges as she brushed Beauregard.

"As if I would ever need him. Not many people you haven't accepted," she mused. "West reckoned a dog's perception of a person was usually accurate. Your judgment is basic, not confused by how folks look or what they say. But, is Hans just untrustworthy and self-centered, or is he dangerous?" She finished his grooming and let him out back.

Beauregard charged out into his yard, doing his standard after-brush roll. She had removed his filthy neck scarf so that gave real impetus to his needs. She had learned to wait until he finished his ritual and settled in for a nap to tie on his clean one.

"I'm trained," she smiled, and turned her attention to Quandary. She realized as she sat down with pen in hand that she had to put a Hans in this story. And a West.

When Seychelle finally gave it up the sun was more interested in coming up than going down. Exhausted but satisfied, she crawled into bed fully clothed, lights burning.

She tried to hide from Beauregard's bark, burying her head under a pillow and swearing, but loud knocking continued. Squinting in the bright mid-day sun that filled the place, she made her way to the front door, opening it a crack. No one was there. She frowned, closed it, realized Beauregard was dancing around and whining at the back door. She hesitated. There was no gate in the fenced back yard but Beauregard seemed to know who was there and it definitely was not Hans.

She pulled back a red cotton curtain and looked up into Brian's wide, enigmatic smile. She unlocked the door and let it swing open to Beauregard's loud enthusiastic welcome. The tall Jamaican squatted to give him a hug and scratch. Seychelle motioned towards the refrigerator. "Help yourself, right back."

She forced herself into relative awareness with a quick cold shower, tied on a clean sarong but left her curls knotted. Goin' native, she thought with a wry smile. The smell of coffee was exquisite when she walked back towards the kitchen.

"You're a good man," she sighed. Toast popped up to punctuate her declaration.

She fed Beauregard while Brian buttered and poured. "Me know too well what you be needin' after an all-nighter."

"Do I look that bad?" she asked, laughing. "Actually, I was just here writing but it was late. So, what's with the back way entry? They after you?" she teased. One side of their fence divided Beauregard's yard from Junior's. She doubted she could scale it, but Brian must have done it many times.

His smile was quick and nervous. "Not yet. They took *Regina* this morning, might have Hans."

Seychelle's stomach constricted. "Oh, Brian. What are you going to do? Won't they look for you here? What can I do?"

"I came to warn you. Every place got eyes and ears. They come askin' questions don' go tryin' to say you don' know us. Be cool, casual. But a better idea is to fly away. Leroy say he drive you to Ocho Rios, you get speed boat to Mo Bay and catch plane, if you want. No good you try from here, not enough flights, and none leavin' Jamaica."

She was fully alert now, thoughts racing. "But I've done nothing."

He sucked his teeth, shook his head. "Don' matter. Guaranteed they know 'bout Geena. The Miami boys come down on 'em every time there's a bust comin' from here. Looks like they not doin' they job, know what I mean? They like the word con-spi-ra-cy, can hold you fo'ever with it. So, I'm gone to mountains 'til tings cool out."

Seychelle took long deep breaths. Think like a scammer. A good scammer. Zachariah had warned of the conspiracy net. Even knowingly concerned could seal her fate. But, running would tattoo guilt across her forehead. Circumstantial. Maybe yes, maybe no. Either way held threats. Yesterday I'd have been gone in a flash, would have grabbed any excuse to head for Murphy's, but what a night it's been. For the first time, I feel that I am a writer.

"Why you smilin'?" he asked.

She looked at him, and with effort gave him her attention. "Brian, you're a good person, I don't want you to get busted. You should go. Thanks for warning me."

"Yeah, what I tell Leroy? He be waitin' in front of Junior's."

"Wish I could just sail away, but I don't have a boat yet. Or go to the mountains with you, but I'd blow your cover. So," she stood and squared her shoulders, "please ask Leroy to wait. I do believe time is right for Beauregard and me to head home."

She stood very still. Where is home now? Where do I belong? Where can I feel safe and relaxed?

Brian gave her a quick hug, left through the back door. Beauregard watched him go, turned back to face Seychelle, and gave a questioning whine.

"All I know for sure is that we have got to get *Wesheena* finished, we've got to get aboard, and we've got to get away from everyone."

Twenty-Three

Seychelle groaned when she looked up at thick black lips curling back from over-sized teeth. Globs of saliva oozed from both corners of his mouth and his tongue was hanging loose, eyes closed.

"You are gross," she said as yet another passing car honked. "And probably a traffic hazard." She laughed as Beauregard's tail gave solid thumps on the seat back but he did not shift position. As soon as they had pulled out of Boudreaux's Used Car lot in their convertible he had taken up his stance with back feet firmly planted in soft leather passenger seat, front paws on dash and head just above windshield. Once they were out making time on the Interstate, wind ballooned his baggy jowls and took his long ears to a 90° spread. He was happy, but she could only guess at the apparition presented to folks as they cruised by.

She laughed again and upped the volume on Santana. She couldn't remember when she had last laughed. Reach Falls and Jamaica felt so far away. She sighed. She'd get off at the next exit and call. She was determined that she would only use pay phones until... until when? Would she ever be free and clear?

"Hello? How are you? Have you heard anything from the lawyer?" she asked when Sky answered.

"Nothing. I called his office about a half hour ago. He is not back from court but has promised to call me. Shall I call you with our friend's phone? Where are you?"

Seychelle had called the public phone, but called the office when no one picked up. She gave Sky the phone number from Trucker's Friend 24hr Truck Stop wall phone, located between toilets and coffee urn. It was the only phone so she took possession, settled in. She was pleasantly surprised when it rang just minutes later.

"Okay," Sky said, "tell all. I'm alone in this phone booth and am supposed to feel safe and confident. I've been told that I should make sure you are not using your credit card and are only using pay phones, though I know there are not many places to use your card in Port Antonio."

"No, I'm not using my card. I'm here, Sky, I've been exploring New Orleans. There were a lot of busts around the Caribbean, and Jamaica seemed the center of it, an associate went down. I was told I should leave. But, I can't leave completely until *Wesheena* is ready. Hey, I did a radical. I was sitting at a stoplight in a taxi when I spotted an old Mercedes 280SL in a car lot. Well, I just stopped that taxi right there and went in and took that little ol' beauty for a test drive, paid for it with the last of West's cash that I've been carrying around and we hit the road. I registered it with my offshore company. Cool or what?" she laughed. "It's in great shape, fun to drive, and Beauregard loves it."

Sky chuckled. "Nothing like going low profile. But, listen, promise to let me take it for a drive. It is the only car I have ever drooled over. Not candy-apple red is it?"

"Classy silver-gray with black top. Of course, you can drive her! I'll probably ask you to look after her for me when I sail away. Everyone okay? Can I talk with Sierra?"

"We're fine, busy. Sierra is out tacking around the bay. Her regatta is tomorrow so we are closing things down and will all spend the day at the Yacht Club eating, drinking and supporting her. Are you going to join us?"

"Oh, I'd love to but it depends on what happens with Geena. I must head down to see her as soon as possible. The only good news I've had is that she's become more than friends with Zachariah's paralegal. So, he's been there to support her. I'm going to pay for the correspondence courses she'll need to get her law degree if she's inside." She sighed. "I mean when. Just pray it is not for long. Sydney said that the sanity-saver is education, the knowledge that incarceration is not wasted time."

"Seychelle, I'm being paged, I've got to get to the office for a phone call. Might be Zachariah. I'll call you afterwards."

"I'll be here," Seychelle said, and felt her stomach tighten. She had accepted that Geena would have to do time, but she was worried about her state of mind. Her guilty conscience over Mamma's death would exacerbate the trauma, as if being locked inside a cell was not enough. Oh God, what kind of women would be there? She envisioned racist bull-dike officers who carried stun guns, but was trying to convince herself it would be more like the British prisons of Chianti's experience.

She jumped when the phone rang, grabbed the receiver. "Was it Zachariah? What happened? Is she okay?" She could hear a tremble in Sky's intake of breath. Seychelle's entire body tensed and her chest went tight as she simply stopped breathing.

"They gave her six years, but Zachariah's appealing," Sky said, rushing on, "and he says it shouldn't have been more than three. He has already filed papers; is sure they will win. Seychelle, are you okay?"

Seychelle swallowed hard, blinked back tears. "How is Geena?"

"Seems she's in shock, is saying she should have gotten more. Zachariah asked that you call him in about an hour on #2."

"Okay. Thanks Sky, I'll call you later." And she hung up. She couldn't talk anymore. She just stood for a few minutes, then walked outside and sat down in her car with six years trampling any change of direction her thoughts attempted.

"Fuck!" she bellowed, slamming the dash with her fist.

Beauregard charged over, stood staring up at her. She stepped out, sat down on the grass and embraced him. He tolerated it for a little while, then licked her salty face and ran off to rejoin three boys he had found to play with in the camper parking area.

She was sweating, though parked in shade. Traffic zipping past on the Interstate was not as loud as Beauregard and his friends. Her nose twitched at the smell of barbecue and she decided they would eat after one more call as truck stops always had great, basic, and sometimes home-cooked food. No matter the situation, Seychelle's appetite was rarely affected.

Returning to the phone, she called in an order for a candy-gram with victory wishes for Sierra, but slammed down the receiver when they asked for credit card number. "Damn!" she whispered, shaking her head. I must think before I do anything. What a way to live.

She checked her watch and headed for a trucker-style feed. If a visit could be arranged, she would go to Miami.

After she feasted on catfish with hushpuppies, and Beauregard had roast beef with mashed potatoes, she returned to the phone and dialed Zachariah's safe phone.

Zachariah sounded tired when he came on line. "I'm sorry, Seychelle, I gave it my all. It's a ridiculous sentence and I'm sure we'll get it below three years on appeal."

"How is she doing? Has any of her family broken their silence?"

"No one. She has suffered, Seychelle, but she is very strong. Tim, my paralegal, has helped her a lot. She is going through the 'I should be punished' stage, which is understandable. I have had my head doctor parlay with her regularly and he saw her as soon as we left court. He reckons she'll be fine, but going through this phase is necessary before she can begin healing."

"Can I visit? Where is she? Have they moved her to a prison?"

"Seychelle, Geena asked that you not come yet. She said, 'I don't want her to see me like this. Let me get my shit together. I'll write to her.' You need to give her some time."

"But, I'm her best friend. I can help her. Where is she?"

"Must honor my client's wishes, Seychelle. Let her lick her wounds. Tim sees her daily. She has the first section of her law course and I believe she will dive in. My shrink reckons that is excellent therapy and he has scheduled sessions with her. She will be in touch soon. Keep sending your letters and I'll get them to her."

"She's not written to me even once. I mean, you keep me up-dated and I know she hates writing letters, but she knows I'm worried. You have given her all my letters, right? And she's read them? Does she talk about me? Have I let her down or does she blame me for any of this?"

"Seychelle, please trust me on this. She has tried to write but says she just cannot seem to get it right. She reads your letters; always says to tell you she loves you and wishes she had listened to you. She reminisces sometimes about stuff you did together." He gave a dirty laugh. "Like the time the two of you went topless in the Mardi Gras parade in Mobile."

She felt her face color. "It was on a dare," she said defensively, "and we were only 18. We wore masks so no one knew us. I've never told anyone."

"Not even West?"

"Lord no, though he probably would have laughed. Zachariah, what about Dolphin Dave? If they hit Geena this hard, what will they do to him? And Charlie?"

"Charlie has disappeared. Dave's case is getting complicated. The coke was pure and they're trying to tie it to one of the big Columbian cartels."

Seychelle noted how his drawl became lazier and softer when he discussed a case so he sounded a real Southern gentleman. How many opponents had been lulled into believing him ignorant? She smiled. She'd played that card, but he had mastered the game.

"Was it simpler to defend when the loads were just grass? Did they go easier?"

"Nobody goes easy on hard stuff. With grass it varies, hung juries are not unusual, intelligent judges who better understand the '60s are more common. I will be honest, it is a whole lot harder for me to defend when drugs are involved, especially when it is being brought into this country. Grass is so much less harmful than alcohol, it's even good for some folks, and it should be legalized. Damned fools keep fighting it. The hard stuff, well I have just seen too many lives ruined. If they would make it legal, they might get some smidgen of control over quality and access. Oh, there'll always be folks needing me and I will defend them because it's my job and you've got to keep your powers-that-be doing their jobs right, following the rules, but my heart won't be in it."

"Do Charlie and Dave know how you feel?"

"They've never asked. Your daddy and I were in accord."

"I know." She hesitated. "Did it affect your defense of Geena?"

"Goodness no, Seychelle. She is not in that business; she just made a stupid mistake. No, I plan on having that girl in my firm. I went at it, guns blazing, but she wouldn't let me use anything that in any way made her family look bad or her upbringing look as if it lacked in any way. That crippled me."

So, Geena had not confided about her first run. Good thing. "Okay, Zachariah, I've got to go. Please give her a hug for me. And take care of you."

"Of course. Listen, your Jerken Jr. has been sniffing around Dave."

"Really? Do you think that means he's after Charlie? I mean, I believe he was the only link between Dave and West."

"No way to know but we will just stay aware. And you will stay away, right?"

"Right."

She attempted three more calls without success so began departure prep. By the time she rounded up Beauregard, raised the top, gassed up and was heading up the on-ramp, she knew exactly where she was heading, where she had to go to turn the page, to move forward.

153

Twenty-Four

A board creaked under her foot and Beauregard growled. "Shhh," she hissed. Has her house always been so noisy? Yes, she had been very aware when she sneaked in past curfew in her teens. Only now did she acknowledge that her dad had most likely known each time. As a child she had thought it haunted. She bumped her elbow on a bookshelf corner and swore.

"This is ridiculous," Seychelle said and straightened up. "This is our house, Beauregard. I parked out of sight of the road but I will not crawl around in the dark like a thief. I just can't believe that creep Jerken is spending time and money to keep watch here."

She found a wall switch and felt better when soft yellow lamplight brought West's room to life. She closed curtains and stood staring at his bedroom. A chill ran down her spine. It was so empty, devoid of warmth and companionship she remembered, longed for. Geena had said that she packed everything in the attic and cleaned his room for her, but Seychelle had not expected this stark, harsh statement of absence.

She turned off the lamp, closed the door firmly behind her and headed for the kitchen, aware of a lump in her throat. The refrigerator was cold but empty so she turned to the sink faucet. She let it run, cupped her hands and splashed her face then slurped that cool, natural well water.

Beauregard was off on his own expedition, checking out smells he knew so well. She wondered what he thought, how extended emptiness had affected scents he picked up. She called him when she got to the top of the stairs.

"Chicken," she chided herself when he charged up, ears flapping, tail wagging. She opened the door slowly, willing her eyes to adjust. The only window faced back through pines and magnolias and it was closed with outside shutters pulled tight. The attic was hot and stuffy, uncomfortable, but dawn was not far off so she left it, pulled the string for a bright bare overhead bulb, and approached boxes that were stacked to one side.

The one marked Pictures and Paperwork was larger than expected so she was relieved to find it only half full. She sat down on a Books box and began going through files, careful to maintain their neat order. She nodded. Geena's organized mind was obvious in this project.

Seychelle began a stack of papers that would go to Zachariah, one for the safe deposit box, and one for disposal. West had evidently sorted most things out before his death, which didn't surprise her. Beneath file folders was a bundled stack labeled Seychelle, in West's angular print. She untied the leather strip that bound them and looked at the birth certificate for Annabelle Seychelle Austin. There followed a photo of her mother, exhausted but lovely, with her newly birthed nursing baby, totally content and secure. A small sob escaped and she automatically touched her locket.

Tears were flowing freely by the time she reached a photo of her and Geena in the front porch swing. They were beaming, arms around each other, diplomas held high. Quickly she rebound West's memorabilia and put them in pile #2. Hot and sweating, she went to the window, coaxed it open and released its dusty shutters.

Night had a pale pink tinge. She inhaled greedily, the soothing fresh scent of conifers a balm to the rough edge of her emotions. Early morning music of birds and insects brought the feeling of home.

"I do love this place, Beauregard. But it'll be a while before…" She stopped. The crunch of gravel as a car approached on the dirt road sent her heart up a gear. She slammed the shutter closed and didn't breath until the car sounds faded away. It had slowed as it went past her house so she did not relax. She closed the window, returned to the box.

The last bundle was small. Geena had labeled it Bedside Table. There was West's thin well-worn notebook titled Enlightened Sayings. Seychelle tucked it into a vest pocket. Next were duplicates of his basic will, house and land papers, etc. Last envelope staring up at her was addressed to West in emerald green ink with a Jamaican stamp. In the upper left corner was one word in neat flowing script. Chianti.

With a trembling hand, she lifted that envelope, her thoughts in all directions. She giggled, realized she was afraid to remove and read the letter. But she was almost drooling in excited anticipation. Beauregard's bark startled her. When she looked up, he gave an out-now-whine, however it took a growl to unfreeze her.

"You're right. Time to go." She slid the precious fat letter into an inside vest pocket that was now empty of all but a few 50's, repacked the box and followed her impatient dog downstairs to the back door. Soft pink was fading into gold and everything was dew-coated but Seychelle barely noticed. She locked up, got the box and Beauregard into the Mercedes and headed for Mobile.

She was on Government Street before she snapped clearly into present mode. She drove past her bank to double-check opening time, then to a 24hour coffee shop in a nearby hotel. She parked in the shade of a Magnolia, took Beauregard for a quick run around the parking lot, lowered windows and left him in the car with dog biscuits and water.

Seychelle found a table and ordered quickly. She did register that her young waiter was quite attractive and flirting with her, but was too involved to care. She had Chianti's letter spread on her table when he presented pancakes and scrambled eggs with free hash browns and extra butter. Reluctantly she shifted the pages, making room for hot plates, but her eyes didn't leave the thin linen sheets where she recognized the script she'd first seen in Chianti's logbook. Hers was a symmetrical hand wasting no energy on flourish. Emerald on ivory. She nodded, lifted the first page to her nose. Nothing. No, perfuming letters would not have been Chianti's style. Not even if it were a love letter.

Was it? Deliberately she smoothed butter over warm pancakes then trickled maple syrup over them. She savored a first bite, and then began to read as she ate.

"Honey-gold Prelude to Full Moon, Port Antonio.

"Hello West! Though you acknowledged the importance of your part in The Business, you called yourself an armchair smuggler. So, strip down and tie that sarong I gave you 'round your hips. Make yourself a rum and coke, leave your shoes off and sit down on the grass in the shade. Now, you are in the tropics with me and we're trying to set up a scam. In truth, it's a typical day.

"Your balanced and practical but spirited counsel would be welcomed at this juncture. I've been offered cargo of both hard and soft nature, with need for very little cash up front due to our good reputation. Oh, and that of my Dolphin connection up there. (Thanks again!) Hard is tempting as it pays over ten times as much, can be hidden away on my boat, and I would be handed cash on delivery. The bulk of grass means I could not stash it so a stop would mean an automatic bust. Moreover, I would have to wait around for payment until it's sold. Probably only a few days, but danger increases exponentially, as you well know. One of our golden rules is that you do not hang around where you do business. Anyway, you see my dilemma.

"Oh, to any intruder who may be reading this letter I wish to avow that this is a work of pure fiction. Ask my lawyer. Amen.

"No luck finding cargo in Sint Maarten; however, I was thrilled to find they had maintained *Cayenne* in the Lagoon. She was as ready as I was to go to sea though it'll be a while before I can do refits she badly needs. Dolphin no longer owns that yard so I bless you for keeping up payments for us. I fear *Cayenne* would have been sold off to cover costs but for you. Though you say you will not accept repayment, I will find a way! The rough emeralds I posted are just to say I'm thinking about you. I received them from the mysterious head honcho of a Colombian fishing boat. Each time they loaded us he sat in the shadows and watched in silence. Third time, just before we cast off, he stepped forward and handed me that velvet bag, said something in Spanish, and kissed my hand. He returned to the shadows and we sailed on to Biloxi, where I first met you. I've not seen him again.

"My decision to come to Jamaica was based on successful past experiences. I had a marvelous voyage complete with intermittent dolphin entourage, but did miss Sydney, yes, I did. However, dwelling on negatives is not my nature. My success will give us a good base for starting over. Yet again.

"What a place! Take a tropical paradise, let the Spanish wipe out most native Indians and introduce African slaves. Then let Brits bring in more slaves and rule for three hundred years so that social stratification and bureaucratic constrictions are firmly established. Stir with a few pirates, hurricanes and earthquakes. Voila, paradise with attitude and big economic problems. First time we stopped here, in Port Antonio, a customs man offered to load our boat with ganja. The one this time tried to get me to bed. On both occasions the refusals were followed by invites to meet families and share their food.

"Know what I missed most in prison, West? Rice and beans. And no one makes them as good as Jamaicans. They also have the best coffee (Blue Mountain), the best rum (Appleton), the best music (reggae), the best breadfruit, and the best ganja. There's a seductive ambiance unmatched by any other Caribbean island. But there's an edge, a volcanic undercurrent I associate with the aftermath of British rule, but perhaps my time inside has left me with a prejudice. The influx of hard drugs is puss oozing from a tropical ulcer that will not heal.

"I spent my first days back here straight, didn't smoke nor drink, intent on initiating contacts. I'm moored at the Yacht Club, a basic and comfortable place set up by a British expat. They have good food and showers and out their front gate is the center of town. Cliffs rise high on either side of the bay and drums converse across water. Night before last I ventured forth. Dare I say that the only thing I remember about coming home was the driver of the tender helping me aboard *Cayenne* as the sun was making its way above cliffs? I assume my aches are from all the dancing I did. Well, I slept the day away, and most of last night."

Seychelle realized her breakfast was getting cold so focused her attention. Thus far all the letter had done was birth more questions. She reasoned that Chianti must have sent the emeralds to West as soon as she returned, while he was still able to drive. Had he taken them and his letter for Seychelle to the bank at the same time, had that been his final deposit in their safe deposit box? Chianti, cool and confident, carried the same tone in her letter to West as in her journal. She was comfortable, familiar with him. Seychelle polished off her breakfast, asked her waiter for coffee.

"The night before my binge I had met my main contact on his yacht. A local guy who works for him rowed me out around midnight in an inflatable. Fewer eyes at that time, and he didn't start the outboard because it would have attracted attention. There were only sounds from creatures of the night, rhythmic bush drums, a few radios, and occasionally the human music of laughter and talk from town. It's actually my favorite time of day in Jamaica. I was a bit tense and night sounds soothed me. Approaching the boys as a lone female in search of a load is a unique situation. In the old days they grudgingly accepted Sydney and I as a team, and were tolerant of our choice of female crews for scams. But that's history. Though I've been out of touch, I seriously doubt there has been a large influx of women in the world of smugglers. I'm on my own now. My contact put more energy into trying to impress me than into closing a deal, but that's not a problem. He's survived here for quite a while, though previously rumor had it that no one worked with him more than once. Anyway, it is he who entices with hard stuff. I asked for a couple of days to think on it. He offered a sample, scraping a few lines from a large white rock. It's been a long time since my last line, but it sure felt pure to me. That's no guarantee of high quality cargo, of course. He was taken aback when I passed on more lines and a bit annoyed when he had to radio for his guy to return to pick me up. Had the egotistical sod really thought I was in for the night? Nevermind. He'll front me a load of toot (good business) or a little grass (as a favor for a friend). I'm not sure what friend he was referring to.

"Today I made my way into those beautiful hills to see an old friend, a grower, a good, beautiful person. His love and life is righteous ganja. He sells several grades but only because it takes time to perfect various strains. Ah, and I did love the sampling! Could actually live out in his fields, I do believe. He will happily front me some as long as I don't carry any hard stuff. Peace and love.

"A hurricane was passing south when we first picked up a shipment from him, however the barometer was rising so we moved quickly to take advantage of that window. A squall blew up just as we lifted anchor but our rendezvous was already scheduled. We motored *Cayenne* to half a mile off the river mouth and hove-to while awaiting midnight delivery. Westerly winds howled, waves grew more aggressive, and bolts of lightning became more threatening. It was quite impossible to spot a small boat in such conditions, so after 30 minutes we jibed and headed back to port. I trimmed sails, then left Sydney on helm and returned forward to keep watch. Just as I took position, thunder accompanied a bolt that lit the entire area. Clearly visible, dead ahead, was a small open boat in which two men paddled madly to move out of our path. Imagine my shock!

"I charged back to Sydney shouting, 'Jibe! Jibe!' He took the helm hard over so we jibed around and eventually managed to pull alongside them. Though both smiled, their relief was obvious. In the radically dipping 12 ft. open boat they carefully timed wave action. When our topsides hovered approximately parallel, they would muscle over burlap sacks of loosely pressed grass. In driving rain, it took superhuman effort. Most of the Jah Red stayed dry, protected by plastic bags. The guys made it home safely that night. We sailed away and made the delivery. It was an auspicious event, early in our career, and reinforced our bond with ganja folks. Next time we visited we took farming tools to them, met their families and even toured their children's schools.

"Who am I kidding? It's a moral thing. Hard drugs are bad karma. Thanks, West. I love talking to you. I can see that almost-smile of yours and the arched left brow. I can't talk with Sydney about this. Besides the fact that they read his mail, he would just worry and tell me not to do it.

"Do hope you're feeling better. I am sure it's more than a relapse of malaria, no matter what you say, so please find a quack of high reputation and get checked out. Remember, you promised to let me take you for a sail on *Cayenne* when I get up there. You'll love her! With much love and positive energy, Chianti."

Seychelle stared at the signature of the woman she had thought she knew so well, unsure of what she felt. She slowly folded the pages, placed them in their envelope. The postmark was smeared, so she couldn't read its date.

"West must have received it just before that final trip to the hospital. Was he worried about her, or was he confident she was fine, that all would go well? Does it matter?" she whispered. "And what do I do now?"

"Anything else for you, Miss?" asked her smiling waiter.

She looked up, took a moment to focus on him. He cleared his throat. "Umm, is there anything you want?" His smile was shy, his dimples cute. "Anything at all?"

Seychelle gave a slow, deliberate nod, steadfastly gazing into his innocent blue eyes. "Yes. What time do you get off work?"

Twenty-Five

Seychelle wiped sweat from her face with a corner of the crisp white sheet and stared at a tranquil farm scene. The watercolor wasn't bad, however they had mounted it in an ornate, cheap gold frame. She looked at her watch and gasped.

"What's wrong?" Her hair muffled his voice. His warm breath on the back of her neck was nice. She felt a small tremor between her legs. Memory of his lips there warmed her. Again.

"I must go," she said, her voice firm, and lifted his hand from her left breast. He tightened the grip of his legs around her thighs and she could feel him becoming hard and ready. Again. "No, really, I must."

"Just let me taste you once more," he whispered and slid his hand down her belly, stroked her hair, made her groan. "You tasted so good," he murmured as he relaxed his legs and slid his fingers inside her.

Seychelle gave herself over to the delicious heat of his mouth as he worked his way slowly down her back, felt her nipples harden as he mauled first one then the other with his free hand, felt her contractions commence as his fingers explored and massaged. Heat from his open mouth on her buttocks inspired loud moans. By the time he pressed his lips to hers she was begging him to enter her, was desperate to have him inside her. Again.

Oh, and it was good, so good.

She finally made it to the shower, her legs weak, her whole being limp, exhausted, satisfied. After a blast of cold water, she had a quick hot shower and emerged invigorated, ready to go.

"Come on!" she laughed and slapped his firm, nicely rounded ass.

He rolled over, smiled. She stared in wonder at his proud erect member. "Oh, no, don't even think about it!" she said with a laugh and began collecting her scattered clothes. She dressed and was out of the nondescript hotel room before her young waiter had finished his shower.

Beauregard welcomed her to the car with enthusiastic licks and barks. She drove away without looking back. She glanced at herself in the mirror. Makeup gone, hair wet and stringy, face flushed, but she was positively beaming. "Thanks, I needed that!"

Seychelle was still wearing a smile when she pulled up in front of her bank. She topped it with sunglasses and stuffed hair under a peaked cap before sauntering in. Within minutes she was being led to the back. The woman remembered her, was very friendly. Though she would have preferred anonymity, it felt good to be catered to. Was that one of the perks successful scammers enjoyed?

Seychelle took her box into the small room, started to open it, and stopped. "What was his name?" she whispered. "Oh my God, I don't remember his name." Amused and embarrassed, she opened her box and began neatly stowing cash in various pockets of her vest and daypack. She placed West's papers on top of a few remaining packets of money and fondled the velvet bag.

Had West made love to her? Her letter didn't have a daughterly feel. Intimate friends? Whatever that meant. She looked at the rough stones. It would take a lot of work to make them worth anything. Who would know how to process emeralds? She decided to ask Zachariah. She couldn't let Sydney see them. How would he feel if he knew Chianti had sent them to West? When had she sent them?

"Get moving," she chided herself. She put the bag into a discreet inside pocket of her vest and replaced the box. "That first few hundred went quickly and easily, I didn't even count. Don't get too carried away with all this hot cash," she told herself as she left the vault.

More subdued, she went to a front teller to purchase traveler's checks. Not fashionable, but handy, she had read, and good scammers don't carry lots of cash. It was a long tedious procedure and she just managed a smile when the young teller wished her a bon voyage. She charged outside to her car.

"Sorry Beauregard," she said and pushed him back when he tried to leap out. "I know you need a run. I'll take you to the beach," she said and reached to close her door.

"You ought not leave him in the car on such a hot day."

His dreaded voice froze her. Her awareness went from the contents of her vest to the minor shield provided by sunglasses and visor against close scrutiny. She cursed herself for staying there so long.

"No, I shouldn't, you're right. I'm taking him to the Gulf right away for a run."

"Yeah," he drawled, "in some places they give tickets if you leave a child or pet in the car, especially on hot days. But I know you love that hound and take real good care of him and I realized you'd left it running with the air conditioner on. You just had lots of business to take care of in the bank."

Seychelle steadied herself, forced a smile. "The lines can just take forever. I should have taken him in with me. This sure 'nough is hot weather and I need a swim just about as much as Beauregard does. So, if you'll excuse me." She pulled the door shut.

"Real sorry to hear about your friend Geena down in Miami," he said through the partially open window. "Real shame about her mamma, too."

She felt real hatred for the sleazy bastard, a feeling she had never experienced for anyone before, and the intensity made her entire body vibrate. "Yes," she said through tight lips. "Mamma was a wonderful person." She started the car. "Goodbye."

He leaned down, rested his hands on the door. "Sure is a nice little car you've got here. Must have cost a lot. Good thing your daddy left you some money. Sure is." He stroked the door and smiled. "Say, you don't know anybody by the name of Derek Shimmerhorn, do you? I believe some folks call him Dolphin Dave, for whatever reason."

Seychelle felt a chill go down her back, fought the urge to throw the car into reverse and stomp on the gas. She slowly looked up at him. "Well, those are both odd names, they sure are. I'm sure I would remember if I'd met him, but I haven't. Why do you ask?"

He gave her a big dumb smile. "A friend of your daddy's. Just thought you might have met him."

"Sorry," she said, shrugging. "Now, if you'll excuse me." With intense concentration she backed out slowly and merged with traffic. She was sweating profusely and her clothes were soaked through.

"Damn, damn, damn! Is he following me?" she fumed. She looked in the rear view mirror, took the next right turn and slowed. No one turned in after her so she worked her way through a series of back streets toward the causeway across Mobile Bay.

By the time Seychelle pulled into a crowded parking lot she had decided someone at her bank must have called Jerken Jr. He was not going to give up.

She left her shoes and vest in the locked car and ran with Beauregard to the gently breaking surf. She was only able to keep up because he stopped to mark most rocks and bushes. Once out on the sand they both rejoiced in freedom, celebrated sunshine. Seychelle howled and Beauregard barked as they ran along firmly packed sand that warm Gulf waters had abandoned. She ran out into the sea, kicked up sprays of salt water for him to chase after and bite.

Eventually woman and dog collapsed in warm soft sand at the base of smooth low dunes. Scattered tufts of grass secured that section of beach from encroaching waves and ordinances protected it from human development.

"The bastard won't find us here," she declared, but stood and cautiously did a slow scan of the area. She could see the top of her car, but nothing suspicious. "No one lurking with binoculars," she said, shrugged and sat down in the sand. She looked out to sea.

"That is where I want to be," she murmured. She stared at the horizon, at what she couldn't see, trying to imagine what the beach would look like from out there.

She startled Beauregard when she jumped up and began running toward their car. "Come on! We've gotta make it happen!"

Seychelle got in and started the car. With Jerken Jr. hot after her the last thing to do was hang out until he tracked her down. Finding a public phone that worked took a while. She dialed Murphy's but got a recording. They had all gone to Sierra's regatta. She couldn't wait, and it was better anyway not to return to Murphy's in case he was, somehow, trailing her. She headed for the Yacht Club.

Groomed lawns fronted the white-pillared bastion of moneyed gentry. Seychelle had gone to a dance here in her teens, remembered clearly a snobbish clique of girls. She looked around but ended up parking beside the road as the regatta had attracted quite a crowd. A glance in the rear view mirror prompted half-hearted efforts with make-up and brush as well as a change of shirt. Her morning rendezvous and beach romp had taken a toll. She shook her head, couldn't believe she had done such an outrageous thing, but could hardly wait to tell Geena, who would consider it a healthy step toward loosening up.

"You'll have to wear a collar and lead, sorry B." She gave him a scratch, hitched up his gear, donned her vest and daypack, and they headed inside.

She went straight through to the patio with hopes of finding them there so she wouldn't have to brave the crowded restaurant and bar. There was quite an array of sails to the South, a race approaching the finish line, she guessed. Sunset had begun so paired white triangles were highlighted by a soft orange glow of the retiring sun.

"Beautiful," she breathed and was momentarily transfixed.

The shore to the North of the club pier was cluttered with sailing dinghies. She headed toward them, eyes scanning small groups. Tall, striking Barry and Sky were easily spotted. She moved through a maze of boats and people, excited to see her friends.

"You came! Hooray!" cheered Sierra. "Did you see me win? Wasn't I great?"

Seychelle gave her a big hug. "I'm sure you were awesome, and I'm not at all surprised, but I just arrived. Did anyone get pictures?"

"Oh, one or two," Barry laughed and held up a video camera in one hand, a small instamatic camera in the other.

Sydney kissed her cheek. "You okay?"

She nodded. "However, I really need to talk. Later, after the awards."

"I was just going to get drinks. Why don't you come give me a hand?"

She nodded, turned the enthusiastic hound over to Sierra, and walked with Sydney into the open bar. "How soon can you finish *Wesheena*? It doesn't matter how much it will cost." She told him about Jerken Jr. "I'm scared. I must visit Geena, if she will see me, but then I'm leaving the country. I'll only come back to get *Wesheena*."

"Let me talk to Barry and Sky. We've had extra hands on it, but I think we can speed up a bit more." He studied her closely, his brown eyes soft and concerned. "Now listen to me. If they had anything solid, they would have pulled you in by now. This guy is trying to build a case and his career on bits and pieces. He's looking to wheedle his way under your skin so you do something rash, connect with someone so he can put the puzzle together. He's trying to prove his theories have grounds. That's the only way they will let him continue to spend time and money in search of the elusive cartel leader he's convinced is at the bottom of ongoing activity. So, you've got the upper hand. Just don't think he has any power over you or he will. Going south is a good idea."

She smiled. "I knew speaking with you was what I needed."

"Now let's get those drinks, folks are waiting. And, I want to see the end of this race."

They rejoined the group and everyone moved toward higher ground as leading boats neared the finish line. Starboard side was marked by the yacht club's trawler and the port side was marked by a large orange buoy. An impressive collection of boats hovered in close proximity to watch the grand finale.

Sky touched Seychelle's arm. "Zachariah called last night. He said he spoke with Geena and she wants to see you. He scheduled a visit for tomorrow afternoon. If you call his secretary, she'll give you details."

"Yes!" She gave Sky a hug. "But I've had no sleep. I will have to fly. And from there I'm returning to Jamaica. Would you mind taking the car? I don't think I should go back to your yard—"

Loud cheers interrupted them. On the water there was action. Two 60 footers had just rounded the point, bearing down on the finish line, beam to beam, sails trimmed to catch fluctuating gusts as they moved from close reach to beat.

"It is the commodore's yacht, *Unscrupulous*, and his main rival, *Grass Roots*," Sky told her.

Sydney moved closer. "It's owned by one of our friends, Pierre the Frog." Seychelle's eyes grew large.

He nodded. "Yes, one of us, as referred to by Chianti. He has been quite successful. Has a place in St. Barth now, plays with the rich and famous, and makes the race circuit."

She frowned. "I assume that means he didn't stick with grass."

He shrugged. "It's the way of the world, my Dear. We purists are a poor and vanishing breed."

"Think he is on his boat?"

"Oh, absolutely. He will be at helm. The business was always just to finance that passion. If he wins, I will introduce you later. If not, he'll just disappear, hates losing."

Sky laughed. "I'm not sure who has the larger ego, but the commodore must be around to officiate afterwards. That's his young wife over there, the blonde with large breasts and diamonds. Rumor has it that she played with Pierre when she went to St. Barth alone on vacation a couple of years back and that was what sparked the big rivalry."

Though there were three boats in close pursuit, the two leaders had everyone's full attention as they edged forward. Seychelle silently cheered as

Grass Roots pulled steadily ahead. One of us. She pondered the phrase. She had become a part of the extended family. Did it feel good because of her lack of family? The loss of West had left her with an emptiness of sorts. The morning session with what's-his-name had filled the space for a while. She smiled at the pun.

Pierre's crew, some wearing dread-locks, were in a frenzy of activity even though the air was light. Reading light wind must be the hardest, she thought, and I'll be good at it someday. She wished she were on board *Grass Roots*, watching Pierre and understanding the reasoning behind his calls. She hardly breathed until his sleek sloop crossed the line half a boat length ahead of *Unscrupulous*.

"Look at that wiry little Frenchman," Sydney chortled. "He does know how to sail!"

Grass Roots glided to the end of the pier and Commodore pulled into his slip along the south side. Ready hands caught and secured their lines. The subdued demeanor of the losing boat was marked by the quick departure of its skipper in his peaked captain's cap.

"The commodore, I presume," Seychelle remarked.

Sydney nodded as the tall lean gray-haired man made long taut strides toward the back entrance of the clubhouse. "Is definitely in a rush to leave the scene. Must be rough to have to stick around and present the trophy."

Cheering, backslapping and hugging aboard *Grass Roots* exploded as soon as lines were secured. She watched as Pierre made the rounds, his posture casual. He was smaller than any of his crew but was obviously the central energy, the driving force. They respected him, liked him, and together they had earned their victory. He caressed his boat with hand or foot each time he stopped to thank and congratulate. Seychelle smiled. She would love *Wesheena* just so. And it wouldn't be long now.

"Come," Sydney nudged her arm. He moved through the crowd to the bow of *Grass Roots*.

Pierre saw them and the smile that was spread across his face widened yet further as recognition came. "Mon ami!" he yelled and grabbed a bottle of champagne as he headed in their direction.

Their embrace was warm when he leapt onto the pier. His angular weathered features reminded her of Jacques Cousteau, on whom she'd had a crush since she had been big enough to watch his specials. West had purchased all of Cousteau's videos for her over the years. She could understand Commodore's wife having a fling with this rogue.

"Congratulations, Old Man! You just keep getting better."

"Sydney, how good to have you with us again, but how sad I am! Our Chianti." He lifted the bottle. "You and I will toast her, her beautiful spirit. We will drink this in her honor." When they embraced again both had tears in their eyes. Seychelle turned away, feeling an intruder. Exhaustion meant her own emotions were at the surface.

She watched the despondent crew of *Unscrupulous* square away decks. They talked amongst themselves and with friends on the pier. Some joking had commenced and tension was lessening as other boats finished and their crews began mingling.

"Seychelle," Sydney said, touching her arm, "meet infamous Pierre the Frog."

Both were smiling when she turned. Pierre took her hand, touched it to his lips. "Sydney's friend is my friend."

"Seychelle found Chianti's life raft and journal. Her search for the person and story behind them has brought her into our circle. Thanks to her I have the journal and at least some idea of Chianti's life while I was still inside. She has met many of our mutual friends."

Pierre's brows were raised. He bowed. "So, you know our Chianti a bit. Then celebrate with us, Cheri."

He tore off foil and was unwinding wire when a pretty blonde grabbed his arm. "Pierre, y'all have gotta go now! He's called the police. I heard him. He said there was definitely somethin' on your boat. They are coming!"

She looked around with obvious fear, squeezed his arm. "Now!" she pleaded, and ran up the pier. They stood watching the commodore's wife weaving through the crowd until she was out of sight.

Pierre declared, "He must have planted something. Merde!" He glanced around, grabbed the arm of one of his crew and began talking quietly to him.

Seychelle turned to Sydney. "I've got to go. Whatever is coming down, I can't be associated with."

"Nor can I," he grimaced.

Pierre interjected, "Well my friends, I'm off."

"Where to?" Seychelle asked quickly.

He shrugged. "Home to St. Barth. Should stop in Tampa." He shook his head. "Cannot believe the bastard would stoop so low."

"Can I go with you to Tampa?"

Both men looked at Seychelle. "I'll explain it all to you later Pierre, but I have a DEA man dogging me and being found here could be disastrous. I can sail, I'll work."

He glanced at Sydney, gave another shrug. "I have no extra foul weather gear or food." He gave Sydney a nod and hopped aboard.

Seychelle's shoulders drooped, her disappointment huge.

"Tout suite, ma Cheri," Pierre called as he stepped toward the cockpit.

She beamed, grabbed Sydney's arm. "Sydney, Sky said she would keep my car. Can Beauregard stay with you?"

"Of course."

She gave him the keys and a quick kiss on the cheek. "I may not be back until *Wesheena* is ready, but I'll call often. I think this is best." She bent to hug Beauregard and climbed aboard just before they threw off the lines. "Thank you, Sydney," she said as *Grass Roots* edged away.

He gave a hint of a salute and smiled, then he and Beauregard began making their way up the pier through the crowd.

People on the pier looked bewildered. Someone called out, "Where are you going? What about the awards?"

Pierre laughed. "There is another race I must win!"

Seychelle stood on the stern and watched yacht club lights recede. She knew to stay out of the way until given an order and was getting oriented to the wind, going over sailing terms and boat parts. Uncertainty about her spontaneous move nagged. What if they sent out the Coast Guard? It would most definitely look worse than if she had simply been one of a few hundred people at a yacht club regatta where a boat was suspected of carrying drugs. However, Jerken Jr. might have shown up and her association with the Murphy's might have come to light. But what if her car and Beauregard were recognized with Sydney or Sky driving? Damn. She would have to wait and call the yard from a public phone in Tampa. Relax, she told herself, they are smart and aware of the details, they won't go driving around Mobile or walking Beauregard down Government Street. Everything will be fine as long as I stay out of the country.

Pierre had the crew maxed-out, getting all they could from *Grass Roots*. He had the sails wing & wing to catch light wind that was behind them. Seychelle assumed he hadn't brought out a spinnaker because it would have attracted too much attention. Her engine was running but it sounded ineffectual, typical of a race boat, there for emergencies but small to save weight. They didn't stand a chance if the Coast Guard came after them in powerboats.

Two crew were searching through deck lockers for whatever had been stashed. Seychelle stepped forward. "Shall I go below and look?"

"Je pense non, mais, pourquoi pas? Go look, Cheri, but do not disturb Seagull. He is navigating us out of this, this mésaventure." His full attention went back to the wheel.

Seychelle had to force herself to move away, to step toward the companionway.

Seagull was hunched over the chart table, wearing earphones. She smiled. His long back appealed to her, she wanted to touch him. Her morning romp hadn't totally satisfied. Following orders, she began lifting cushions, using a flashlight to look through the lockers beneath them. The packet wouldn't have needed to be big to insure a bust, so she checked all corners. Luckily, weight considerations meant that a minimum of equipment was carried so spaces were not filled.

When she came up for air from her search of the engine compartment Seagull was sitting with his back to the navigation table, smiling at her. "Nice ass," he teased.

She laughed and walked over, leaned down and kissed him without reserve. He returned her intensity, running a hand down her back and pressing his knee between her thighs. She stepped back to catch her breath.

He took her face in his hands. "What are you doing here?"

"I could ask the same. I didn't see you at the club."

"I'm the navigator. I had just finished logging out and stowing charts when Pierre came down to tell me the change in plans. And you?"

"The DEA man accosted me at the bank today and I was paranoid he would show up at the club. I had just met Pierre with Sydney so asked if I could sail south with him. Doesn't seem very intelligent now, leaping onto the boat that was about to be searched." She gave an embarrassed laugh. "But I am happy to see you. I was afraid you had been locked away. Dolphin Dave was concerned."

He kissed her again. "And I wasn't sure I'd see you again. I was supposed to crew for Dave but I had unexpected guests, thanks to Yolande, so I've been living aboard *Grass Roots* since then. Coming up here with him was probably not very intelligent either," he said and sighed, "but mahn, me do love dah racin', me do."

"If they stop us, will you be arrested?"

"Don't know, just may be so," he said with a chuckle, sounding truly West Indian. "All be circumstantial but gathering storm clouds for Dolphin Dave. I be wid him many a time." He shrugged, his eyes reflecting his far away thoughts. "They tie with Sint Maarten, can be a plenty tight string."

Seychelle watched his thoughts return to the present. He studied her. "Why do you think they are after you?"

"It is a very long story that begins with my father. But my tormentor thinks I'm the link he needs to the big cartel boss. He is nosing around Dolphin Dave as well. I need to get to Miami to see Geena, then out of the country and stay out until they finish building a boat for me at Murphy's. Then I'll sail away, and I suppose it doesn't really matter where, long as I don't go home."

"Disobeying orders?" Pierre barked. They both jumped, turned guilty faces to him. He stepped down the companionway steps, flashed a quick smile. "Relax. You reached?"

Seagull nodded. "Bonehead is on his way." He turned to the radar and zoomed in on their area. "He'll be at 87°40'W x 30°10'N at 0200, and he said, 'Tell the amphibian midget that's power-time not hot-air-time. The Wolf will wait all day but I have fish to catch.' He did agree to radio stand-by on the hour in case there are any changes."

Pierre chuckled. "Ah, the fish-killers, they are amusing, no? Okay mes Amis, let us examine the situation. I will board that fragrant commercial vessel and be deposited near a friend's farm in Florida. He will fly me to Panama City and from there I will fly home. My motivation is of no concern to you. You do not wish to be aboard my beloved *Grass Roots* if there are visitors. You may go with me, mais, I cannot promise that my friend will be able to help." He shrugged. "As you wish. My crew will not stop in Tampa as planned, but will meet me in St. Barth." He gave a nod and disappeared up the companionway.

Water rushing past the hull filled the silence. Seychelle wanted to follow Pierre, to shadow him and learn. She didn't want to play hide and seek with Jerken Jr. She wanted the honesty of weather fronts and currents and full sails and ocean depths. She wanted to keep sailing.

Seagull stretched, folded his long fingers behind his head. "So, do I stay in the pan and assume the Coast Guard won't go to such lengths on suspicion, or do I leap into the fire and hope Wolfman can get me out of the country before the forces close in? The problem is that I don't know what they know." He laughed without mirth. "Precaution or paranoia, which will guide me?"

Seychelle shrugged. "Wish I could provide counsel. Is that Wolfman from the old gang?"

Seagull nodded.

"I'm glad the ties are still there. Do you see him often?"

"He dropped out years ago. A hard-core grass man, a connoisseur, grows his own for a select clientele, I hear. He's a good man. I'm not surprised he's willing to help. Your kind of person." He paused, took her hands in his. "How is Geena?"

She began the long story, stopping when he turned to plot their course on the well-worn chart. Pierre interrupted a couple of times to check course and weather updates.

"Why do you have three records?" she asked. "Everything is recorded in your logbook and double-checked, and the course is traced on the paper charts that you are laboring over. Plus, you are typing it all?"

"Times they are a-changin' and our Pierre will not be left behind. Everything on this boat is updated perpetually. This," he opened his arms as if in embrace of the knobs and screens before him, "is the latest from IBM. The positions, observations and radar info are all recorded on these." He hit a button and a three and a half inch square flat black diskette popped out. He smiled. "Seriously, a computer is the future, said to replace logbooks and charts. Me, no, give me a sextant, radar, chart and logbook. The pleasure and security derived from tracing our progress across a chart can't be matched. My logbook is the personal touch, essential, I reckon. There is no better read on a rainy night—" He was interrupted by a radar alert.

There were several blips on the screen so Seychelle just watched, feeling rather dumb. When the radio crackled to life Seagull put on earphones, listened and responded, then charged up on deck. He returned with Pierre. While they studied and conferred over radar and chart, Seychelle contemplated how very little she knew about navigation. Oh, she would be fine with a compass and chart around the Mobile area. But how grandiose was her ego. She was having a boat built, even contemplating ocean cruising! Oh sure, West had taught her basics and she could sail, but she was far from comfortable with a sextant. She felt like a fool.

Pierre disturbed her self-chastising. "What is your decision, Cheri? Our taxi will be alongside in about five minutes. There approaches from the coast what we assume to be a boat filled with your gendarmes. There are enough boats around to confuse the issue and we generally do not show up well on radar. Luck is an element, of course."

Seychelle hadn't expected such rapid deployment. She felt like a deer mesmerized by the headlights of an on-coming car.

Pierre murmured, "Merde! I am on deck." He unlocked a drawer beneath the nav table and put some things in a backpack, then went up.

Seagull put his arm around her. "Seychelle? You okay?"

She could almost see the panic that was trying to consume her. Deep breaths. Are you with me, West?

"You don't have to go, Seychelle. I think it's best for me, but we'll see. Only you can decide for yourself." He kissed her on the cheek, tucked his logbook into his backpack and moved toward the companionway.

"I'm coming," she said, her voice hoarse, a croak. She willed her feet to move forward, took the hand he offered.

As soon as they stepped on deck and the cool breeze struck her face, she revived. The throaty throb of the fishing boat diesel was alongside as they kept pace with the broad-reaching sailboat. No lights burned on either vessel but her eyes adjusted quickly. Seagull led her amidships to the port shroud. She stepped over the lifeline, bracing with one hand on the shroud. The boat moved in close and she leapt over, watching only that there was a deck where she aimed her foot. Hands closed around her arms, she was lifted and pushed into more waiting arms.

She looked back just as Seagull was moved through in the same manner. Pierre hugged each of them. "Come meet my friend, Captain Bonehead. I brought a fine Chablis to compliment the fresh fish we will eat."

Seychelle breathed in overpowering smells of fish and diesel, listened to her companions laughing and jibing, and looked up at glittering stars. She could almost hear Chianti laugh and say, "I love this life!"

Twenty-Six

Fiction. "Can think of nothing worse than getting to the end with regrets of things undone. So, life to its max, I say! Have difficulty talking with people who profess boredom or make excuses for why they haven't pursued their dreams. I'm not searching for the meaning of life, I'm reaching for its fullness." Chianti.

Seychelle closed her journal, which she'd named Quandary. "That was her first entry in their first logbook. With time she found humor in the naiveté of her view of people and their situations, but she still had little time for those with no perceptible lust for life."

Wolfman's trademark mass of hair and beard gave a faint hint of a nod. He had picked them up at Fish Café, across a red gravel road from the pier where Bonehead had deposited them. They dropped Pierre and Seagull at a farm with a small plane in its barn and a dirt runway across its cotton field. Now they were driving south and there was sufficient daylight to appreciate his intense, intelligent indigo blue eyes. She was enthralled. His just-another-day attitude had taken tension out of their situation.

She studied him. "I don't know how well you knew Chianti. She mentioned you amongst their extended Caribbean family, but didn't give any details. Why did you ask me about her? Do you know anything about her disappearance? Why didn't you get in touch with Sydney?"

"Sydney and I were casual friends, never actually working together, though I believe we participated in some deliveries without crossing paths. Chianti added positive energy to operations in the Caribbean. From all I've heard about you, Seychelle, you would have been close friends."

He glanced at her startled face, smiled. "Zachariah is my brother, though no one knows except West." He nodded. "I introduced The Boys to Zach when we were just starting operations and he was struggling to set up his own law firm."

She could only stare, was unaware her hand had automatically gone to her locket.

"I was in the Philippines with West and Charlie and Bonehead." When he looked at her this time he burst into deep, pure laughter. "I was delighted when Pierre introduced you. That is why I volunteered to drive you down to Miami. I wanted to get to know West's daughter who has come to play a part in this sequel to our bodacious escapades."

"Bonehead? But he's such a, uh…"

"Tobacco-chewing-hick? Uneducated redneck? Loud, smelly old fisherman? Yes, he's all that. And he's wily, has a nose for danger and an uncanny ability to avoid it. Loyal and trustworthy, too."

"But, he's old. I mean, you were all in the Navy together, right?"

"He's about the same age as West and Charlie, just very weathered. He has fished all his life. Kicked out of the Navy when he lost a lung in action. Charlie was injured at the same time. I was a medic, and got to know them then. West was the officer assigned to their case. Things were fairly relaxed in the Philippines and I was always high. When West walked in on Charlie and me sharing a spliff one day, Bonehead just talked him into ignoring it. Charlie was a hustler, and could read people. It wasn't long before he dared West to take some grass back to the States when he went home on leave. Charlie knew he could do it and would like the challenge. The rest is history."

Seychelle scoffed, "For you maybe. Me, I'm downright discombobulated. I keep getting hit with new, shocking bits of info about my mild-mannered father's adventures, his secret life. I'm almost afraid to meet anyone new for fear of what they may add, of how much more deeply entrenched I may be."

Wolfman turned his full attention to her, and was only drawn back to driving when his wheels complained of hitting the gravel curve. "I'll take that as an exaggeration," he said, his voice soft but firm. "You want me to tell you everything, but I can't. Some I don't know; some would compromise others. Suffice to say we all kept in touch after returning here. Besides philosophizing over world problems in our idle hours, we had done a lot of brainstorming over the dilemma of poor quality grass at high prices back home. And even that was in short supply. I had a friend at school, we'll call him Jose', whose father was from Colombia. He could get good grass in large quantities, but obviously could not bring it into the States in Colombian fishing boats. Bonehead reckoned he could pick it up from Jose's boats off shore and bring it in safely

176

and quickly in some of his family's fleet of fishing boats. After a time, he began bringing up regular shipments from Jamaica as well. Charlie was our marketing man, and had plenty of connections. West had access to long-term financing and our overhead dropped dramatically when bulk buying. So, there we had the basic formula for success: better product, better service, and lower cost. Few businesses can boast all three. In the '60s there was only grass really. Some coke was flown in for high-rollers, but all hard stuff was tied to crime. Basically, it was bales of weed, seeds and all, and that was what we were interested in."

Seychelle absorbed every word, suppressing her multitude of questions but for one. "Why did you say you had a friend, this Jose'?"

Wolfman looked at her, his furrowed brow barely evident between the sections of salt & pepper hair that sprouted forward. "I'll not ask why you inquire." He signaled and turned into a service station.

"Jose' used to accompany every boat up, but he was arrested by Columbian military. They're funded by our government, who only make the in-fighting worse with their lack of comprehension." He turned off the engine and all was quiet for a few minutes. Seychelle forced herself to wait in silence.

"He was tortured and his father was executed. Their group supplied us for a while. But it fell apart. So many ganja growers were closed down. Cocaine was easier to transport, easier to hide at higher altitudes, and provided more profit. Bonehead, West and I pulled out. Charlie has done well, but even he is fed up. He has gone into hiding, only emerges when necessary, and tries to do business with what remains of Jose's family. Says he's going to get their marijuana fields going again. Hard to picture him as a farmer, but we'll see." He got out to pump gas.

From envisioning New York Charlie in overalls, Seychelle veered into West securing loans from a small-town Southern bank manager for grass shipments, and then to a cannabis-laden fishing trawler with a swarthy captain in the shadows. Was it Jose' who had given Chianti the rough emeralds?

"Why did they start using sailboats?" she asked as soon as Wolfman returned to the car.

"Too many straight red-necks working around fishing fleets, and too easy to keep tabs on commercially licensed vessels. Recreational boats are varied and difficult to track, the wood or fiber-glass sailboats often don't even register on radar. Fishing boats still play a small role, like in your case last night, but they won't usually chance it unless there is big money, and that means hard drugs."

He began asking questions about both Geena and Chianti. They were pulling up in front of the prison before Seychelle had a chance to ask, "Why didn't you come to West's funeral?"

"And who would have benefited, Seychelle? What could I have done for him or said to you? When he learned he was dying he notified Zachariah and secured arrangements for your future. To me he sent a case of St-Emilion Grand Cru. His note said, 'With no regrets I bid adieu. Grow only the best, Wolf. I'll be watching. West.'

Seychelle shivered. With no regrets. "And that's what you're doing?"

"Doing my best," he said with a beatific smile. "West had notified Bonehead when Chianti told him she was heading north, but neither lookouts before nor searches afterward were of any avail. She is the only grass smuggler I've known to be lost at sea."

"You've done the run. What do you think happened?" she asked.

He shrugged. "She was a good sailor, from all accounts, and I know she was cool, even-headed. If her radar was out or she fell asleep, she could have hit a rig or been hit by a tanker in that area. She could have hit a container. They are lost off ships with surprising regularity. Really, there are so many possible scenarios you can play out. Accept that we will never know. And that one of the attractions of The Business is that you combine dangers inherent in sailing with those of breaking man's laws."

He sighed. "I miss it sometimes. The legality pressure is ever-present, but watching weather developments for your crops just doesn't compare with confronting it in a small boat."

"Is it right?" she asked. "Do you think it is right to break the law? I mean, for the good of the majority, that's the basis of laws, isn't it? What gives you the right? Or West, or Chianti? Yes, grass should be legalized, but there are always lots of folks who think things should be changed before they actually are. So, just go do it? The Klan thought they were right to string people up because of their color though the law said no. Where do you draw the line?"

Wolfman's smile was almost paternal. "I believe that West would say that you know that answer in your heart. The right of the individual, Seychelle, that is what it's all about, whether grower, shipper, dealer or user. And always there is the absolute dividing line of not hurting folks."

Seychelle turned away, stared at the high prison walls that confronted them. Who was hurting whom?

"Rounds of barbed wire have been replaced by razor wire, more effective at ripping flesh of would-be escapees," Seychelle said through clenched teeth as she stared up at the 20 ft. wall. "But, they say, health care has improved, more educational courses are available, and a fortune has been spent on physical fitness programs. They're only cons, and they'll be back in before long, so why waste money? That attitude usually wins out over do-gooders who don't seem to have the right plan either. Most are privately run, for profit. God, what kind of world is she in? Hopelessness must permeate this place."

"Stoke your positivity before going in, don't add to negative energy. You've not had much sleep. Relax, get centered." Wolfman pulled an engraved silver and turquoise cigarette case from his pocket and offered one to Seychelle.

She frowned and shook her head. "I don't smoke."

He smiled. "It's my best home-grown. Just take a few puffs, as if it's a cigarette. It will take the edge off."

She took one of the perfect joints, gazed into Wolfman's sympathetic eyes while he lit it for her with his matching lighter. She had been unable to sleep during their drive down, was too anxious to ask questions, to learn more about her father's other life and early days in the Caribbean. When they stopped for lunch, she'd called Zachariah to make sure she could see Geena.

She took a long drag, closed her eyes as soothing smoke circulated. "Zachariah said she was stabilizing but vulnerable. You're right. I've got to be an upper for her. Speaking of which, this stuff is great!" She took another drag.

Wolfman glanced around at guard towers and double gates. "Don't look like you're enjoying it too much or they might want some," he said and chuckled. "Bastards probably supply inmates with hard stuff." He shook his head. "Geena is lucky to have you as a friend."

Seychelle gently stubbed out the joint after a third toke. "Strong shit," she smiled. "Best not get too relaxed. Zachariah was surprised when I told him I was riding with his brother. He was quick to assure me that he had not compromised my confidentiality. Would his position with your cartel, if you will pardon the term, be considered knowingly concerned by powers-that-be if he were investigated?"

"He has covered the legal loopholes but you can never be sure. Suffice to say, Dolphin Dave is a situation that is making everyone nervous. Your Jerken Jr. seems to be a focused bounty hunter. The quilt he is piecing together could form a pattern, but hopefully it will remain a pile of scraps."

Seychelle jumped when her Casio sounded off. She sighed. "Wish I could just hang out and sample more of your quality herb, to be honest." She did a quick make-up and hair check, sprayed herself heavily with perfume, as Wolfman suggested, and popped the mint he gave her into her mouth. Without a backward glance, she got out, squared her shoulders and walked up to a black metal door with ENTRY painted in large red letters.

After being searched by a grim, armed female guard she was led through two locked doors to a large barf-green room. A male guard with discolored teeth and buttons straining over beer-belly directed her to a table, told her to sit in one of the blue chairs. She tried to keep a smile, and was determined to remain undisturbed by surroundings. She sat and studied people around her. They were tense, trying too hard to be cheerful, these families and friends of jailed women who sat in dirty white bolted-down chairs wearing faded orange jumpsuits. Kids were loud, unable to sit still, needing attention where there was none to spare.

"Seychelle."

"Oh, Geena!" she cried, jumped up and threw her arms around the diminished body.

"Be seated please," ordered a flat, nondescript voice.

Neither looked around. They just released each other and sat down, eyes locked, tears flowing. Seychelle could only think of starving people pictured on aid posters. She searched her friend's face for the spirit, the devilish defiance she loved.

"You look great but tired," Geena said. "Too much sex and drugs?"

Seychelle hadn't been prepared for her wretched appearance or the flippant remark. She surprised herself by leaping into a recount of her romp with the nameless waiter and continued in a lowered voice with the yacht club scene as well as the night's adventure at sea.

Geena was hungrily hanging on every word. They were alone, it was like old times, girls laughing and sharing, both leaning far forward in their chairs, their hands almost touching.

"But why?" Geena asked.

"Why? Well, he was cute and I was horny," Seychelle quipped.

She laughed, "No. Why hop on the boat?"

Seychelle looked at the friend with whom she had shared everything, from whom she had never had a secret. "Geena, I can't give you details here and now. Just trust me that you are going to love my story when I can lay it all out to you. But the problem is that bastard, Jerken Jr. He has been following me and now is trying to pull together bits and pieces to tie me to Dolphin Dave and you. I'm terrified he will make a connection with Sierra's family."

Geena scowled. "A sister across the hall from me offered to contract. Says there are brothers who'll do white cops real cheap, just 'cause they like doin' it."

Seychelle's horrified expression provoked a cold burst of laughter from her. "Just joking, Seychelle. Relax."

"Sure. Uh, I've had some pretty radical thoughts myself. There must be a lot of tough cookies in here."

Geena shrugged. "Most are in for drugs, few for violence-related crimes. I'm one of the few who come from good homes." She looked away.

"Sierra sends love and a big hug," Seychelle said quickly. "Oh, and you must write to her. She does adore you. At least congratulate her on winning her regatta for the third time."

Geena's eyes watered. "I'm not sure I'm a good person for her to know."

"Now you're being silly. You made a stupid mistake. Move on. She has lost Chianti; she can't lose you or me now." Seychelle watched her friend withdraw. She took a different tack.

"Hey, my boat will be ready soon—" She got so wrapped up in telling her about the boat and Sydney and Jamaica that she didn't hear the end of the visit call.

Geena interrupted her. "Time for you to get back to the real world."

Seychelle groaned and grabbed her hands. "I'm so worried about you, Geena. Zachariah reckons your sentence will at least halve on appeal and he wants you to work for him when you get out. You'll get your law degree through the course, and will probably breeze through with all this time to study."

Geena withdrew her hands. "That's not allowed." She stood. "Thanks for coming," she said in a flat monotone.

"Geena, I wasn't going to tell you until launching, but I'm going to name my boat *Wesheena*, for my two favorite people. Okay?" she asked, desperate for approval, a smile, anything.

Geena stood. "You should save all your good deeds for someone who deserves them. And besides, you sure wouldn't want anyone to connect you to me." She turned and joined the group of prisoners being searched before being herded back to their cells. She didn't look back when Seychelle called her name.

Twenty-Seven

SCAMMIN'...
What's one to say of the thrill of a scam?
There's nothing to compare.
It's more than proving to yourself
that you can take the dare.
The friendships that arise are tight,
though odd they sometimes seem.
The price paid for a mistake is high,
so carefully do we scheme.
The plan is laid out, there is no doubt
that this one will succeed.
Connection made, cash up front,
then can we proceed.
"Quick, load it up, you're taking too long
in this dark bay tonight!
I hear a boat roundin' the point."
"Shhh! Fool, douse that light!"
"Okay, all's well, let's get out of here.
At sea's where I need t'be.
A nice sail North while sampling the goods
then a careful, safe entry."
Each plane is surveillance, each boat Coast Guard.
"Chill, have another warm beer."
Who's rowing out after four long nights?
"Relax, the off-load's here!"
Chianti.

Wolfman's laughter was full, rich with pure pleasure. "Aye, she captured the feel of it. Makes me want to get on a boat. Those were the days," he said with a sigh. "Listen to me, I sound like an old man. But I tell you, I probably would have done the same as Chianti, had I been unlucky enough to land inside."

Seychelle made a note in Quandary before tucking it away. She would accredit her fictional hero with those sentiments. "I'm understanding attraction to The Business for sailors, but being land-bound, like West, it must have been a form of torture."

He topped up both their glasses with Chateau Mazeris. "It is very close to St-Emilion, but not quite so smooth. Such pleasure your dad's gift provided. I regret I couldn't have taken you by my place. I have one bottle left. I think I shall save it and perhaps we will be able to share it at some point in the future." He lifted his glass. "To West!"

Seychelle was surprised to find she was beaming with pride as they touched glasses.

"It was sweet torture for him, I believe. Ah, we loved regaling everyone with details of our voyage as we ate and drank at each after-scam bash. West was a willing ear, with enthusiastic questions. He experienced it through us. Of course, we thought all involved were just hungry to do what we were doing, that the smuggling world revolved around us." He chuckled. "But I do believe West was content, that he loved his life." He reached over, took her hand and raised it to his lips. "Having met you I can appreciate that you were the center of his life, that he didn't need much more."

She felt a warm flush move over her body as she slowly moved her hand back to her glass. At a loss for words, she took a sip, shifted her gaze to the menu.

As if on cue, Zachariah appeared beside their table. "Hope you saved a glass for me," he said as he bent to kiss her on the forehead. "Has my renegade brother been entertaining you with wild tales?" His thick brows were bunched in mock disapproval.

Wolfman shook his hand. "He wouldn't be seen associating with me in public if it weren't for you," he said to Seychelle with a smile.

She studied the men as a waiter bustled around. Gentleman lawyer and cannabis aficionado, each was amongst the upper echelon of their respective trades. They had quite a lot in common, actually, and probably would have been friends even if blood had not united. She could see West forming bonds with both, and could imagine them laughing and talking together.

"How was Geena?" Zachariah asked as soon as their waiter moved away.

"Not good at all. She's down on herself and there is an aggressiveness I've never seen."

He frowned. "I hoped your visit would help. She has refused to see Tim or our shrink this week."

"Is there any chance I could see her again tonight? I couldn't get a flight until after midnight."

"No evening visits allowed, and from everything you told me on the phone you shouldn't delay departure. The doctor isn't concerned. He says she has progressed and it is normal to slip back into self-recrimination at times."

"I'll send her some Yellow Submarine socks and underwear," Wolfman said. Both glared at him and he held up his hands in defense. "I'm serious. One of the boys was suffering through intense cold turkey in a state prison and unsuccessfully cut his wrists. He's told me several times that my gift saved his sanity. He would look down at the Blue Meanie on his crotch or Yellow Submarines on his feet and laugh. Can't get too serious about doing yourself in if you're laughing. They make them for women as well."

Seychelle and Zachariah looked at each other. He had voiced their worst fear and opened a channel of action, frivolous though it seemed.

"Good idea," Seychelle said. "We used to watch Soul Train, MTV or Saturday morning cartoons. Geena said the Beatles didn't have soul, but the first time we got high we watched Yellow Submarine and she was converted. We went on to watch it so many times, an obsession of sorts. Can we go by a bookstore on our way to the airport?"

When Wolfman nodded the waiter approached, taking it as his signal. Zachariah chuckled when Seychelle specified no meat in her eggplant Parmesan and he proceeded to order his usual bloody filet mignon. When they were again alone with their glasses topped up, he said, "I have accepted that Wolfie only eats creatures from the sea, but don't tell me you are becoming a vegetarian because of one bad ham bout."

She shrugged. "Chianti and a little girl I know are starting to affect my choices. What's happening with Dave?"

He frowned. "Ongoing criminal enterprise, conspiracy and importation were the opening salvo in court yesterday. And, they have issued an international arrest warrant for Charlie."

Wolfman asked, "Don't they need solid proof for that?"

"All they need to do is convince a judge, and there are some who will accept circumstantial evidence if there is enough mud. Your Jerken was in court."

Seychelle cringed. "I wish you wouldn't refer to that vermin as mine."

He smiled. "Sorry. I put dawgs on it when you first told me about him so his is a sub-file within yours. One of my researchers pointed him out lurking in the back of the courtroom. They had trouble sniffing out any information on him at first, but he was a prime witness in a drugs case in Atlanta a few years back so that gave a clue. In his teens he and his brother had been part of a gang there. His brother died on some bad coke so their gang killed the dealer. Jerken turned state's evidence that brought down the dealer's main suppliers as well as part of his own gang. He disappeared then, we think he went into training and then went undercover, and only resurfaced for that Atlanta bust. Though he wears Coast Guard guise, they don't pay him. How and where he is paid remains unknown. We do know he has been in the DA's office several times during the past couple of weeks."

"So, he's not a lucky lightweight who is guessing, is he?" Wolfman asked. "Seychelle gave me an outline of his appearances thus far. If we add the fact that Charlie grew up in Atlanta, we now have a possible link, don't we, Counselor?"

"Well now, little brother, I do believe you have just made a valuable contribution," Zachariah drawled.

"No, Charlie is a New Yorker," Seychelle declared.

Wolfman nodded. "He told us some great stories about running away to The City in his teens. Survival meant getting rid of his Southern drawl as well as out-thinking guys on the street. He even got me saying you guys rather than y'all," he laughed. "But his family was in Atlanta and he went back regularly, though he said it was mostly for business. The first shipments we brought up went there."

"I didn't hear that last statement," Zachariah declared and flashed his brother a look. "Now, if we assume Charlie, or some of his family, was connected to the drug business there, then we have a possible connection, a vendetta or some such. And in following the path he turned up various players, like West and Dave."

"Okay, but how can that help in defending Dave?" Seychelle asked.

"Ya gotta think like an opossum to trap one, our papa used to say, and those words of wisdom have served me well in the game of law. Jerken has spent a lot of time, and therefore money, trying to trap Charlie, we will assume. Dave will have to do time for the importation; however, I'm guessing it is the Jerken evidence that is the foundation for the other charges. Can we discredit his evidence, whatever it is, due to his personal involvement? Or, can we get him to back off if he thinks releasing Dave will better lead him toward Charlie? He obviously knows Charlie has left the country, though I doubt he knows where to find him. I'll update my team tomorrow and we'll see what direction to take."

"I take it you don't think he will try to follow me to Jamaica. I was just one of the many routes he tried in pursuit of Charlie."

"The most they can do is subpoena you, but finding you to serve it on is not a realistic prospect if you've departed for parts unknown. Oh, and I don't want to know exactly where you are going, better for both of us. They would be hard on you in the witness box and telling the truth would mean tying all the pieces together for them. Not good for any concerned."

While their meals were being served Seychelle thought over what he had said. Zachariah was an example of the old Southern statesmen. He was just a bit outside the box but of good heart and intention and he possessed sensitive insight into folks. "Do you think he will try to get to Geena?" she asked. "Can he question her without you there? There is no telling what the outcome would be in her present state."

"Official questioning would require that they notify me first. If he asks and she agrees, then he can visit alone, however she is too smart for that, our Geena. Keep faith, Seychelle, she needs you to believe in her, especially when she doesn't."

They ate in silence for a while. Seychelle laughed aloud and they both looked at her. With effort she composed herself. "I'm about to sail away single-handed into the open ocean, though I don't really know what I'm doing, in a custom yacht I'm having built with dirty money inherited from my father, who I'm just now getting to know though he raised me. I'm basically on the run from the law, though I've actually done nothing, and I'm leaving my best friend rotting in prison. Funny, don't you think?"

Wolfman put his hand on hers. "You're caught up in—"

"An energy flow," she interrupted. "Yes, I know all about how one just gets swept along." She gave a sweeping gesture with her other hand and knocked over her wine glass. Horribly embarrassed, she watched the waiter rush in, feeling tears trickling down her cheeks. She wanted to hide, but equally wanted to overturn their table and break dishes and punch a few of the happy, secure diners around them.

"Sorry," she mumbled. "Too much wine and too little sleep."

Zachariah ordered coffee for them while Wolfman produced a handkerchief. She tried to laugh when he explained it had been with him on every scam, so she couldn't take it with her.

"What are you naming your boat?" he asked.

"*Wesheena*," she replied with effort.

"West would approve. I wish a lovely lady would name a boat after me. Listen, if you will accept me as crew, I will teach you all I know. You said West taught you the basics, and you love sailing, so you just need some pointers from an old sea dog like me to prepare you for reading traffic, open ocean sailing, stocking provisions, and the like."

"It's one thing he is good at," Zachariah said. "Take him up on it. And, he knows boats. He can help you shake her down."

Wolfman leaned toward her. "I know the Caribbean intimately. You said *Wesheena* would be ready in December. Perfect time to take her south, and I will be free until spring."

"I don't know for sure, I've not called Sydney to confirm when she'll be ready," Seychelle said. "You are really sweet, but I—"

"Shh," he interrupted. "Just think about it. Know that my offer is sincere and that West would not want you heading out unprepared. Damned foolish, he would say."

Subdued but appreciative, Seychelle sipped coffee and listened to sailing stories. They finished the meal with Key lime pie and much laughter.

Twenty-Eight

Seychelle cupped a hand over her ear to block out airport noise. How she prayed she had not heard correctly. "Sky, what did you say?"

"Last night, after you left, Sydney went out to drive your car home. Your Jerken Jr. waited until he started the car before stepping out and demanding information about you. Sydney told him that he had heard at the Yacht Club that you were trying to sell your car, cheap, and he was checking it out, that he didn't know where you were going, just that you said you'd call him when you got back. Anyway, he demanded full identification so we are lucky that he had Grandpa Lee's address on his license. Jerken made it clear that he didn't believe Sydney. Thank goodness we brought Beauregard home with us!"

Seychelle's dream flashed vividly before her, the kite dripping blood on everyone she knew. She groaned. "Oh, Sky, I am so sorry. I curse the day I entered your lives."

"I'm trying to be philosophical, everything for a reason. Barry's mother took Sierra and Beauregard to a cousin's farm where she can ride horses. We told her it was a reward for winning the regatta. Mother Murphy knows something is going on, but didn't ask questions, bless her."

"What is Sydney going to do?"

"Something between low profile and disappearing. He drove the car up to Grandpa Lee's, is going to leave it there, and will bus back here tomorrow. I've searched this place to be sure there is no sign you or Geena were ever here, though some of the workers may identify you if presented with a picture so am unsure of the right direction to take. I tried to call Zachariah but he's not called back."

"I'll call him right away. Did anything happen in the club?"

"Within a few minutes of your departure a couple of police arrived. They asked a few casual questions of some people who raced, but nothing really. Much ado about nothing, it would seem."

Seychelle wasn't so sure but said nothing. "Stay close to the phone, I'll get Zachariah to call you right away. You can tell him everything, Sky. The more he knows, the better."

She hung up and called Zachariah at home, and was surprised to be told by his service that he was at his office. He had left them at the restaurant declaring that he was unplugging his phone and allowing himself the rare luxury of spending a whole Sunday in his pajamas. She dialed his office and he answered on the first ring, took her number and told her he would call shortly.

She waited, hovering over the public phone lest someone try to use it. When it rang, she leapt right into an account of all Sky had told her, ending with the plea that he call Sky right away.

"I will, but we have a more immediate problem. There may be a subpoena out for you. You do not want to be caught trying to leave the country. It sounds like you are in an airport. At this point I am required to recommend you contact officials or direct me to on your behalf."

She stood frozen, hearing nothing but her own breathing. I am the key, the lynchpin. If they have me, they have everyone.

"Seychelle? Are you understanding?"

She cleared her throat. "Yes, Zachariah, actually my head is the clearest it's been for a while. But something else has happened or you wouldn't be in your office. Tell me." She consciously planted both feet firmly on the floor.

"The yacht *Grass Roots* was boarded in territorial waters and coke was found aboard so she was confiscated. The owner, whom you know as Pierre the Frog, and an unnamed West Indian were arrested when trying to take off from a private airfield in North Florida. Pierre called me. I will be representing him."

She waited for him to say more. The silence answered her main question. "Well, counselor, I'll see you when I see you. But tell me, why unnamed?"

"There is a good chance they had neither a warrant nor justification, are holding him under suspicion, so can't release information yet. When I see Pierre later today, I will know more. Why don't you call me tomorrow, from wherever you are?"

"Thank you, Zachariah. Good night."

Seychelle stood by the phone just long enough to make sure no one was looking at her suspiciously, then ducked in a restroom. Cold water in the face and some make-up as she was looking decidedly ragged. She pulled her hair into a bun, tied a scarf around her head and changed shirts for a slightly different look. Okay, let's see how a professional skips the country undetected.

Wolfman seemed deeply engrossed in a newspaper that hid most of him. When Seychelle sat down beside him he said nothing for a moment, then handed it to her. He pointed to a short article on the third page titled, Noose Tightens on Tri-State Drug Cartel. It quoted a reliable source as saying the on-going effort of federal officers in conjunction with the police of Florida, Georgia and Alabama was bearing fruit. Two more players, thought to be a Frenchman and a West Indian, were picked up this morning when trying to leave the country by plane from an obscure landing strip on a farm in NE Florida. The pilot, thought to service the cartel regularly, was also arrested. A racing yacht, owned by the Frenchman, had been boarded a few hours earlier and found to be carrying cocaine. Though the reports were unsubstantiated, so names could not be released, the source had proven accurate thus far. The trial of Derek 'Dolphin Dave' Shimmerhorn, thought to be a cartel bigwig, has begun this week. The rest was bravado about how the paper would keep the public informed.

She folded it neatly and calmly asked that they step outside. She took sunglasses from her vest and, though she felt a bit silly, donned them since she couldn't help glancing around constantly. He stayed at her side and as soon as they were out the revolving doors, he took her hand and led her to a taxi. They rode in silence, hands clasped, and disembarked at a Holiday Inn. From there they took another to a car rental company.

"Won't they be able to trace you?" Seychelle asked as they drove away in a black BMW.

"Tricks of the trade," he smiled. "Now, tell all."

She recounted her calls without interruption. When he made no comment, she stated the obvious. "So, I guess I'm relying on you to get me out of here. And I do apologize for the, uh, imposition."

His burst of laughter startled her. "Y'all are fresh," he mused. "Let us be honest. Dear Seychelle, I must save both your ass and mine."

She frowned. "Of course, how stupid of me! They must have followed us or they had the place staked out and saw us there. Have you used that pilot before? There isn't any chance they have been watching you, is there?"

"The pilot is a friend. He'll probably get off. Were they interested in me? Well, now, I sure enough am hoping that is not so, but stranger things have happened, sure enough they have."

Seychelle noted he had lapsed into a drawl, and that seemed uncharacteristic. Not that she would know after only one day in his company. Has it really only been one day? Perhaps the drawl was the contemplative state for both brothers.

"Well, where are we going?" she asked with a mighty yawn.

He patted her hand. "Roll your seat back and close your eyes. You need some rest, though you only have a few hours. You are going to have to trust me, daughter of West. I will get you to safety."

She did as told and was immediately asleep. Wolfman looked over, smiled. The innocence, the trust, but she was intelligent. He must go carefully with this one.

Tampa Bay seemed huge but claustrophobic. Seychelle wished Wolfman's connection had been located on the coast. Sunshine Skyway was barely discernible in the distance and they had to pass beneath its bridge before indulging in any sense of relief. Only then would they enter the Gulf of Mexico. She shook her head as she took another turn on the jib sheet winch. They were hours away from safety, from sailing outside US waters.

"Why did you just play skipper in the Caribbean? I mean, you were one of the bigwigs, the planners. Was there more money to be made blue-collaring than orchestrating?" Seychelle squinted into midday sun, her sunglasses not up to the job, and turned away from the winch to face him.

"I wanted this," he spread his arms in an all-embracing gesture. "Wouldn't you?"

"Well, yes, but the most vulnerable, in possession the longest, are boat crews. So that's part of the appeal, right?"

Wolfman smiled, "See, you catch on quick. Now let's see you get sails trimmed so that this windvane will hold a course. It is not great, but should do the job. I would have replaced it if we hadn't been in a bit of a rush."

"That's good, don't sheet it in too tight or it won't draw. Remember, just off the wind is faster. That's footing, and we are hot-footing it out of this bay." He chuckled. "Damn, but I've missed this!"

Seychelle watched him stand and stretch to tighten the mainsail leech line. He was in good shape, though a slight paunch curved above his jeans. Not quite

6 ft, sturdy but not athletic, his movements were sure and smooth. She would have thought him in his mid-thirties were it not for sprinkles of grey in his great bush of hair and the fact he had been her father's business partner in the good old days.

"You believe this boat is safe, right? That she will make it to Jamaica without worry, right?"

"Oh, I've sailed a lot further in a lot worse. It's a production fiberglass charter boat, Seychelle, built to take abuse. Not impressive but not a dog. We'll average four to five knots, with any luck, and not have an abundance of equipment failure, though something always goes. Sails are in good shape, seacocks are solid and show no signs of leakage, bulkheads haven't moved, and we've got a full set of charts. I didn't have time to inspect all 35 ft. of her, but I feel confident. I trust we won't starve?" he asked.

Seychelle had fallen into deep, exhausted sleep in the car and he had shaken her awake after securing the sloop that morning. Pressing money into her hand, he had stuffed her into a cab and told her to find a market and get four weeks of food.

She feigned indignity. "I learned from Chianti and she learned the hard way."

He gave a dramatic sigh. "Ah, I well remember their first run. They had us very worried, but they survived. We teased her mercilessly. I mean, some crews just took peanuts and Cokes on their Stateside runs. No one planned on baking bread and growing sprouts, but Chianti did. I sailed Bradford's boat, *Serendipity*, on that one. I had a case of canned tuna, crackers and vitamins."

He smiled in memory, shook his head. "He went down a few years ago, lost that beautiful wooden boat. A sin really. They probably auctioned it off for pennies. He's a good man, never got out of the grass trade, but he thought he was impregnable in his New England woods. A lot of people in that area earned good money with him. After Bradford's bust, Charlie centered his attention on the South. He said Southerners were easier to understand."

"We are a plain and simple folk, and have no need for adventure," she said with a smile.

"Right. Well listen, I'm wired and will keep watch for the next 12 hours if you'll feed me, and I am easy. It is obvious that you need sleep. Deal?"

She nodded, saluted, and went below. She had loved the pressure and responsibility of the market run with a time limit and the threat of The Man ever-present. Her Puerto Rican cabby had been a willing ally, pushing carts as she flung in boxes and cans. He helped loading everything into his car, and unloading into the boat's salon. Her healthy tip and promise they would see him in a month ensured his silence.

In short order Seychelle handed Wolfman a bowl of ramen noodle soup laced with hot chilies and garlic, a bottle of water, a thermos of coffee, and a bag of chocolate cookies. He was smiling happily when she descended into the forward cabin. Her thoughts as she dozed off in a snug, dry sleeping bag were again of Chianti's, "I love this life!"

She awoke to his kiss on her forehead. "You must wake up, Seychelle."

Desperately she struggled to move. Where was she? She tried to get up but he was holding her shoulders. She shook her head. She opened her mouth to scream but he clamped his hand over it.

"Seychelle, wake up!" Wolfman said firmly. "Listen, we've not much time. Are you okay?" He removed his hands as she focused her eyes on his.

Slowly she nodded, fighting down the panic and nausea that had engulfed her. She was sweating, moving out of her nightmares.

"We may have visitors. A Coast Guard boat cruised by, waved congenially, but they are making a big circle. There is no tax sticker on this boat so they may just want to issue a ticket, but I don't trust the bastards. Y'all be cool, thinking clearly, okay? We've got to play it like a nice couple out on charter."

"Yes," she said, clearing her throat as she sat up.

"Okay, my name is George W. Johnson from Miami. You are you, don't try to change that. We are just cruising down to Key West, getting you used to the open sea. You get seasick, are afraid, whatever. You with me?"

"I'm fine, George." She tried to smile but it became a grimace when they both heard an outboard rev. Wolfman winked, patted her hand, and went up the companionway.

She heard his hearty greeting. Their replies were muffled by wind and outboard. She stood up shakily, conscious of how much she wanted to go back to sleep, let happen what may. At least if they locked her up, she'd be able to catch up on sleep.

"Stupid girl!" she swore and slapped herself. The outboard was getting closer. She had a vision of Jerken standing in the boat, staring at her, and had to force herself to put her foot on the first step.

"Y'all are welcome to come aboard," Wolfman drawled. "I never trust these darned charter boats, but since I can't quite afford to buy my own yet, well, y'all know how it is. I'm tryin' to convince the little lady that it's so much fun that we ought to buy one instead of a wedding ring."

On cue, Seychelle popped up. "He's got lots of other jokes, but I doubt y'all want to be subjected to them," she yelled across to them. The two clean-cut men smiled politely at her. Her relief that there was no Jerken was quickly squelched by the realization that their boat was only 10 feet away. They were being boarded.

The older man hopped over when close enough, leaving his partner to hover behind them. "No need to drop your sails," he said with a smile when Wolfman offered. "Just want to make sure the boat meets specifications. For your safety. I'd like to see your papers for the boat, please. Oh, and identification, if I may."

Seychelle's stomach contracted. What if they have my name? Not a thing you can do about it so be cool. She talked about the weather and her seasickness, getting a touch graphic, while the officer read over papers George had given him.

"I'll take a look down below, if I may," he said as he refolded them. "I'm going to issue a ticket to the charter company, they're late on tax, but I won't make you go back as long as it meets safety requirements. Identification?"

George produced his driver's license and captain's license from his wallet while Seychelle fumbled in vest pockets for hers. "Too many pockets," she mumbled. She forced herself to stop and think, don't betray nerves. She unzipped the appropriate pocket and removed the transparent pouch that held her important papers.

"Ah, your passport is fine," he said and extended his hand. She handed it over immediately, fearing her hand would shake if she hesitated. She glanced at Wolfman who looked completely relaxed as he pocketed his wallet and chatted about the problems inherent in chartering a boat.

"Jamaica is a nice island," the man stated matter-of-factly as he made notes in his small notebook. His sunglasses regarded her as he returned the passport. "Shall we go below?"

Seychelle commenced bolstering herself. If I had weed hidden below, what state would I be in? I'm only this shaky because of lack of sleep. Think. What's wrong with this picture? Everything depends on me.

She turned to face him. "Officer, please take this place apart." She glanced at the companionway to ascertain George wasn't listening, lowered her voice. "Find something, anything to say we have to turn back. Oh, he's promised me a nice hotel room and a whole wardrobe when we get to Key West, and he's a good man, he'll honor his promise. But, Sir, I am just plain old terrified of getting any further from Tampa."

"Can you show me your lifejackets, Ma'am?"

She pointed to jackets in the quarter berth. "He examined this boat end to end before chartering it, knows his boats, but surely y'all can find something. I don't want him to know how scared I am, you see. I mean, he takes care of me, he sent me to Jamaica when I wanted to get tanned. You know how it is after a long winter." She smiled and shrugged.

He cleared his throat, and was obviously uncomfortable. "Is there a holding tank?"

She followed him into the head and kept talking about how they were going to get married, then began questioning him about his marriage. It didn't take long. She followed him up the companionway into the cockpit where he quickly raised his arm to summon his escape.

"Good luck, Mr. Johnson," was all he said before stepping into the Coast Guard boat as soon as it came alongside. He didn't look back as they pulled away toward St. Petersburg.

Wolfman kept looking at her but she would say nothing until they were out of sight. She started giggling then and her laughter verged on hysterical. Finally drying her eyes, she sat upright in the cockpit and told him about her ploy.

"You see, I thought that if he found we had no clothes he would get suspicious. And time spent in Jamaica, well that automatically raises brows, doesn't it? So, you're a sugar-daddy, of sorts."

"Your father would be proud of you," he said with a smile.

"Now, as long as my name doesn't flash red in their system, they won't come charging back from over the horizon. But, by the time they return to the office and enter our info, we should be clear of the causeway, shouldn't we? Though I do appreciate we'll still be vulnerable until 12 miles off the coast."

"Oh, they call themselves protecting commercial rights up to 200 miles off the coast, though the world disagrees. However, no good wasting time and energy worrying about possibilities over which you have no control. Right now, the captain orders you to your bunk. I'll call you when it is your watch."

She nodded and went below, clasped their minor success to her breast and fell into a dreamless sleep.

Twenty-Nine

Seychelle awoke with a start, sat up, almost fell. Her first clear thought was of the head, dictated by her pressing need, but a heavy cloud of foreboding shrouded her waking. Her clothes and sleeping bag were soaked with sweat and the harsh glare of sunlight through the salon hatch told her it must be late morning. Surely not. She had crawled into the forward berth before sunset.

She stripped down and stepped into the small shower, gave her face and body quick sprays of cold water. The boat's motion was so jerky she had trouble standing and had to hold on.

"We must be in the wake of a ship. How long have I been asleep?" she asked her puffy-eyed reflection. She squinted at her watch. "Holy shit!"

She grabbed tee-shirt and sweatpants from the trash bag of clothes she had indiscriminately filled when getting groceries. Grabbing any available handholds for balance, she scrambled up the companionway.

"I'm sorry, Wolfman," she began, but her apology froze on her lips. He lay sprawled across the cockpit sole like a discarded doll, his head rolling loosely from side to side with each dip of the boat.

"Wolfman!" Seychelle shouted, lowered herself onto her knees and moved aft until she was beside his shoulders.

"Wolfman?" she whispered, staring at dried blood beneath his nostrils and under his head. She took a deep breath, lifted her hand to the side of his throat. She could feel nothing. Her stomach tied in knots. Don't Panic flashed like a neon sign in her head. She moved her fingers around, prodded gently and kept calling his name.

There! She felt it. She pressed her fingers to her own jugular, then back to his. Weak, but it was there. His skin was clammy, but so red. How long had he lain there in the sun? What had happened? She looked up at the sails. They were on a broad reach but the genoa was back-winded and the main flopped about with boom swinging loose, the traveler set to port. Guilt flooded over her. He must have tried to go dead down-wind with both sails out, wing & wing. It was the fastest point of sail, but the most difficult to maintain. He was too tired, but had been trying to give her a long sleep. He must have fallen or been hit by the boom. Lucky their mast hadn't come down, she supposed.

Okay, think. Make the boat safe and then attend to him. She looked at the compass. They were heading SW, steering 230°. She shook her head. If I turn to retrace the route to Tampa, we will have wind right on the nose, I think. But, no way can Wolfman take a beat to windward. Besides, reentering Tampa Bay is probably not a good idea. So, get as gentle a ride as is possible toward the coast. I'll figure out our next move when the boat and Wolfman are secure.

Seychelle looked around, saw no other boats, moved the traveler amidships, brought the genoa over and secured the boom so they were heading southeast. That would do for now. She looked around again and went below, grabbed a blanket and pillows off aft bunk and returned to the cockpit. Again, she felt for his pulse. Barely there, but he was alive.

"Come on Wolfie! You're tough...don't you dare die! How did you let this happen?" She was sobbing as she positioned pillows around his head to keep it still. "Is your neck broken?" She covered him with a blanket and forced herself to begin a gentle examination of his head. She moved her fingers slowly through his thick hair, following the structure of his skull. She gasped when they found the indenture above his right ear.

"You were facing aft when it swung and caught you. Look at this blood," she said as she parted his hair. "Either you are still bleeding or it didn't happen that long ago." Was that what woke me? The sun would have dried that beneath his nose quickly.

She went below and looked at the radar. There was nothing close enough to worry about. Wolfman had marked their position on the chart just an hour before. Good. She then gave full attention to the sails. Not so difficult really. She loosed the mainsheet a touch and sheeted in the genoa, bringing her bow up to a close reach. She kept glancing at Wolfman. Their ride was smoother as *Wanderer*, she just remembered the boat's name, took chop at a steady angle but the change had shifted his body. She shuddered.

"Please live through this," she pleaded.

She stood close to the tiller while the windvane jerked side to side in efforts to settle into its new assignment. She had watched Wolfie set it up, but she neither understood nor trusted it. It took a few adjustments, and a near-jibe, before they were steering a steady course and she used the time to study clouds. In frustration that bordered on debilitating fear, she acknowledged they told her nothing. They were more thickly massed toward the coast but she doubted that signified anything. One reassurance was that radar said there were no big ships in any direction. Maneuvering through traffic was a terrifying prospect.

She took a last look around then knelt down beside Wolfman. His pulse felt stronger, though she couldn't be sure, and his body temperature was definitely closer to normal. She cursed herself for not paying closer attention in first-aid classes at school.

"Elevate his head!" she exclaimed as a curtain pulled back from one of her storage cells that was rarely accessed. She ran below and stripped the forward bunk. With the cushions Seychelle carefully insulated his body from sliding sideways. She folded sheets and towels, slid them with greatest tenderness beneath his head and shoulders, layer by layer, until she was satisfied. Another bunk was stripped before she was sure he was completely secure from movement.

Searching turned up no first-aid book of any kind. With a wet towel she wiped his face with care, squeezed some drops between his lips and laid it across his neck. Another forage turned up two small trays of ice that she bagged and secured with new white tee-shirts, fashioning a turban. Now only his nostrils and eyes were visible but the sun was brutal. She couldn't find his sunglasses, so smoothed some cream over eyelids and every bit of skin she could see amongst all that hair and laid a sail bag over his face. She tied one side to starboard toe rail and stretched it across, swearing at a lack of available points for attachment in the cockpit. Finally accepting the lopsided configuration was the best shade she could manage for him, she scanned the horizon for boats, then sat back to assess their situation.

"Well, West, my first time actually at sea on my own, but what a mess. Your friend is as secure as I can get him, though I don't know how extensive his injuries are. Looks bad. Luckily, we're less than 20 miles off shore. Just wish it were some Caribbean island coast, not Florida. I like him, West, and I don't want to lose him. Sort of a combo of the type of affection I felt for you and basic hot desire like the waiter inspired."

She giggled. "Bet that shocked you. But, listen, I've got to put his life first, worries about getting arrested second, right? It's just that your extended family is in danger if I'm taken. Oh, I would have no qualms about lying to protect them, but it is against everything you taught me and I wouldn't do it well, would probably make it worse for everybody. You raised a virtuous, honest daughter who is having trouble discerning smudged borders between right and wrong."

Frowning, she stood and did a short pace on the windward deck, trying to force ordered reasoning to replace emotions. She stopped and stared up at the top of the mast. "Damn boat, can I trust your radar, when you don't even have a pair of binoculars? Hope none of the rigging breaks. Wolfie's jibe could have done damage and I'd not have a gosh-darned clue."

Her attention was drawn to port. A ship had come into sight on the north horizon, very distant…3 miles? "If I get on the radio or send up flares, they will probably come to see if they can help, whatever kind of ship they are. But, what can they do? How many ships come equipped with doctors? We can't move him to another ship." She stepped below and searched until she found a flare pistol, loaded it and stepped up on deck. No ship in sight.

"I wasn't below that long! Did I imagine it?" she demanded. "If I call Coast Guard on channel 16, they will come with a medic and air-lift you to hospital, which might be what is necessary to save your life. Will you thank me if you awake under lock and key? Will the others thank me if I present the prosecution with their star witness, me?"

"Damn you, West!" she bellowed. And the tears flowed. She sat down on deck and let them.

Her lapse into self-pity was disturbed by a splash. She shook herself, moved back to the cockpit to make sure Wolfman was still there. Stupid, of course he is! She lifted the bottom of her tee-shirt to blow her nose and realized her exposed arms and face were very burned. Fool. Sun was lowering but they were at least an hour from the evening's cool relief.

"Oh great, nighttime navigation!" She sighed, disgusted with her ignorance. Bending down, she extended her hand under the sail bag to check if there was still a pulse. The negativity of her thought struck her when she realized that, yes, there certainly was, and it was stronger. She stared at his face, willing those blue eyes to open.

"You can't tell me what to do, nor can West, though he tried, he most certainly did. But I reckon I was just plum denyin' the reality of his condition, and was sure he'd always be with me. Nope, now it's my turn." She stood, staring out into the endless blue, and shouted, "Get your shit together Annabelle Seychelle Austin!"

With that repeated as mantra she went below, located sunburn lotion and slathered copious amounts on every exposed inch of her body. She was pulling on her long-sleeved shirt when she heard another splash. A rush of adrenaline had her on the bow in a flash, just in time to see two dolphins leap to starboard. Her smile pulled at the taut burned skin of her cheeks.

"You are a weak, sniveling girl," she said, "but you can do this." She watched them frolic, diving and gliding, and with their dance she calmed.

She checked Wolfie again. He was out, but he was stable, she reasoned.

"I am a smuggler, and you are my illegal cargo. I will get you ashore safely," she vowed.

But time passed and she questioned each decision she had made. Finally, sitting at the nav table, Seychelle got thoughts organized and started plotting their course to Florida's coast. She jumped at a noise, throwing down the protractor and pencil. It's a radio! Where are you? Static. Aft cabin. Where's the damn light? Wolfman's bag! She unzipped and up-ended it.

"Whiskey motel, y'all copy?"

She knew that voice! "Bonehead!" she shouted, fumbling to hold the black radio up and find the talk switch.

"Hello?" she yelled, breathless. "Uh, over!"

Silence. She moved into better light, was relieved she was pressing the transmit button, and released it in a panic. Static.

"Oh, please," she pleaded. "Wolfman is hurt!" She released, pressed. "Over!"

"And who you be?" the man asked cautiously.

It was him! "Bonehead, thank God! This is Seychelle, you gave me a ride." Static.

"Ya said 'nough," he growled. "Stay close."

"Bonehead! No, wait!" She stared at the radio, wanted to throw it overboard, wanted to scream.

With effort she returned to the nav table, clutching Wolfie's radio to her chest. Relax, she told herself, take your time and get facts ready. He'll call. That channel wasn't safe. Bonehead's the only one who can help now, you're very lucky he radioed. Wolfie must have arranged it. It hadn't even occurred to her that Wolfman might have a radio with him. She found a DC charger in the pile on the bunk, plugged it in next to the radar.

The Business. She sighed, studied the radio to make sure she knew how to use it, kept it on channel 23, where Wolfie had it, where Bonehead had known to call. She put on her vest, for its security-blanket feel as much as for practicality, and sat staring at the radio while watching for traffic on the radar screen. She smeared more cream over her cooked face and neck, and realized her skin was as thirsty as that radio battery. She returned to figuring out their first possible landfall when an alarm sounded. Seychelle jumped, swore, checked radar. Nothing.

"What?" she demanded and charged up into the cockpit, forward to the bow. There was nothing about to hit them and nothing they were about to hit. That she could see. Damned alarm. She gasped, turned, ran below and grabbed a flashlight.

The steps were easy to remove, as was a large panel that hid the engine. Wolfie had pointed it out when they first came aboard but where are the controls? A small flashing red light confirmed her fear that power was low. Was there enough to start the engine? She hit a button marked START but nothing happened.

"Shit, shit, shit!" She searched the area. Ah, an on/off switch. She turned it to ON, turned the red battery knob to ON, hit the button and held her breath when it began turning over. But it wouldn't catch, it sounded like it was growing weaker. She stopped, sat back.

"Think!" she bellowed, staring at the pile of metal that sat before her. "You are a diesel engine. Ahh, you need juice, a drink of diesel. But, Wolfie filled up before we left. Of course!" She jumped up, scraped and bruised both legs climbing out without steps, crawled over to the controls beside Wolfie's head, made sure they weren't in gear and shoved the throttle forward. Her descent was careful, thoughtful. She even located the oil stick and checked the level. She gave the Volvo a caress.

"You are strong and handsome. You will do your job and get us to shore. But right now, all I ask is that you juice us up so we have a radio, instruments and lights." Carefully she put her finger on the button and pushed. Once, twice...six times it turned over, weakening. "Please, please, please...Yes!" Oh, that glorious roar!

Seychelle replaced and secured steps, lowered revs and gave a hoot of pure pleasure. "I can do this!" she said and placed both hands on the boom. "We can do this." She felt such affection for *Wanderer*. How totally obsessed would she be with her very own *Wesheena*?

After ritual perusal of their surroundings for traffic, checking for lights now as night had settled, she checked their course and the set of the sails, and then sat down beside Wolfman, felt his pulse and updated him.

"I'll get Bonehead to call Zachariah, that number I do remember. We are steering due east now and should be at Big Sarasota Pass entrance by 0800. Hopefully he can arrange for someone to be there to lead us in since we don't have a detailed chart. Surely there is a fishermen's network or some scammer's link he can tap. If not, it'll be up to Zachariah's money and/or connections. Wind has stayed below 15 knots and there have not been any ships or fishing boats. Let's hope our luck holds."

Seychelle sat contemplating the luck concept, and was startled by the radio. She charged down to the navigation table. "Whiskey motel here. Over."

"Where is he and how bad's he hurt?" Bonehead demanded without preamble.

"He's been unconscious for at least eight hours. The boom hit him across the right side of his head, a deep indenture above his ear. Some bleeding there and from his nose, but it has stopped. His pulse is steady, and has strengthened a bit. He's warm and I've secured him in the cockpit." She talked as she stared at the radar screen. She gave him their coordinates, well her guesstimate, and ETA, though it was an uneducated guess, and then awaited orders with pencil in hand.

"You ain't radio nobody?"

"Well, no. I didn't know he had a radio until you called and the Coast…"

Static. She hushed and waited.

He finally came back on with, "I know. Ya did good, Girl. Head elevated?"

"Yes."

"Gotta talk to some folks," he drawled. "Keep 'er sailin'." And he was gone.

Seychelle stood with mouth open. In her head began the recriminations, so much she should have told him. Thoughts turned to Zachariah. And what of his brother? Precarious position or not, he had to know.

She sat clutching the radio, taking long deep breaths. Never use names on the radio, be careful what you say. Never use names...her eyelids were heavy, her face hot, and she felt so very tired. She leaned back, just needed to relax, but was jerked to attention. "Zachariah?" Her heart was pounding.

The radio growled. "Was I dreaming?" She stared at it, pushed. "Whiskey motel here. Over." She tried to calm her breathing.

"Where are you and what is going on?" Zachariah demanded. "Over."

After giving him a complete rundown on Wolfie's condition she said, "You don't want me to tell you where we are, and I can't call the Coast Guard. But there is a mutual friend who is going to help us get him taken care of. Over." Silence.

"I know him, of course. He knew your father and my connection to you, but not to your passenger."

She understood, but the silence went on too long. "What else has happened? Over."

"Your agent was shot a couple of hours ago. He is dead."

"Oh my God," she breathed. Her thoughts went immediately to Geena, but surely there wasn't time. Would she have gone so far? She pushed. "Who, uh, who did it? Over."

"They don't know. He was here in this city. It looked like a professional hit. Over."

"Maybe it was revenge, someone from that last bust he witnessed," she said, willing it so. "Over."

"They will examine all possibilities, of course, but immediate attention goes to my case." He cleared his throat. "There are subpoenas to be served on both you and your passenger, though no warrants, as far as I know. That may change at any moment. If you do not come in now, if your innocence is not established now, you may never be able to return. Please think very seriously about your decisions. Your future may depend on them." The silence after this declaration stretched.

She had never felt so alone. "I wish you could lay aside your job and advise me like my father or your brother would," she said in a very small voice. "Over."

"Just because neither of them would have walked in and faced the system, well, that doesn't mean you should emulate them. You are young, and have done nothing wrong beyond knowingly concerned, as far as I know. I doubt you will do time in prison, though confiscation of assets is a certainty. I cannot ignore the fact that my brother's life may be at risk, though he has most certainly chosen his lifestyle and the inherent dangers. Over." There was no drawl, the facts, just the facts.

She had honestly not thought about the money. "What about everybody else?" she mumbled. She stood. "I have to go. I'll call you as soon as I get him to a doctor." She turned the radio off and returned it to the charger before he could reply.

After a glance at the radar screen she went up, looked around. Such a dark night, no stars visible. There were no lights, hence no boats, and that was good news, a good omen. Hopefully.

"He's feeling the pressure, Wolfie. If they try to pin knowingly concerned on him, he's finished. Career, reputation. They wouldn't even have to prove it. I'm sure he has himself well covered off-shore, but his high profile would make him a prime target."

She stepped below, turned the radio on, tuned to 23, full volume, and returned to Wolfie. She pressed her fingers to his throat, smiled at the steady throb.

"You are going to be okay, I can sure enough feel it in my bones." She leaned over and kissed him gently on the lips. They were dry, cracked. She took a tube of cream from her vest and carefully smoothed it on his lips, nose and eyelids. The radio made her jump. She charged below, grabbed it.

"Whiskey motel here. Over."

"How he be?" Bonehead asked.

"The same, but I do believe his pulse is just a little stronger, though that may be me willing it so."

He gave a little chuckle. "Sometimes ya need the strength of other folks ta help ya through, so ya just keep on a willin' him ta git over it. Now, Capt'n, at 0800 I want ya ta have y'all at 27° 16.7 N x 82° 34.4 W. A 20 ft. trawler'll be waitin'. Have ya sails down an' ya radio on 33. He'll say, 'Welcome back,' and ya answer, 'I been missin' ya,' then he'll lead ya in ta a li'l ol' pier and an ambulance'll take 'im ta a private clinic. If ya wanna go with 'im, the boys 'll watch ya boat. But I wouldn't stay 'round too long if I was you. Friends 'll keep an eye on our boy for ya. Over."

"We'll be there. What have you heard? What's happening? Over."

"Cain't stay on. Ya git a report there."

Seychelle cradled the silent radio to her breast.

Thirty

"I cried when he pronounced Eleven Years.
Flat, without emotion, stated.
Tears were my expletives. But I look back and say
of that chapter, as with all now past,
I have no regrets!"
Chianti.

Seychelle could see three fishing boats that seemed about the right size. Chianti's accounts of their nighttime rendezvouses had made her thankful for morning light, but now she felt naked, much too visible for comfort. Every inch of her was taut, all senses peaked. She kept checking their position on the radar, trying to keep *Wanderer* in exactly the right spot. God, it seemed they had been there for hours. Had her watch stopped? It could not possibly have been only 20 minutes.

"Oh, Chianti, be with me now. I wish I had your stalwart philosophical outlook. But maybe that comes with experience. Or hindsight. It's 0756. What a night! I curse the Yank logic that preserves red right return navigational lighting. West said it would remain forever as the symbol of the US refusal to get in step with the rest of the world. I think…"

"Welcome back! Over."

"Yes!" Seychelle punched the air and bolted below.

"I've been missing you," she stated clearly. Oh, should I have mimicked Bonehead's slaughtered English and slathered on the Southern drawl I've worked so hard to discard?

She tugged and twisted a fat strand of hair, stared at the unresponsive radio. Belatedly she keyed it and said, "Over." Her face warmed with that blatantly amateur act.

"You comin' or not?" was the bemused reply.

She stuck her head up and saw one of the boats had turned its stern toward her. Attempting to regain her dignity, she stepped to tiller, disengaged the windvane and put her in gear. She had been motor-sailing for the last four hours and the engine had behaved just fine, but she still did not trust it. West had instilled a healthy cynicism. She clearly heard his oft-repeated admonition, "Always think you'll have to sail out of the situation you're putting yourself in, as engines are not reliable." She certainly needed no other worries at present, but forced herself to re-assess her position. The process actually relaxed her.

A white-uniformed man was waiting on the short aluminum pier. Her landing wasn't smooth, too fast with the incoming tide, minimal though it was, but she tossed the stern dock-line to him and he got it on a bollard. By the time the boat was secured it had a few new scrapes, but nothing serious.

Seychelle stepped over the lifeline onto the pier and extended her hand. "Thanks!"

He returned her firm shake and gave a slight bow of his handsome head. "Dr. F. Kennedy Lopez. Please tell me every detail you know about our patient," he said as he stepped aboard.

As she turned to follow him, she noted the fishing boat had tied off to some trees a few hundred feet away and two men were very involved stretching and arranging nets on deck. Reassuring.

Another uniformed man got out of the only vehicle in the small clearing that served as a parking lot. He opened double back doors of the white van, rolled out a gurney, shouldered a large framed backpack and headed toward them. He joined them on board as Seychelle began explaining.

Dr. Lopez examined Wolfie while she talked, asked a few questions, and disassembled the backpack. It became a stretcher with blankets and a multitude of straps. The two men maneuvered it under him with great care and then stabilized his head, neck and shoulders with a self-inflating brace that formed to his body.

Seychelle stood by, feeling quite useless, but mesmerized by the entire procedure. Though neither man was nearly as large as Wolfie, they managed to lift the loaded stretcher up from cockpit to deck. She released and dropped both lifelines, enabling a fairly smooth shift over onto the gurney. Once they had him in the van, they immediately attached two drips and a heart monitor.

"Carlos will drive us to our clinic," Dr. Lopez said. "You can ride back here with me. Do you need anything from your boat?"

"No. Oh, damn! Wait!"

Seychelle ran back, jumped aboard, scurried down to aft cabin. She had included everything from Wolfman's pockets when she repacked his bag before they docked. She had also emptied and repacked her daypack and was quite shocked to find Seagull's logbook in the bottom. When had he slipped that in, and why?

She grabbed their bags, looked around in case she had forgotten anything. "Thanks for getting us here, *Wanderer*," she whispered and ran back to the van.

Thirty-One

Seychelle had no idea how long their trip took, and hadn't a clue as to where they were. Dr. Lopez had been talking into his wrist monitor, perpetually checking Wolfie, adjusting his drip and flow of oxygen. He had interrupted the process only to give her a cursory checkup.

"Smooth this over all your burned skin, drink this, all of it, and lie down," he ordered, handed her a blanket, and turned back to his patient.

She forced herself to stay quiet, to follow orders, to ask no questions. There were no windows, no siren, just the perpetual hum of equipment, engine and Dr. Lopez's calm voice. She fell asleep immediately.

Seychelle awoke with a start when the van doors were thrown open. She jumped up, grabbed their bags and stepped out, awkward and dazed. She tried to stay out of everyone's way. Dr. Lopez and Carlos wheeled Wolfie out and down the ramp where two uniformed men took over. Carlos closed up the van and was driving away when Dr. Lopez took her arm.

"We will take care of Mr. Johnson while you freshen up."

She glanced around. They were in a warehouse with no windows. Several trucks, cars and vans in various states of disrepair filled most of the area and her first feelings of foreboding surfaced.

"What are we doing here? Where are we? Where are you taking Wolfie?" she demanded and jerked her arm from the doctor's grip.

He frowned. "Nothing to worry about, this is our clinic," he stated. "Come with me, you will see. We need to get inside, take care of your friend immediately."

Seychelle looked at him, shook her head, tried for clear thought. "Did you drug me?"

Dr. Lopez gave a hint of a smile. "Yes, actually. You are suffering from exhaustion, dehydration and sun exposure. You are not in danger, but Mr.

Johnson is, therefore we must temper this panic you are feeling and attend to his needs." With that he turned away from her and rushed after his patient.

Seychelle felt as if she'd been slapped. She caught up as the steel warehouse door rolled up into its frame. Her gaze went from her silent sheeted friend to the carved wooden doors that silently dropped through the floor as his entourage approached. Star Trek, she thought, and fought down giggles that threatened to erupt into tears.

She accompanied them into the entry sector where they were sprayed with light, slightly antiseptic-scented mist. All removed their shoes and even Wolfie's sneakers were left. In the next room she put his bag in a locker and kept the key. She refused to leave her vest and daypack, so Dr. Lopez let her keep them but insisted each pass through a metal detector, as at an airport. They even rolled Wolfie through. Reasonable, she thought, since they probably took care of politicians, rock stars, criminals, and outlaws like us.

They passed through into a tastefully decorated foyer. "Through the door to your right are guest facilities," Dr. Lopez told her. "You can freshen up and relax. I should be able to give you a full report before long."

"But what is your initial assessment? What are you going to do? Are you going to operate? Is he in a coma?" She couldn't hold back her questions.

He gave her a tolerant doctor's smile. "I would say he's unconscious but stable. We will do a scan and our neurosurgeon will evaluate the situation. Now, if you will excuse me."

Seychelle stepped over and touched Wolfie's parched lips, kissed the small red naked space between thick brows. He looked so vulnerable. Like West had at the end. She stared at the huge elevator that yawned ahead of him. Would he ever come out?

She turned and made her way into her assigned space, unaware of the sumptuous greenhouse she entered. Sobbing, she stumbled down stone steps and collapsed onto soft grass. Tears flowed as self-recriminations dominated thought, until she lay spent, weak.

Eventually, when her nose demanded attention, she acknowledged that she must pull herself together. "You're no good to anyone in this state," she admonished and sat up. "Well my goodness gracious!" Wide-eyed, nose dripping, Seychelle studied her surroundings.

Trees, bushes and flowers formed a jungle with Southern inclinations. She was sitting on the grassy bank of a pond, well, it had to be a pool actually, she reasoned, since they were indoors. She blinked, rubbed her eyes in disbelief as she stared at an amazing array of colors. Lilies, azaleas, orchids and tulips covered a small island in the pool's center.

"Okay," she sighed and stood, "I am hallucinating, too much sun, but I have got to find a bathroom." Seychelle wasn't sure if she felt more like Alice or Dorothy, but this most certainly was not Alabama.

"Well my goodness," she said again and sniffed when she looked up. There was no ceiling, just a large green dome through which sunshine filtered. She finally spotted a door with a large elaborate 'L' and tried to head for it with some modicum of dignity. The thick etched glass door slid aside as she approached, revealing the foyer of what bore semblance to, and even smelled like, a spa.

Seychelle blinked, rubbed her sunburned eyes. A delicate, lovely woman stepped forward and gave her a gentle, almost shy, smile.

"Hello Seychelle, I am Rochana," she said, and handed Seychelle a large, soft tissue. "You must be so very tired, yes?" She turned away while Seychelle, bewildered but obedient, blew her nose.

"Would you like first a bath, shower, massage or sauna? Ah, no, you must need something to drink first, or something to eat. We have an excellent chef," she said and smiled. "He is my husband, but I am honest, he is very capable." She gave a chirp of a giggle.

Seychelle roused herself with effort. "I, uh, I need a bathroom and a shower, I think, and to wash my hair. And, water, no, uh, iced tea, do you have sweet iced tea?"

"Of course! Silly me, you are a Southerner. I can get for you. I am from Thailand, but now I like your custom and I too drink sweet iced tea with lemon. Follow me please."

She followed without question into a bathroom and a shower room beyond any she had ever imagined.

"Water, water, how I love thee!" Seychelle whispered as she luxuriated in the multitude of jets that pounded her body from every direction. With a touch of her finger she could choose aggressive, gentle, hot, cold, pulsating, stimulating. She groaned with pleasure, could feel knots releasing, her body aching as it processed. How long since she had known such pure, unquestionable pleasure? Was it in the womb? No, I had to get very worried, exhausted, stressed…I had to experience life on the edge to fully appreciate this moment of pleasure.

She stretched, crouched, stretched, did breathing exercises, then stepped out, wrapped a huge, soft towel around her body and consumed three glasses of tea. I will not just survive, I will thrive, she decided.

When she opened the door Rochana appeared. "Come," she said and led her to a small room. "Relax on table, soon you will be like new!"

Seychelle started to protest, but hushed and what followed was pure ecstasy. He had large, sensitive hands and used a luscious oil to maul, probe and stretch every inch of her body. She fell into a deep, delicious sleep.

She awoke with a jerk and a surge of guilt. As soon as she sat up soft lights came on and Rochana came in with a big smile.

"Better, yes, you look better!" She gave her another glass of tea, put some clothes on the table beside her and left. Seychelle drank up and quickly donned soft cotton underwear, designer tracksuit and sneakers. She didn't question how Rochana knew her size, nor did she ask about price since she was fairly sure she didn't want to know. But she did need a report on Wolfie and she did need food.

Rochana appeared as soon as Seychelle stepped out of the room. "Dr. Lopez will join you in the galley as soon as he can. Tell me what you want to eat."

Seychelle felt so good, so renewed, that she didn't question her guide about anything. She even accepted that she did not know who was in charge of this situation, where she was, or what was going to happen.

"Two eggs over easy with grits and toast, and peanut butter. And watermelon, if you have it, and a cinnamon roll, warm with butter please. Oh, and I would kill for a cappuccino!"

Rochana's laughter was like tinkling bells. "Come," she said and spoke rapid Thai into a small radio as she led Seychelle out into the humid greenhouse.

Raised, layered planters hugged all outer walls. "We grow almost everything we eat, and we can grow all year long," she said with obvious pride. "We have special lights if we need, but the Florida sun is good sun. Experimental solar panels so always we have power. Friends bring food from the sea."

Seychelle stared in awe at tall, laden okra plants and fat watermelons amongst tangled vines that covered a 20 ft. section. "Well, I won't worry about my friend starving if I leave him here with y'all."

Except for the grass-covered bank where she had cried, the pond was completely surrounded by coconut palms and fruit trees.

They approached a break in planters where a clear glass door slid open. "Our galley," Rochana said. "You can make your cappuccino and there is melon. I will come back with your food."

Seychelle had so many questions, was totally overwhelmed even before stepping into the state-of-the-art galley. All stainless steel and glass-fronted, from espresso machine to wine rack, every wall was decked out, the coolers displaying a multitude of choices. And, much to her surprise, her daypack and vest occupied a chair.

She had settled at the table, melon and pecan pie and cappuccino nearly finished, when Rochana appeared. She placed the tray before her and smiled. "You keep eating and drinking. Dr. Lopez says it is very important. He will come soon."

Seychelle ate with gusto, savoring each bite, groaning with pleasure at times. She wiped butter from her chin and laughed. Has food ever tasted this good? Somehow it doesn't matter if he's a great chef or if I've just awakened. West, are you watching?

She was so involved that she jumped when Dr. Lopez walked in. She watched him, forcing herself to remain quiet while he made an espresso.

He sat down across from her and locked his dark eyes on hers. "He would like to see you."

It took a second for his words to sink in. Her mouth formed a slow smile and she let out a war whoop, began laughing. "I knew it, I just knew he'd be fine."

He placed a hand on her arm when she started to stand. "Let me explain his condition to you."

"No!" she wanted to scream, but perched on the edge of her chair and stared at him. Fear and anger gripped her. She should have called the Coast Guard, should have gotten him off that damned boat. She saw the kite dripping blood on him. Limp, she settled and leaned back.

"Mr. Johnson has temporal lobe epilepsy, has had for many years, possibly due to an injury when on active duty. All he remembers is that he had commenced bringing the mainsail around for a controlled jibe, and then he became dizzy. What probably followed was a trance-like state, though only a few seconds or minutes in duration. The blow itself may worsen his seizures or make them more frequent. There is no way to know. The cranium is damaged and surgery will be necessary, however our neurosurgeon needs to examine reports from his previous injury before proceeding. We should receive those tomorrow."

She started to protest, but he raised his hand. "Trust me, everything is totally discreet."

She doubted there was any possible way to get Navy records discreetly, however that was not the issue. "May I see him now?"

He nodded, downed his coffee. They took an elevator down two or three floors. "Are we underground?" she asked.

Dr. Kennedy just smiled and led her from the elevator, down a silent hall, past numerous closed doors. He stopped and inserted a card in the door with the letter J. There was a hint of a click, then a buzzer sounded from within and it opened.

The nurse gave a warm smile. "He's been waiting for you. Just press that green button if you need anything at all."

Seychelle watched them leave before approaching Wolfie. She was nervous, shy, guilty, lost. Tubes, wires and monitors put her back in West's hospital room.

"Well at least give me a smile. I am alive thanks to you."

She looked into those clear blue eyes and laughed. "Good thing you have epilepsy or I would have accused my self-appointed sailing guru of being a careless, half-assed sailor!"

His smile broadened. "I'm a great teacher. You got us here, didn't you?"

She took his hand and leaned in to kiss the space between his eyebrows. "You know, they are going to have to get rid of all this hair so they can see what damage you've done. I can hardly wait to see you bald."

His demeanor changed. "Now listen to me, Seychelle. I fade out at times, so don't interrupt. You can't stay here. Bonehead called a little while ago. He promised he would get you wherever you want to go. The guy who was after Charlie was shot but there's a good chance he gave everything he had gathered to the DA who's prosecuting Dave. You, daughter of West, are the missing link for their case. Dave will do time, but everyone, including Zachariah, could go down if you do. Without you or Charlie it will probably unravel into so much circumstantial evidence. I'm going to be here for a while, so I'm safe, then I just might head on down and join Charlie. I know when to move on. Take the handkerchief." He put his hand on the green button. "Go now." His smile became a frown, the door opened, his eyes closed, and a nurse was ushering Seychelle out into the hall.

Dr. Lopez was one of three people who rushed past her into his room. The nurse who had been with him earlier walked her back to the lounge and promised to get her if he regained consciousness. Shaken but clear-headed, she went straight to the phone.

When Zachariah's secretary asked her name, she said it was the topless girl from Mardi Gras. Her call went right through.

"Tell me."

"He's in a private clinic, top of the line. He was clear and lucid for a while, but is unconscious again. Their neurosurgeon will evaluate today. They think he will be fine but his epileptic seizures might be worse. I don't know if that means more debilitating or more often."

"Epilepsy?"

"From an old injury. He knew he had it, but a seizure came when he was jibing. Listen, he is going to leave the country as soon as released from here and advised that I leave immediately, which I will. We agree it is better for all concerned, including you. I will have his doctor call you as soon as they know what procedure is needed."

"I cannot tell you how relieved I am. And I apologize. I should have had more faith in you. I have covered my legal obligations, so let me say that I am here for you no matter what you need."

"Thanks. How's my friend?"

"My paralegal is there now in response to her invitation, so I take that as a good sign. You know the importance of keeping in touch with her, no matter where you are, and the method we have been using is best. Your other friends called. I have connected them with a trusted lawyer in their area who will confer with me. They are concerned about you."

"I'll call them. Can you put their legal costs on my account?"

"If that is what you want."

"Yes. And, they will present a bill for the project they are doing for me. Please settle it immediately, okay?"

"No problem."

"Also, I want to set up a trust fund for their daughter, sort of a miniature of the one you set up for me."

"Just send me the details." He chuckled. "Anything else?"

"No, uh, well, do you know anyone who works with emeralds? Who can process rough emeralds into finished stones?"

"Hmmm, I might. Location may be a problem. You will need to give me time on this one."

Seychelle could hear her name being paged. "Gotta go. I'll call you when I can."

She rushed out the door and crashed into Bonehead in the foyer.

"Whoa, little Girl," the big, weathered man said evenly. "Ya gonna hurt somebody, rushin' 'round like that."

"Sorry, I thought they were calling me for Wolfie, that he was conscious again."

His lined face looked like a hound dog's, with the same soulful eyes. He put his arm around her shoulders and they turned back to the door. "Now, that boy is gonna be fine. He's tougher'n most an' ya won't find better doctors nowhere."

Obviously familiar with the place, he went straight to the bar and got a Coke, then to the phone and made a call. Seychelle watched him while she mixed herself a rum and coke with lime. She was going to have to trust him completely, as did Pierre and Wolfman. As had, it seemed, West and Charlie.

He stared at her as he walked back to the kitchenette. "Yeah, you're his young'un. I see it now that I know. Most especially when ya got questions rollin' 'round your head." He nodded his head slowly, still staring at her, pulled out a chair and sat across from her at the table.

"Yo daddy wuz one of the finest men I've known. He couldn't stop 'em kickin' me out after I was hurt, but he made the bastards pay me, stood up to 'em he did. We thought alike 'bout lots of things, him 'n me."

"Like cannabis?" she asked, giving it as innocent a tone as she could.

He gave a bark of a laugh. "He'd ask questions in just that same way when he wuz diggin'. Yeah, 'bout that. 'course, he weren't as ferociously ag'inst drugs as me, but he sho' didn't like 'em. By the time I met West I'd done seen too many men blowed ta smithereens in Nam 'cause of heroin. Ya smoke pot?"

She shrugged. "Sometimes. He didn't like hard drugs because my mother was addicted. I'm equally anti. I've not smuggled, but inadvertently have gotten tied in with this circle. Not all are purists, as you know. But the guy who was shot, Jerken, was after me because he was after West as a link to the head honcho. We're assuming he was after Charlie. You know about all this stuff?"

He was opening another Coke. "Didn't know 'bout yor mamma. Sorry ta hear it." He took a long drink. "Heard Jerken had a lot of shit on a lot of folks. Wuz undercover for DEA, lookin' ta bust the coke connection ta Colombia. Most likely damn stupid ta pop 'im cuz ya know he'd of filed all the shit. Maybe shoulda' been done sooner."

They both sat silently contemplating their drinks and present situation. She knew he would help her, and that was the bottom line right now. "Is there a warrant out for me?"

"I hear it's in the makin'. Don't mean they can serve it," he drawled and his mouth curved into a slow grin. "Now the way I see it is we ought ta leave that rag-boat to the boys. It'll prob'bly sink anyways. My cuzin's waitin' outside. He'll take us ta hiz speedboat, an' where ya wanna go will determine which trawler he deposits us on. Ya with me?"

She felt like hugging him, but just nodded and stood.

On the way out Seychelle stopped at Wolfie's locker. She took his handkerchief, wrote Brian's address on a piece of paper that she slid into his joint case, and stuffed one rough emerald into his wallet.

"You'll give this key to Wolfie for his locker?" she asked.

"Don't know what else I'd do wid it," Bonehead replied as he stashed it in his pocket.

Thirty-Two

"Quieten down!" Bonehead hissed at the two fishermen. "And kill tha damn light," he growled when one lit a cigarette. They were evidently new at this.

Seychelle sat on the bow, senses at full alert. West had often interrupted whatever they were doing to make her stop and be aware. "Close your eyes," he would say, "and tell me everything you feel or hear or smell." Sometimes she had treated it like a game, sometimes like a nuisance, but there were times when it had registered as an experience. Detecting wind direction had not been a problem for her at any point when sailing and she now recognized that had been his intention.

"Where's the wind?" he would ask. She would point, and was rarely wrong. "And what direction is that?" She had gotten better at that one with time, and now felt quite confident.

Tonight, they had *Big Mama* pointing into a NE wind, tugging on her anchor. The 10 knot breeze was almost cold. Time to head south, she thought. The trawler's years in the dead fish business was overwhelmingly evident in its odor. Seychelle made herself ignore it. Concentrate.

"This rendezvous must be a success," she whispered. "I can't ask more of anyone."

"He's late," Bonehead grumbled at her shoulder.

"Shhh!" She was sure she had heard the clank of a halyard. She closed her eyes. Yes. She pointed to port, at about a ten o'clock angle. There, the low rumble of a small diesel and halyards slapping mast. Slowly her eyes opened and strained to detect a hull shape or ghost-like white haze of full sail. So ready was she that the form was perceived before actually seen.

"*Wesheena!*" Seychelle whispered.

Her long sleek profile presented itself as she turned to round *Big Mama's* stern. Seychelle's eyes watered. She stood staring for a moment, then followed Bonehead aft to position fenders along starboard rail. Their two crewmen took

220

positions on bow and stern to catch and secure lines. Wind and 3 foot chop meant they would need to time it precisely as the sand atoll they were anchored behind gave minimal protection.

She advanced from aft of *Big Mama*, slowly moving parallel into position for rafting up. And then it began. He had been in *Wesheena's* cockpit, but when the sight or scent of Seychelle reached him, Beauregard went nuts. He barked, he howled, he turned circles, he whined, he charged up and down the deck.

Seychelle felt renewed. "Beauregard! I missed you!" She yelled, laughing.

And he jumped. The boats heaved in, met just as he disappeared from sight. "No!" she screamed.

Bonehead grabbed her arm, pointed toward the stern. Later he would say, "I wuz just tryin' ta show 'er where tha damn fool dawg would cum out."

But for Seychelle there was neither thought nor hesitation. She dove from the stern. Her water resistant vest meant it was not a smooth, deep entry, as was her norm, but she recovered. With head above water, eyes open, she searched and called. She kept telling herself the fenders would have kept the boats from crushing him.

Waves pushed her back, she was several feet behind *Big Mama's* stern now, and just even with *Wesheena's*. Sydney had put the boat in neutral as soon as Beauregard had gone down, so her prop was disengaged. The two fishermen were struggling to get lines secured in response to Bonehead's shouted, "Don' le' go of the bastard!"

"Beauregard!" Seychelle shouted. She registered movement beside her, on *Wesheena's* swim platform, but her eyes did not move from the area before her. There! No. She cursed the deception of waves and shadows.

Bonehead centered *Big Mama's* spotlight in front of Seychelle, on the gyrating, mismatched hulls. This time the lump that appeared above the surface was solid. She opened her arms to embrace the dog, but his frantic paddling and clawing defeated her efforts, pushed her away and down.

Suddenly, from her right came the shout, "I've got him!" and she realized Beauregard was being lifted out of the water. She looked up at Sydney's straining face as he pulled on the wet dog's collar. Seychelle lunged forward, clamped her hand onto the stainless-steel bar that formed a swim platform at the base of *Wesheena's* transom, and pushed the dog's rear end with her other hand.

All she could think was, "Thank you, Chianti!" as she scrambled up after him.

"Good thing we weren't in the North Atlantic!" Seychelle said as she rubbed and massaged the trembling dog. They sat on the salon sole while Sydney prepared hot chocolate on a two-burner gimbaled stove. "Nice design," she said.

He nodded. "Chianti had some really good design ideas. If I had missed him from her swim platform, I would have slid open her transom and launched her aluminum dinghy. It contains a sealed survival kit."

"Let's hope we never need the kit!" she said and hugged Beauregard. He began a renewed assault of licks.

Bonehead had tied *Wesheena* aft of the trawler and ordered Sydney, "Make sure tha damn fool girl 'n 'er dawg are awlright. We're watchin'. Leavin' in 20 minutes. Cain't keep hangin' here."

Seychelle looked at Sydney. "There aren't enough words to thank you. Saving Beauregard, designing and building one of the great all-time boats, rushing her to readiness, bringing her out." She stopped when Sydney put his finger to his lips.

"She is not ready, there just was not enough time. Radar and depth sounder are the only working electronics, but everything you'll need is here. All manuals and equipment are in the aft cabin. Compass, sleeping bag, flashlights, plastic bottles of water, and bucket for toilet will serve you until you get to Jamaica. I'm sure Brian will help you get connected."

"Sort of the way you and Chianti started out."

"Sort of." He handed her the warm drink. "Luckily Sky had time to stock for you. There is plenty of food that doesn't need cooking, though there are several canisters of gas for her two-burner. Her solar panels will keep microwave, lights, radar, and depth sounder in operation. Her sails are the latest design Kevlar, tough, light and very fast. Her Volvo is new, and should have no problems."

"Don't y'all worry, Sydney. We'll be fine and Brian will help. You know I would love to have you come with us, but it seems like I just sort of radiate bad luck. I feel awful about the car incident. What do you think is going to happen?"

He shrugged. "Whatever happens, I cannot help believing we are all better off without Jerken around. I did think about joining you, gave it serious thought. However, I need to build Chianti's boat and the Murphy yard is the only place I can make that a reality in the immediate future. Creating *Wesheena* has been so good for me, and has felt right in so many ways. Also, the yard and family are a healing experience, a normalizing. Oh, in the canvas satchel you have your boat papers, a letter from Sierra and one from Zachariah, as well as a plain brown envelope that came in the post." He gave her a quick tour, with a cursory explanation of gear and rigging.

He was showing her how to adjust her transom-mounted windvane so *Wesheena* could steer herself when his hand-held VHF radio crackled.

"Le's go," Bonehead drawled.

Beauregard barked and jumped around, revitalized. Seychelle threw her arms around Sydney. "I am so lucky to have gotten to know you and Chianti. I love you both."

He returned her hug. "I wish you fair winds and following seas!" he said and stepped up on deck. Seychelle took the helm. She powered forward to the trawler's stern so that Sydney could release their bowline, let *Wesheena* drift back, then pulled up alongside *Big Mama* slowly, with intense concentration. Sydney looked back, gave a salute, and jumped over onto the trawler. Seychelle was shocked to see Bonehead leap across onto her boat at the same moment.

"Circle whilst they lift the anchor," he shouted. She did as ordered, very confused.

He stepped down into the cockpit and stood beside her, watching her for a minute. Then he threw his head back and gave a great roar of laughter.

"By God, yer his, fer sure." He reached into his jacket and pulled out a plastic bag. He tossed it down the companionway. "Later."

"Why have you taken so much trouble to help me?" she asked. "For nearly a month you've hidden me, shifted me around on boats, stayed with me, though there were certainly safer ways to stash me while I waited for *Wesheena*. You've endangered yourself. I don't believe it was just for West and Wolfie."

Bonehead turned and spit over the side, looked up at the rigging, gave the deck a cursory survey.

"It'll serve ya fine, I reckon." He spit again, motioned for her to pull up alongside *Big Mama*. Resting his hand on the boom, he faced her.

"The way I see it is, you haul ass outta the country, an' they figure there's a reason, maybe don' look so hard at ever'body else. An' like, with Charlie gone, maybe not so much hard shit be comin' in and they don' look so hard at the folks bringin' grass. Oh, I know thangs won't ever be tha same as it wuz, but I just cain't watch it all go ta hell an' do nothin'."

And with that cavalier proclamation he turned and spit, then leapt over onto *Big Mama*.

Seychelle watched the trawler fade away into the night.

She was left with a myriad of questions, but all took a back seat. She was on her very own boat, her *Wesheena*. She raised her mainsail with one reef and rolled out her headsail to about the size of a Yankee. She was tired, knew the Beauregard episode had taken a lot out of her, so opted to sail conservatively even though she desperately wanted to get to the declared 200 mile territorial limit as soon as possible.

Getting sails balanced and windvane set up took time, but she was thrilled with the way *Wesheena* sailed, even reefed down. On broad reach she was cruising at seven knots and sailing on her feet, so her ride was smooth with virtually no heel. Morning was draped in pale yellow when she finally went below to find food.

She made a fat sandwich with banana, honey and peanut butter, and added a scoop to Beauregard's dry food.

"Look at all this food! We have to send Sky a thank-you note." He was too busy with peanut butter to respond with more than a wag. Seychelle understood, took a couple of bites before sticking her head up to have a look around. All clear and the radar screen agreed.

With instant cappuccino and sandwich, she settled at the table and opened the canvas bag. The first letter, the one from Sierra, brought tears.

"Since I must accept that Chianti can't be here, then I would like to have you as my next Godmother. Please, if you don't mind. I had thought about asking Geena as well, since she was having so much trouble and I thought it would make her feel good, but I just can't do it. You see, Sky finally told me why Geena is in prison. What she did is bad, Miss Seychelle. Hard drugs kill people. I will write to her sometimes, but I can't love her so much. Please write or call me as soon as possible because I want everyone to know you are my Godmother now, if you say yes."

"Oh, Beauregard, what if she finds out about her own father? I mean, look how I'm being affected by West's actions. But he didn't go against his own 'ngs, and I can't say I disapprove of what he did. Anyway, I am a

Godmother. Great, I like it. Hey, maybe you can be her Goddog." She laughed but he ignored her.

The plain brown envelope made her nervous. Who would have sent her anything at the yard? Resolutely she pushed it aside and ripped open the one from Zachariah that included two letters from Geena. He said Seagull had been identified as being on Pierre's boat and neither had officially cleared into the country. Possibly Sint Maarten police were looking for him as well as Charlie. Seychelle took a deep breath, felt the lump in her throat. He went on, "I will try to keep you updated when I forward Geena's letters. The murder will affect all present cases. Wolfie is stable, his surgery went well. He will be in touch. Bon voyage, Seychelle. You will do just fine; of that I am sure."

Geena's first letter was short, the handwriting jerky. It had been written the day after her last visit. She apologized; said she wasn't herself. The next was three days later, assuring Seychelle she knew nothing about the murder, but admitting she was glad he was gone. Her handwriting was normal, her tone closer to the Geena she knew, but Seychelle's disquiet was not alleviated. She touched her locket.

She went on deck to check all was well. Golden globe was just peeking over the horizon and she stood appreciating its warmth. Her thick hair was not quite dry. She should probably give it a fresh water rinse. What had Bonehead been saying? Was she a pawn, being manipulated for the greater good? Had Wolfman actually been part of the plan, for her to take the fall in absentia? Great way to show respect for an old deceased friend, use his daughter as the sacrificial lamb. But, in honesty, could they have had any hand in the progression of events? Doubtful. Just made practical use of the end situation.

She took another look around, checked the compass she now wore on a lanyard around her neck, and went to her navigation table to enter their assumed position on the chart.

"Our first chart," she whispered. She entered time, date and position on the opening page of her logbook and noted, 'First position on first chart in maiden voyage of *Wesheena*.' She slipped her log into the rack next to Seagull's and Quandary.

Pretty exciting. Through Bonehead she had gotten a full collection of Caribbean charts and navigation tools. He had even given her a few basic lessons with a sextant. However, she had read that satellites were being set up that would track boats, simplifying navigation and ensuring accuracy. Soon, she hoped, but was quite content with radar, depth-sounder, and her collection of charts for this section of the world. She hadn't asked Bonehead how he got it all discreetly loaded onto *Wesheena* while she was still in Murphy's Boatyard.

She set up the 'fuzz buster' Bonehead had given her to help look out for large ships. "Insurance," he'd said, "cause they might'n see y'all so good."

Then she looked for the bag he had left. It was under Beauregard, who was snoring. Easing it from under his warm body provoked a groan and a couple of tail thumps.

First thing she fished out was a rather beat-up black and white photo. She guessed it was from around fifteen or twenty years back. The Boys celebrating a successful scam, their first? They were sitting around a table that was littered with empty Dom Perignon bottles and over-full ashtrays. All beamed at the camera, glasses raised. Bonehead was rough, unshaven, in jeans and tee-shirt. He looked old, even back then. Charlie looked much the same as he had in Sint Maarten but with more hair and less wrinkles. The Latin-looking fellow was handsome, must be Jose', with an unbuttoned shirt and too many gold chains on smooth chest. Wolfman was just as hairy, but seemed very young, sort of a hippie. And then there was West, the West she hadn't known. He looked the sophisticate of the bunch, neat and conservative, but just as drunk as the others. Beside his right hand lay, yes, she was sure, it was a stack of money. She got a flashlight to determine what was sticking out of their pockets. No! Out of every visible pocket was protruding a $100 bill! What a brouhaha this pic would have raised with Navy brass! She had to laugh. This one she would keep with her forever.

She went up and looked around. Not a ship in sight. Beauregard's whine reminded her he would need help until he learned to maneuver his long body and short legs up and down the companionway steps. She boosted him up.

"This is our world now, Beauregard." She picked up her soggy vest. As soon as she and Beauregard had begun to tremble, Sydney had thrown blankets over them, presented her with a change and ordered immediate action. She had discarded the vest and all her clothes in the cockpit in the rush for warm dry replacements.

"Well, I'm sure I'm not the only woman they've all seen naked. Hey, I don't have to wear clothes out here!" Beauregard lay down to sleep in the morning sun while Seychelle stripped and threw her clothes below. She sat down, picked up her vest and emptied out each of the pockets to see what damage was done, then put it in a plastic bucket and poured in a bottle of fresh water to rinse out the salt. She had sealed in plastic bags her passport, cards, house and bank keys, money, Chianti's letter and West's book, Enlightened Sayings. All were fine, and had been secure within zipped pockets. But the emeralds and Wolfi's handkerchief had fallen out, and were somewhere on the bottom. She sighed.

"Oh, Chianti, I am so sorry." She could picture the green velvet bag laying on the seafloor and tiny, brightly colored fish investigating. She shook off the regret. "Turn the page. Starting a new chapter."

Below she dug again into Bonehead's bag and yelped. There was a sack of grass! She ripped the duct tape off and smelled sweet, red-haired weed. There were even rolling papers and a lighter. "Wow, Bonehead, nice gift!" She wasted no time, rolled one.

Seychelle sat on the aft deck with her first big fat joint, a bag of Oreo cookies, and the plain brown envelope in her lap. She regarded her world with a contented sigh and lit up. Exhaling slowly, letting her tension float out and fade with smoke, becoming part of this world.

"Bless you, you old redneck."

She only smoked half the joint before ripping the envelope open with a great flourish. It was addressed to Annabelle Seychelle Austin, with no return address, and Mobile, Alabama postmark.

"Let's see what grand surprises this one holds, Beauregard."

Inside she found a newspaper and a plain white sealed envelope that she opened a bit more sedately. From it she pulled a stack of photos.

"Oh my God," she groaned. In the top photo she was sitting with Geena, Yolande and Seagull on his boat in the lagoon at sunset. That was the first day she had met Seagull. It was obviously taken with a zoom lens. The second photo was darker, but it was easy to make out the profiles of her, Charlie, and Seagull in his living room. The next was taken the same night, when she talked with Yolande and Seagull on the little dock behind his house.

"I wish you had bitten the bastard, Beauregard!" she fumed. The last two made her stomach feel queasy. Their Reach Falls afternoon looked far from innocent. Two poses she, Brian and Geena had struck in their naked mushroom frolic suggested an orgy in progress.

"Hans!" she bellowed. Beauregard jumped up and growled, so loud and angry was her exclamation. She looked at him. "You knew he was bad, didn't you?"

"But, why? Was Hans working for Jerken? Had he set up Geena? I left my camera in Brian's house!"

Then she opened the Sint Maarten newspaper. Emblazoned across its front page was the headline, 'Teacher Declares War on Hard Drugs'. Beneath was a picture of Yolande standing beside a grave with the quote, 'I've lost a promising student and an aunt to the drug trade. I want it stopped!'

The interview ran on for two pages. Part of it was the story of how her cousin, a law student, had come to visit from the US and been lured in to play mule, and how it had literally killed her mother when she was busted. She lambasted, 'The Yank they call Charlie' and listed some of his lackeys, including Seagull. In the last paragraph the reporter said the DEA had finally sent someone down to investigate. That before they had just asked for police reports, but perhaps now the Americans would see what their growing drug market was doing to the citizens of Sint Maarten and other Caribbean islands.

Seychelle tossed photos and the newspaper into the Gulf of Mexico. She pressed her dolphin locket to her breast as she watched them disappear in *Wesheena's* wake.

Then she paced and thought. She trimmed and re-trimmed sails. She finished the joint and made cappuccino and rolled another. She studied her charts and the 'Ocean Passages of the World' book Sydney had given her and read Chianti's account of passing through the Panama Canal. She made notes in her logbook.

Seychelle had set her new course by the time the sun was settling into the horizon directly ahead of *Wesheena*. She took the bottle of champagne, sent with love by Barry and Sky, to the bow along with Enlightened Sayings. She popped the cork and declared, "Socrates reckoned that if you know what good is, then you will do good. I'll drink to that."

She took a long drink and poured remaining bubbles over the bow of *Wesheena*. The empty bottle she tossed into the sea contained no message.

…and she sailed away into the sunset…

CPSIA information can be obtained
at www.ICGtesting.com
Printed in the USA
LVHW012125010921
696650LV00004B/80

9 781647 504144